THE ODYSSEY GENE

KFIR LUZZATTO

PINE 10

CONTENTS

DEDICATION

To Eti, the companion of my journey.

BOOK ONE

W e hold these truths to be sacred and undeniable; that all men are created equal and independent, that from that equal creation they derive rights inherent and inalienable, among which are the preservation of life, and liberty, and the pursuit of happiness.

Thomas Jefferson, "Rough Draft" of the
American Declaration of Independence

CHAPTER 1

"**M**ay I join you?"

The passenger sat all alone by the table on the main deck. He lifted his head and gazed at the young woman before him. She wore a crew member uniform; a name tag, neatly placed above her shirt pocket, advertised her name and position: "Dana, Entertainment Officer."

"Go ahead," he answered uninvitingly. "My name is John," he added with a belated spark of politeness.

If his tone and lack of interest hurt her feelings, her face didn't show it. Her smile remained steady on her lips, and she slid her thin body between the table and the chair in front of John's.

"I noticed that you have been sitting here alone during the last few days, and I thought I might offer you some more interesting options to pass the time," she said. She moved elegantly, even when sitting down, and her voice harmonized with her motion. "We have quite a good music library, movies, books, and more. Are you interested?"

"Not really, thanks," he answered flatly. "I'm comfortable here, and anyway, we have only a little more than a week left before we reach our destination."

Her face dropped, and she waved her hand in despair. "It's very frustrating, you know," she said. "This is my first assignment as an Entertainment Officer, and I want to do a proper job of it, but nobody seems to be taking me seriously. I tried to talk to that group of mining engineers over there," she added confidingly, pointing with her chin at a group of people sitting at a table at the edge of the hall, "but they are busy all the time studying and exercising, and they don't need my services. Apart from you and them, all other First Class passengers are either older couples or government officers who keep to themselves. All right," she concluded resignedly. She let out a quick sigh and pushed her chair back a little, preparing to get up. "I won't keep bothering you," she said bitterly.

She stood but didn't walk away. John looked at her, his interest aroused by her behavior. Dana stood there, seemingly unbothered by his piercing gaze.

"You are not bothering me," he said at last. "Please sit with me. A little company won't hurt me, but I'm not in the mood for entertainment right now."

"Talking to passengers is also part of my job," she answered earnestly. Her face showed her relief at the invitation as she sat down again.

John studied her delicate features, amazed at his audacity in fixing his eyes on her so openly and directly but feeling no embarrassment. Dana's body language had made it clear that she didn't mind.

"How old are you?" he asked.

"I'm twenty-three."

"And what brings you to this ship?"

"Well ... I thought flying to another planet and seeing things I have only heard about in school would be exciting. But in reality, so far, it has been a big disappointment. I'm cooped up in this box all the time and see nothing at all. I hope that New Australia will be as interesting as they say."

"What do you know about New Australia?"

"What everybody knows," she answered mechanically. "Until about one hundred and fifty years ago, the planet served as a prison, to which dangerous criminals were exiled from Earth. With the establishment of the New Nations Organization, the practice of exile was discontinued, and the planet became a member of the NNO. The truth is," she said, her expression changing from the scholarly mechanical back into her previous lively one, "I am excited at the thought of landing there. I hope to return with many interesting experiences to tell."

"You know something about the history of New Australia all right," John admitted. "I hope you also know that the planet is dangerous and that you'll have to take good care of yourself there."

Dana sat up straight and waved her hand in a discounting gesture as if the dangers were no concern to her. "The crew, and I among them, have been told all about that before we took up the job. I don't plan to go into the savage Newist territories, although they say visiting them is an amazing experience. And you," Dana asked with open curiosity, "what's the purpose of your trip? Are you an NNO observer or something?"

"No. I wish ..." He looked at her, then immediately moved his eyes to the corner of the table. "The truth is that one month ago, I took the test and came out D-positive."

Dana's expression turned from excited to grave, and John could scarcely hide his surprise in seeing that she looked even more beautiful when she seemed concerned.

"Oh, I'm so sorry," she said, and her voice had an unmistakable ring of genuine sympathy. "It must be terrible for you."

"It's funny, but in a sense, it's great. To be immune to that horrible disease, I mean. Do you know anything about the Davies Gene?"

"I know what they teach you in school. I know about the pestilence and about the limitations imposed on those who, like you, are D-positive."

"I understand that you are D-negative ..."

"I haven't been tested yet. I'll do it as soon as I return from this trip, but there isn't a chance in the world that I'll test positive. Both my parents are negative, and nobody in my immediate family is positive."

"I'm sure it'll be okay, and I don't want to worry you, but do you know that one-half percent of those with no family history for the D-gene turn out to be positive?"

"It's a very low percentage, and I've never met anyone like that."

"I'm like that."

"Oh, that's terrible! How did it happen?"

"As you know, everybody has to take the test before age twenty-five."

"Or earlier, if he is a candidate for a classified job or wishes to marry," she pointed out.

"Right. I was doing well at my job and had my entire life before me until ..."

John looked above Dana's head, far away in time and place. The images returned to him with a quality of unreality, like a movie in which somebody else played the leading role. He started describing the pictures etched in his memory to Dana – or perhaps to himself – in a low, flat voice...

Nothing appeared out of the ordinary the day the head of the Critical Computing Division summoned John to his office, except the interview itself, a new experience for John, who had never before stepped into the office of such a powerful man. He had only met him briefly during the rare visits to his department or when the department had visitors, which was seldom.

After a short wait, John was ushered into a spacious room featuring a vast desk, empty but for a computer terminal.

"Sit down, John," said the Division Head. John walked hesitatingly toward the chair, sat down, and waited for his boss to speak. The Division Head was a man of kind manners, soft-spoken, with long white hair. Notwithstanding his important position and heavy duties, he never forgot to smile at his staff, and they loved him for that. Now, too, as he spoke, he smiled gently.

"I've heard good reports about you, John," he opened the conversation.

"I'm glad to hear that, sir," John answered with some embarrassment.

"Not just good ones, but outstanding ones. I'll go straight to the point, John. One of our Department Managers–the Department of Census–is retiring because of health problems, and we need a replacement. I want to infuse young blood into the department, which has not developed to my satisfaction during the last few years. I have asked around, and everybody pointed to you as the best candidate for the job. So, if you want the position, it's yours."

John couldn't believe his ears. This job offer represented a meteoric promotion, unheard of in the organization.

"I ... I don't know what to say ... I wasn't expecting this."

"What about saying 'thank you'?" asked the Division Head with an ill-concealed smile.

"Thank you, sir. Thank you very much! This is a great opportunity for me. I promise that I won't disappoint you."

"I'm sure you will justify my trust in you. We didn't pick you just like that ... your record speaks for itself. Now, go celebrate and let me do some work," he added, this time with a broader smile.

John stood up, still incapable of fully digesting the news. "Thank you again," he repeated, his hand already on the door handle, an expression of joy and shyness on his face.

"Ahh, one more thing, John," the Division Head added as an afterthought. "I almost forgot. Have you taken the D-test already?"

"Not yet, why?"

"It's needed for your new job. It's a classified position. So get it over with because I don't want that to delay us."

"No problem. It's only a formality anyway," said John and left the room.

That night, John and his family–his parents and two brothers–celebrated the news of his promotion at John's favorite restaurant. Everyone beamed with pride at his achievement, particularly his two elder brothers, who were also doing well in their careers.

The following day, John woke up early and took the brief train trip to the nearest branch of the National Laboratories for "D" Control. About ten young people, looking tense, sat waiting for the test. After a brief waiting period, a laboratory employee led them to a small lecture room, where an authoritative-looking man in his forties greeted them.

The room was bare. Simple chairs sat in three orderly rows before a small lecture stand on a high podium. Behind it, John noticed a whiteboard of the type used to project images and to scribble on. The flag of the NNO hung majestically at the edge of the podium. The room was freezing, but the man seemed at ease despite being lightly dressed; none of the others dared complain about the excessive air conditioning.

"Good morning, everybody," the man greeted them once the last visitor had seated himself. "My name is Dr. Martin, and I will be your instructor for your test procedure today. It consists of three stages. In the first stage, where we are right now, you will receive a brief but complete explanation of the test's history and legal aspects. The law requires the laboratory to ascertain that every tested person knows and understands the importance of this test. We will take care of this matter momentarily."

"At the second stage, you will give a blood sample, which will be used to run the test, and at the third stage, you'll receive the test result. The last two stages take place individually, in separate rooms, and we take great care to safeguard your privacy. Questions?"

"Yes," asked a young man who sat at the edge of the first row. "What happens if someone refuses to take the test?"

"Thank you very much for your question. I was about to come to that. Legally, we can't force you to take the test, except as a condition to issuing a marriage license. However, if you reach the age of twenty-five without taking it, it will be considered as if you had taken it and were found to be D-positive. All your rights and limitations will be exactly the same as applies to a tested D-positive person. Anybody can take the test after the age of twenty-five but will have to pay for it. If the individual tests D-negative, the record will be corrected accordingly. But you should know that the test is expensive, and it is rare for a citizen to take that route, which offers no advantages. More questions?"

The young crowd sat quietly and asked no more as if asking the next question might be dangerous. John could feel the tension in the room.

"All right," continued the instructor, "if you have no more questions, let's move on to the lecture." He turned his head to scan the room and continued after a brief interval. "As you know, exactly seventy years ago," the instructor said, checking his watch as if to find there the correct date, "a pestilence known as the 'Watson-Davies Epidemic,' or simply the 'D-Plague,' killed millions in a matter of weeks. All the scientists of the New Nations engaged in research to discover the virus and find a cure for it, but to no avail. However, after a few weeks, an important fact emerged–certain ethnic groups appeared almost totally immune to the virus."

Dr. Martin paused for a moment and swept the room with his eyes, perhaps to gauge the effect of his tale on his young audience. But since all had heard the same lecture many times before, in school and at work, they simply sat there patiently, waiting for it to run its course.

"Here," he continued after a brief pause, "begins a dark chapter in the history of the New Nations—the epidemic, which many believed would be the end of some ethnic groups, induced panic. Panic fostered the spreading of many tales, all similar at their roots, according to which the immune ethnic groups were the ones who had spread the epidemic.

"These false accusations started a bloodbath that spread around the world, resulting in the slaughter of tens of thousands of humans. Thousands of others, men, women, and children, were imprisoned by their governments in research facilities where ruthless scientists used them as guinea pigs in an attempt to characterize the virus and find a cure for it.

"Pretty soon, it became apparent that no conspiracy existed and that the reason for the immunity of certain groups resided in a gene that imparted resistance against the disease. That gene–now called 'Davies Gene' after the scientist who identified it, or simply 'Gene D,' is the gene for which you will be tested here today."

Dr. Martin paused for a second, pulled his sleeves, glanced from right to left, and continued.

"Even after the epidemic subsided and no longer threatened to obliterate humankind, many still requested sanctions against D-positive groups. This resulted in harsh laws that took away civil rights from the immune population and, in practice, turned them into second-rate citizens. This phase lasted about twenty years until fifty years ago when the Supreme Court of the New Nations abolished those laws but allowed two limitations to stand. The first is the prohibition for D-positive individuals to marry D-negative partners. The reason for this limitation is that it is scientifically proven that half-breeds are much more apt to contract the disease than the rest of the population. This means that if we let many half-breeds be born, the epidemic may return with such strength that we may not be able to fight it. Today, the disease is less common than other contagious diseases, such as AIDS or tuberculosis, and is no longer considered a global threat.

"The second limitation has to do with the ban on D-positive workers in sensitive governmental positions. The Supreme Court accepted the government's view that it is necessary to prevent the infiltration of D-positive elements to key positions because it is feared that 'negative elements' who are both immune to the disease and in key positions might spark a renewed pestilence for their own purposes. Beyond those two very reasonable limitations, D-positive citizens enjoy all the rights of every D-negative citizen.

"I hope that now," he concluded theatrically, "you appreciate the importance of the civic duty that you are performing today by taking the test. Questions?"

"What happens if a 'pure' and a 'positive' still wish to marry?" somebody asked.

"That's a bizarre idea–a perversity, I would even call it. According to law, the woman may undergo a sterilization procedure, or the couple may sign an a priori waiver of the baby. In such a case, if the woman reports her pregnancy in time, it will be terminated. Otherwise, the baby will be taken from its parents and sent to a confined facility, which it will never leave as long as he or she lives. We only know of very few such cases. More questions?"

The girl who sat to John's right raised her hand, and when the instructor nodded in her direction, she stood up.

"I wish to understand," she said hesitantly, "why are those persons who turn out to be D-positive punished? And you will agree that the limitations you spoke of are a form of punishment. They certainly didn't choose to be positive ..."

"Yes," the instructor answered with open disdain, "just like a poisonous snake didn't choose to be born a snake. Nevertheless, when we meet a poisonous snake, we kill it; we don't sit beside it and discuss its bad luck with it. What's the difference?"

The girl lowered her gaze and sat down. Nobody asked any more questions, and after a brief interval, the instructor sent them, one by one, to a small room where blood samples were taken from them.

John killed time waiting for the test results by watching a documentary about the pestilence and its roots. After another wait, the tested youths were called one by one to a small room, in alphabetical order, to receive the test results.

The girl who had asked the question was third in line. John watched her enter the room with a bowed head. He hoped for her that she'd test negative, but her countenance made her tension clear. When she left, walking fast and containing her tears, John understood that her fears had materialized and she had tested positive. He couldn't help feeling sorry for her. In contrast to many of his friends from "pure" families (as it was customary to call those families that sported negative D-test results for all their members), John never felt that he was better than any "positive" and never considered them his inferiors. Two positives worked in John's department, and he treated them as equals.

John was so deep in thought that the clerk standing at the door had to call his name several times before he heard him and got up. He walked into the small room almost entirely occupied by a desk covered with documents and stood before it.

"Sit down, please," said the clerk politely.

"You know, I'm in a bit of a hurry, sir. Perhaps you could just give me the certificate of testing and let me go?"

"It's not so simple," answered the clerk, who had seated himself heavily. "Sit down, please," he repeated.

John sat testily. He wasn't new to the waste of time that went with official procedures—a well-known trait of every public servant, but this was becoming aggravating. Still, like every experienced citizen, he had learned that letting the clerk go through the prescribed procedure was often the shortest way. He shifted in his seat with a sigh and waited for the clerk to go on.

"I am holding your family's file in my hands," he started. "I see that they are all pure, right?"

"Absolutely," said John with satisfaction. At least the clerk had taken the trouble to find out who he was dealing with.

"You received a full day of instruction today. Of course, you learned that pure families can give birth to a positive subject, although chances are very low."

"Yes. Less than a half percent."

"Correct. And have you appreciated the dangers of cross-breeding between pure and positive individuals?"

"Of course, and not for the first time. What is this, a pop quiz?"

"No," the clerk answered without looking him in the eyes, "I am giving you the test results."

"What are you saying?" John asked, doubt clutching at his heart.

"You tested positive. You are not pure," stated the clerk.

John heard the words, but his brain refused to record them. He got up with a jerk and stood there, shaking his head in disbelief, his body trembling uncontrollably.

"But ... it must be a mistake. It can't be true ..." he murmured.

"I'm sorry," said the clerk and handed him a piece of paper with the result written on it. He looked embarrassed but went on speaking in a businesslike voice. "Our test is never wrong."

John mechanically took the paper the clerk had been holding before him, turned away, and left the room without another word.

CHAPTER 2

The corner of the main deck was empty of passengers. John and Dana sat quietly, without looking at each other, the last words of John's tale still ringing. After a long pause, Dana spoke, breaking the silence that had become oppressive.

"It must've been tough for you," she said. Her voice betrayed sorrow and sympathy.

"Yes. I admit it came as a blow, particularly because I wasn't expecting it. I only said to myself that I'd go and get rid of the nuisance of getting tested. I didn't think for a moment that the answer could return positive."

"Would you like me to get you something to drink? Your tongue must have dried out from all the talking."

Dana got up without waiting for an answer, perhaps to move on beyond the embarrassing point the conversation had taken them. John was thankful that she had managed to keep the conversation on a normal chitchat level. It must have been her first encounter with someone who had tested positive and talked openly about it–an embarrassing experience, if not a shocking one.

"Yes, thanks," he answered politely, "but on condition that you'll drink with me—consider it a part of your duties."

"No problem. I'm allowed to keep you company and drink with you. What would you like?"

"Anything you're having. I don't care what."

He watched her walk gracefully to the small bar open to first-class passengers and pour a pinkish liquid into two tall glasses. John thought that how she had reacted to his tale was admirable, considering her young age and lack of experience.

"How did other people react to the news?" Dana asked after she placed the glasses before them and sat down again.

"Oh, I learned a lot about human nature from the reactions of my nearest and dearest—and also of strangers."

"Did you have a girlfriend?"

"Yes, and she was the one I went to first, still in shock from the news. Her name is Maya, and she's a talented physicist. We met in school, and although we hadn't said so in so many words, we knew we were meant to spend our lives together, marry, and bring children into this world."

"And how did she react?"

John's face froze as those minutes came back to him.

"How, indeed ..."

He had walked from the laboratory, who knows for how long, but certainly over one hour. He must have decided subconsciously to walk toward Maya's house because when he lifted his head, which he had kept bowed all along, he saw the well-kept garden before her home. She lived in an elegant building; hers was a well-off family.

"John? What are you doing here? Come on up," said Maya when John pushed the intercom button.

John walked heavily toward her, and his countenance made it plain that something was wrong.

"What's the matter? What happened?" she asked, and when he only shook his head, she pointed at an elegant sofa at the edge of the sitting room. "Come here, sit down," she ordered. "Do you want me to bring you some water? I'll be right back," she added when John nodded faintly.

"Now tell me what's going on," she pressed him when John had finished gulping down the water. He hadn't realized how thirsty he had been. He wanted more, but he saw that Maya had grown impatient and understood there was no way to put off his tale any longer.

"I went to take the test today ... because of the new job offered to me," he hesitated.

"Yes, and–?" Maya asked with a furrowed brow.

"I tested positive," John almost whispered the terrible words.

The atmosphere of the room felt frozen. Maya looked at him and then moved her gaze to the window, looking far away as if trying to digest the news. John watched her without speaking and waited for a word of consolation, longing for her warm touch to lift some of the pain that hurt inside. He recalled as if it were yesterday the only time when, during his studies, he had flunked a test and how well she had comforted him then.

"You understand what this means?" Maya asked in a low, quiet voice, without moving from her chair that seemed far away from the sofa on which John sat.

"Of course I do. It's a blow, but together we'll get over it."

"No, I meant what it means for us. There is no longer any point in our relationship. We should end it now."

"But ... I'm sure that we'll manage ..."

"Yes? How?" she asked bitterly. "We'll never be able to have children, and I want children. Do I deserve to be married to a second-rate citizen? I don't think so."

"But ... but you haven't taken the test yet," John appealed to her, clutching to the last straw of hope. "Maybe you'll test positive too."

"Is that what you wish me? Don't be stupid. I come from a pure family, and there's no chance in hell that I'll test positive."

"I, too, come from a pure family. Who knows? We don't need to decide now. Let's wait until after you take the test."

"I'm not going to do anything of the sort! Besides, I have more than two years until I have to take the test, and I won't take it a day before the legal date. I'm sorry, John. It's bad luck, but here we are."

"Then, this is the end?"

"Apparently," she said flatly, looking at him in a detached, estranged way. "You'd better go now," she added.

He got up, trying without much success to keep an erect bearing. Maya watched him walk to the door and leave the apartment; she spoke no more. She hadn't touched him even once. She watched him go as if he were no longer alive.

"What a bitch," Dana exclaimed when John finished his tale.

John swallowed twice and tried to hide the perturbation induced by his memories of that day, which had come back so forcefully to him. Then he noticed the glass in front of him as if seeing it for the first time, lifted it, and slowly sipped from it. Dana sat there without looking at him as if wishing to safeguard his privacy.

A burst of laughter came from the mining engineers sitting at the lounge's corner. John looked at Dana.

"Yes," he answered. "I admit that I didn't enjoy it. But in a sense, she made things easier for me because I no longer felt any love for her after the way she acted."

"And what happened at work?"

"That surprised me. I was very nervous when I went to relay the test results to the Division Head, but he already knew them."

"Come in, John. Come in and sit down," said the Division Head when John hesitantly opened his office door. "I'm very sorry about the test result," he said in a fatherly voice. "I tried to find out what can be done, how to promote you anyway, but I haven't found a way to circumvent the law."

"I'm very grateful, sir," John said emotionally. "You didn't have to do that."

"Right, I didn't have to. I don't have to do anything at all at my age, and in my position, I don't have to pretend that I believe in the idiotic laws that won't permit me to enjoy the services of a talented young man like you. You can quote me on that."

"I thought that the law was meant to protect the citizens," John reacted in surprise.

"Yes? That's what they sell you and all citizens. I can tell you there is no scientific proof that being negative or positive means anything once the epidemic has passed. The weak ones died, and the strong ones became resistant, including those who didn't have a natural gene for it. A few weak people will always die; we have no reason to believe the pestilence may return. It's all a bag of nonsense," the Division Head concluded heatedly. "Unfortunately," he added, "I don't have the power to go against the law. But I haven't given up."

"What can you do?"

The Division Head lowered his voice, passed his fingers through his white hair, and fixed his eyes on a point far away above John's shoulder.

"I've spoken with colleagues and friends who are influential in various committees, and they promised to work to lower the security level of your new job to one that is allowed for a D-positive employee. Until then, the deputy will continue to fill in, and I won't appoint anybody else for the position. The job will wait for you. I have been promised that changing the security level won't take more than two years. I know how disappointed you must be, but two years is not an eternity."

For the first time, John lifted his head and met the straight gaze of the Division Head.

"I don't know how to thank you, sir," he said, his voice trembling with emotion, "but right now, I am a little confused and don't know what to do with myself."

"It's only natural. Take a holiday—a week that you deserve anyway. Rest and let time do its wonders, then come back in one week, and we'll talk about the future. Okay?"

"I'm grateful, sir. I really am. Your support is very important to me."

"Bah," said the Division Head dismissively, "don't mention it. Just keep in mind that you're not alone in this. Your friends at work think highly of you."

Before he closed the door, John looked at his boss again. He was shaking his head in anger, and an expression of sorrow darkened his features.

"I drew great strength from that conversation with the Division Head," said John, smiling sadly. "I felt much better after it."

"But, your parents and brothers surely supported you."

"My family is the main reason I am on this ship right now."

"How come?"

"It's a long story," said John sadly.

"You've still got a full week to tell it to me," Dana retorted, making it clear that she wasn't going to give up.

"I'll tell you what. If you agree to have dinner with me, I'll tell you the whole story."

Dana checked her wristwatch and the board hanging from their table, listing meal times. Although the exact time had no meaning in space, all the activities, including meals, took place according to Earth's time to maintain a comfortable routine for the passengers.

"The next is in less than two hours. I'm going off duty in a few minutes, and I'll have enough time to spruce up before dinner. Shall we meet a few minutes before then?"

"Deal!"

Dana rose and smiled broadly, making John's heart pound. "See you later, then," she concluded. She started walking toward the door. John watched her slim body move, still held spellbound by the harmony of her motion. She stopped and turned back to him.

"Dress up," she ordered, still smiling, and walked out.

John was surprised to discover that he felt like dressing up for the first time since his test's fateful day.

CHAPTER 3

John spent the first three days after the test as if in a dream. He sat alone in his room and spoke to nobody. Most of the time, he stared at the ceiling, playing the images of that day in his mind again and again and examining them dispassionately, from afar, as if they didn't concern him.

The atmosphere in his home was one of mourning. His parents did not approach him or speak to him. When, now and then, he left his room to quench his thirst or to try to eat something when his hunger became insufferable, he checked first that the ground was clear to avoid imposing his presence on his family.

The worst moments of his life were when he had to face his parents and tell them the test result. When he got home, exhausted and confused after a walk of who knows how many hours, he found them in the kitchen, drinking tea. At the sight of John's expression, his father got up quickly and stood frozen beside John's mother's chair, taking time to digest his son's words.

"It's not the end of the world," he tried to comfort him at last. "We stand by you, John," he said in a choking voice. "It's not important to your mother and me. It doesn't have to influence our daily life at all."

Brave words, but words that sounded empty while John's mother wept, her face in her hands, and mumbled, "What shall we do? What have we done to deserve it?" and similar lamentations.

"Thanks, Dad," said John weakly and ran to his room away from the embarrassment of that moment.

On the fourth day, John's father knocked on his door and entered when a weak "come in" came from John. He found John unshaven, the rancid smell of stale sweat emanating from his shirt, and his unkempt hair standing partly on end. His father sat beside him on the bed, fondly hugged his shoulder, and then straightened up and spoke to him.

"How do you feel now, son?"

"I've been better."

"I'm sure. But we can't change the facts, so now it's time for you to get yourself together and move on with your life."

"What kind of life can I expect to have?" John asked bitterly.

"A wonderful life! You will have a few limitations, that's true, but in everyday life, you won't feel them at all."

"Thanks for the encouragement, Dad." John felt better already. At least his miserable condition hadn't scared away both his parents. "I know it won't be as easy as you make it sound, but I'll manage eventually." He became quiet as a thought suddenly worried him. "And how is Mom coping with it?"

His father moved his gaze to a far corner of the room and spoke slowly, measuring his words. "This is very hard on her. She can't understand how this could happen in a respectable family. I mean," he corrected himself quickly, "in a family where everybody is pure. But she loves you, and she'll come around. Don't push her right now; give her the time she needs."

"I understand," John said sadly.

"Now, I suggest you get up and take a good shower. Dinner will be ready in twenty minutes, and it would be good for all of us if you'd come and sit with us at the dinner table."

"I'll be ready in time," said John, watching his father leave the room with bent shoulders–the shoulders of an old man.

In the shower, John prepared himself for his meeting with his mother. He felt a little as he did as a child when he had broken a window and had to come and justify himself to her. He knew that he had done nothing wrong this time but derived no solace from the thought–the apprehension at the coming meeting remained as strong as before.

Despite everything, John's mother managed to summon enough strength to create a normal family atmosphere. She spoke to him as he entered the dining room: "Hi, honey, good that you're here," she said. "Can you help me with this heavy platter? Great. Come on, sit quickly before the soup gets cold."

John followed instructions, thankful that his mother was not allowing any moment of silence that might become embarrassing. Then he remembered the traditional Food Prayer, which had been universally adopted since the first days of the post-pestilence period, which every family said at the dinner table. The prayer included supplicating to God not to inflict illness on those at the table and their families and to preserve the genes' purity. The prayer that was said in their home at every meal hadn't helped them, and now its words sounded like a mockery of their misfortune. John panicked, waiting for his father to say the prayer. He glanced at him, a silent and wise man, but did not allow his countenance to reveal his thoughts.

"Good appetite," his father said and started sipping his soup.

For the first time since his voluntary exile to his room, John felt a smile trying to surface. He controlled his impulse to thank his father openly. The meal passed in a quiet atmosphere and symbolized John's return to a semblance of normalcy. From that moment, he and his parents never mentioned his "handicap" again. During the following week, their life seemed to be going back to normal. John returned to work, where nobody mentioned his situation, although obviously everybody knew about it. He often wondered if the hand of the Division Head was in that.

In an attempt to find a new direction in his life, John started going out at night to places he had never been before. He sat alone in bars, particularly bars frequented by "positives," and drank more than he was used to. He recalled someone at work–he couldn't remember who–telling him that "positives" got together and developed social relationships in certain bars. At the time, he hadn't paid too much attention to these tales, which hadn't concerned him, and now he was reluctant to ask his colleagues direct questions about them. He didn't know what "developing social relationships" meant exactly. Could those be some sort of forbidden relationship, perhaps conspiratorial and underground? Or maybe the positives sought a social environment where they could feel better? He didn't know the answer but realized that his drive to seek the company of people who felt the same as him would only grow with time.

John couldn't remember the name of a single bar for positives. Still, everybody knew that the positives preferred certain city areas over others, so he decided to spend time in clubs in those areas.

One evening, his quest was rewarded as he sat at the bar of a dark club he had already visited in the past, which played relatively quiet music. The place was packed with merry couples at all times, giving him a pleasant sense of anonymity. From where he sat, he watched a small crowd moving on the dance floor and relaxed, drinking a cocktail with an exotic name. He was annoyed when someone climbed up on the stool beside him and blocked his field of view. John looked up and saw a young man, more or less his age. After a brief sip, he ordered a beer from the bartender and turned to John.

"Good music, what?"

"Ah-ha," John answered noncommittally. The test results had changed him from an open person to a reserved one, and he was wary of conversing with strangers. He sized up the young man, trying to decide whether he was pure or positive. No external sign existed that could give away his genetic makeup.

"I've seen you here before," said the young man. "Do you come here often?"

"Not really," John answered politely, "this is the second time."

"You know, of course," the stranger continued, "that this is a club favored by 'positives'?"

"Really?" John answered with a neutral voice, fixing his look on the floor.

"Yes, and I think you knew that," said the stranger, looking straight into John's face. When John didn't react, he put out his hand and said, "My name is David, and I am positive."

John considered the outstretched hand, finally shook it, and said in a low voice, "I'm John, and, as you guessed, I am positive."

"Nice meeting you, John. You can feel at ease. I don't think that there is even a single pure here."

"How can everybody here be so cheerful?" John wondered, looking at the couples dancing and laughing.

"You have been tested recently, right?"

"Right. Only a few days ago. How did you know?" John asked in surprise.

"You look depressed, and I can tell that you're confused. Besides, you don't know anybody here. Positives who have been around for a while and have come to terms with the situation get back to 'business as usual' and live a normal life."

"A normal life ..." John repeated bitterly. "How can you talk about 'a normal life' when you are not normal?"

"No problem. I found out that I was positive five years ago. Today, I go to work, go out with girls, and have fun, just like before. I don't let the limitations imposed on us keep me from enjoying life. You'll see that you will also learn to come to terms with them."

"I'm sure I'm capable of getting used to it. That's not the problem. The problem is that I don't want to get used to it."

"Shh ... don't say things like that out loud. Coming to terms with your limitations is an important part of your duties as a positive. Only on this condition will society suffer your presence. If you become labeled as a 'rebel positive,' it may be very dangerous." John sensed that David meant every word he had said.

"I don't understand. The rights of thought and freedom of speech were not among the ones that have been taken away from me."

"No. At least, not officially. However, the government does not like rebels, and those unwilling to accept their reduced social standing are viewed as a real threat to public order. I've heard many stories about rebel positives who have disappeared without a trace. Although most cases have not been corroborated, people who know their way about don't dare make such statements out loud."

"I can't believe my ears," said John. He felt a chill running down his spine. "Do you mean ..."

"Just a second," David checked him. "Why don't we take a nice little walk outside? It's a lovely night, and this place is stuffy."

David's expression left no room for doubt that he wouldn't go on talking in the club. John nodded, paid for his drink, and followed David on his way out.

Outside, David walked quickly, chatting about the weather and the stars, and every minute or so, he turned back and checked the empty street. After five minutes, he slowed down and turned to John, speaking in an undertone.

"I hope you understood why I didn't want to go on talking in the bar. The police always keep undercover agents in clubs frequented by positives, and certain conversations are better not held there."

"You're starting to sound like some revolutionary or something." John smiled at him.

"I'm no revolutionary, but, like you, I am not one of those who think that our inferior status is something we should take lying down."

"But what can we do? It's the law."

A young couple approached them in the otherwise deserted street. David kept silent until their paths crossed, and they got sufficiently far away. When the couple disappeared behind a corner, he went on explaining.

"Do you know what Andania is?"

"I heard about it. Isn't that some settlement in New Australia?"

"It's much more than a mere settlement. It is an independent state established in New Australia by positives and for positives. In Andania, every positive can live a full life based on equal rights."

"But, as far as I know, New Australia is a primitive and dangerous place, and the opportunities for a civilized life there are quite limited."

"This is part of the disinformation that the government spreads among us. In Andania, you'll find the best scientists and a quality population living an independent life. The New Nations Organization maintains extensive commercial ties with Andania because of the sophisticated electronic elements manufactured there, using the rare metals found in New Australia's mines. But the NNO can't impose their laws there, so they prefer to keep quiet about Andania as much as possible. For instance, they don't want you to know that positives get married there and raise families, if they so desire, with pure citizens."

"Are you serious?"

"Dead serious."

"And what about all the stories about the dangers and the wars that plague New Australia?"

"Those are facts, but the problems with the original settlers don't stop the positive population from developing a great society. Andania is indeed a country of pioneers, and dangers are attached to that. But on the other hand, a positive can live a free life there."

"Mmm…"

"Andania has an Interests Office here, which, among other

activities, provides information to people who wish to consider emigrating to Andania. This is the address," said David, handing John a small plastic card with an address printed on it. "You may want to visit them and hear about the options."

"If it's so good, why aren't you there?"

"I am there, in principle. I am with the Interests Office and recruit positives who wish to live a life of freedom, like you. When I feel my work is done here, I'll take the first ship to Andania."

John stood on the sidewalk, his mind in turmoil from the thought of a renewed freedom. On the other hand, a decision to emigrate to Andania would signify the end of his life, as he knew it now, including all the safety and convenience.

"I ... I don't know. I'll think about it."

"Don't hurry. There is no pressure of time. Sleep on it, and if you feel like checking out the options–without any obligation–you can call the office and come for an introductory meeting."

"I can't promise anything. I'll think about it," John murmured.

"Don't miss the opportunity," David concluded.

During the week after the meeting with David, John kept his usual routine and forgot all about Andania and the plastic card with the address in his wallet. At the end of that week, their home bustled with feverish preparations for John's mother's birthday party, to which all her best friends and family had been invited. On the birthday eve, John was in the sitting room reading a new book when the phone rang. His Aunt Claire's voice sounded at the other end of the line.

"Oh, hi, Aunt Claire. How are you?"

"Unfortunately, not so well. I called to tell your mother I won't be able to attend her birthday party tomorrow. I've got the flu. Will you wish her a happy birthday for me?"

"Oh, I'm sorry to hear that. Get well, Aunt Claire."

"Yes," said his aunt and hung up.

John turned around and saw his father standing in the doorway.

"That was Aunt Claire, Dad. She says that she's very sorry, but she's sick and won't be able to come to the party. A pity, but we'll party without her."

"There will be no party, John," his father said in a tired voice. "Nobody's coming."

"What do you mean?"

"I mean that your aunt is the last one to call. Everybody else already said that they won't be coming. One is sick, another one had to go on a sudden trip, and I can't remember what excuses the others made."

John walked away from the telephone, sat in the armchair, and closed his book. Then he looked straight at his father.

"It's because of me, isn't it? Because I'm positive, our relatives and friends are ashamed to come to our house."

"They are stupid. Narrow-minded. Ignore them; they don't deserve your attention. Let them stay away. Who cares?"

"Thanks, Dad, but it's my fault."

"Don't talk nonsense! Nothing is your fault. You didn't choose to be positive." His father's anger at the world was evident in his voice.

"I'm not at fault for what happened, but I'm responsible for what will happen now. I need to think ... forgive me," John added, walking to his room without looking back.

John sat on his bed for a long time and thought about his situation. Only now did he realize that his brothers hadn't called him and hadn't come home to support him since he had tested positive. His mother, whose love for John was beyond doubt, walked the house like a ghost of herself and barely spoke to anybody. His strong and proud father moved around with shoulders bent by the burden of keeping the family united, at least outwardly.

It took him a while, but eventually, his confusion cleared up, and John knew what had to be done. He lifted the telephone receiver and dialed the number from the plastic card David had given to him.

"Andania's Interests Offices," a voice answered almost immediately. "What can we do for you?"

"I would like to come for an introductory meeting," John said.

"When would it be convenient for you?"

"May I come right away?" he asked.

The Andanian office's door was at the end of a long corridor in an old building that housed both offices and apartments. John might have missed it, but for a sign that identified it. A security guard opened the door and accompanied him to a small waiting room. After a brief interval, the door opened to admit a man about fifty years old, who introduced himself as the senior deputy of the Andanian Office's head.

"My name is Bander. Welcome," he said. "I understand that you asked for an urgent meeting. What's the rush?" he asked after he and John had seated themselves near a small table in a windowless room. A glass of cold water had been placed before John.

"I ... I don't know. You must forgive me if I sound confused, but I don't know exactly what I expect from you. Someone–David is his name–said that he works for you. He suggested that I should come here."

"Yes, John. We know a little about you. David reported your meeting to us. You are a computer programmer, right?"

"Right."

"I've certainly got good opportunities to offer you, but first things first ..." The door opened, and a young woman in a white robe walked in. "Will you agree to let us take a sample of your blood? This office works for positives only, and we must verify that you test positive."

"I have no objection," said John as he rolled up his sleeve, "but I don't understand the need for this. I took the test a short while ago, and I am positive."

"The reason," said Bander, "is that we want to ensure that no pure ones infiltrate us pretending to be positive. Some extremist organizations that work against us may want to infiltrate our ranks. Perhaps the police may also have an interest in it. We will have the results within fifteen minutes," he added as the woman left the room with the blood sample.

"Okay," said John. "But meanwhile, do you mind telling me what this is all about?" He buttoned his shirt and waited for Bander to speak.

"Of course. As you know, we formally represent the interests of Andania here on Earth. Anyone who wishes or considers the possibility of emigrating to Andania has to come through us. We will check his record and find a suitable job so that he will fit in immediately upon his arrival in Andania. We are also here to help those who need to wind up their affairs–for instance, to sell property–and do everything we can to make things easier for him or her. Some have no money, and we lend them an initial sum to help them settle in Andania. Do you have any particular problem?"

"No. I don't own much property, and the little I have can remain with my parents–but wait! I haven't decided yet that I want to consider moving to Andania. I think we're rushing things."

Bander got up.

"Of course. Here, look first at a movie that illustrates life in Andania. Later, we can talk about the details."

The lights went off as an image appeared on the wall. The movie was a short promotional film. The first frame showed an aerial view of a metropolis in a broad valley–Andania City. The view panned toward smaller settlements at the edge of the enormous valley, between twenty to forty miles from the city's edge. A voice explained in each of those settlements, a few scores of families lived. There, vegetables and cattle were grown to supply the demand of the inhabitants of the city.

A map appeared beside the picture, and arrows moved on it as the narrator's voice explained the geography of the Andanian Valley. Its furthest settlements were found a few hundred miles from Andania City, and the coast provided a rich and varied seafood supply. The camera moved on to the end of the valley, flew above a chain of high mountains, and reached an immense, endless-looking plateau dotted with several settlements. The narrator explained that those were towns in which the original inhabitants of New Australia–the so-called Newists–lived. Those were descendants of the criminals exiled from Earth in the past– heirs to thieves, murderers, and rogues. They maintained a low living level, and a few worked in the mines operated by the New Nations Organization. Many of them, however, were bums who had never worked a day in their lives.

The Newists had an ongoing conflict with the citizens of Andania that had started on the very first day the positives had settled in the valley. All attempts on the part of the Andanian pioneers to convince them that cooperating would only bring advantages to everybody produced no results. Also, although most of the planet was empty, the Newists refused to come to terms with the pioneers' presence. They resented the higher level of life and the better technical expertise of the Andanians. This led to armed confrontations and victims from both sides. There was no sign that the Newists would consider anything other than keeping up the conflict, although the level of hostilities had been low for a few years.

"Are they ... the Newists ... as savage as they sound?" John asked when the movie ended.

"Yes," said Bander gravely, "but that's not too bad if you are organized to handle the problem like we are in Andania. You must relate to it as a natural calamity, like the rain or the heat."

"Mmm ... "

The door opened again, and the woman in the white robe approached Bander and whispered something in his ear. Then she left without looking at John.

"Welcome, John," said Bander, smiling at him. "You passed the test. You are D-positive."

"Yes, I knew that."

"Now it's official. Now we can talk about the details of your emigration to Andania."

"Hey, don't push me! I'm not emigrating yet."

"You will."

"But, I told you ..."

"You wouldn't be sitting here if you weren't ready to emigrate."

John stared at him in silence. He knew that Bander was right.

CHAPTER 4

Dana gazed into John's face. She didn't prod him to continue his story and, instead, waited patiently. John swallowed once or twice, playing with his knife and fork. The food was good, but he had let his mind wander so much that he couldn't remember exactly what he had eaten.

"You know," he said quietly, "you are the first to hear the whole story, and when I tell it, I understand for the first time that it is reality–more than I've ever realized before. That's it–my former life is behind me for good."

"I know the feeling. It's like when someone you love dies. When my grandma died, I didn't tell anybody at school because I felt that in that way, she'd stay closer to me–more ... how should I say–more alive if I didn't admit that she had died. A month later, I told my best friend about it, and only then did I start to grieve. But the good news is that it'll get easier for you now that you've admitted to it openly."

"You may be right, but I still struggle to grasp. So little time has passed."

"What happened after you visited the Andanian mission?"

"I went back home and spoke to my parents. I told them I had decided to try my luck in Andania and would be going soon. Bander, the man from the Andanian office, said that this ship would leave in a few days and that I could leave on it or the next one four weeks later. I decided to go right away ... I think my mind was made up before leaving his office.

"The relief at home was immense. My parents were sad to part from me, but they understood that I had made the right choice for them and me. Even my brothers showed up and came to support me—I think they worried that I might change my mind and stay. They wanted to make sure that I was really going.

"The following morning, I went to work and submitted my resignation. The Division Head summoned me to his office and gave me his blessing. He also permitted me to withdraw my salary and all the money due to me immediately, and that's how I could buy a first-class ticket on this ship."

"A good investment," Dana remarked, smiling.

"A great investment," commented John, "seeing that I met you."

An embarrassed silence ensued until John went on, speaking fast.

"I've seen the conditions in tourist class. I don't know how one can suffer through such a long flight, and I think most emigrants have tourist-class tickets. Maybe they're the smart ones, not squandering their money on a flashy ticket but saving it for tomorrow, but I wanted to feel that I was leaving Earth with a raised head ... going in style, you know?"

"Good for you," said Dana, "but you are kind of wasting the advantages of a first-class ticket when you sit all day alone, doing nothing. You must take advantage of the luxury for which you have paid."

"I'm doing it right now. I'm using your services," John smiled at her.

"At your service always, kind sir," Dana answered, bowing

slightly without getting up from her chair. "And how did you spend the last days before the flight?"

"I mainly used them to wind up personal affairs. I went through my things and threw away a lot of stuff, especially letters and souvenirs from Maya. Then, I selected a few memories I wanted to bring with me. As you know, the weight of allowed baggage is limited, and I had to be choosy. The rest I gave to my family and the few people I could still call my friends. I left my room empty, free of anything that might remind someone of me. That's how I wanted it to be–a home sterilized from John, which will not remind my parents of me all the time. If they want to think of me, they can open the photo album, and maybe we'll talk over the videophone now and then if I have the money for it."

The waiter placed two coffee cups before them, and John glanced at them with surprise. He didn't recall having ordered coffee, and if asked what stage of the dinner he had reached, it was doubtful that he could have given the correct answer. His mind was immersed in past images, as it had been since he boarded the ship.

"And what are your plans now?" Dana asked.

"The truth is that I haven't bothered planning my future yet. I've been too busy thinking about the past. But you know, I think this is a covert form of self-pity, and I must put an end to it. From now on, we won't talk about the past, but only about the future," said John excitedly.

"So, what will you be doing in Andania?"

"I guess I'll work in my field. Bander explained that when you reach Andania, you must take a one-week basic training, which helps every immigrant integrate quickly and naturally into the Andanian society. After the initial week, they will offer me a few positions suitable for my talent, from which I will choose. I understand Andania is in great need of computer programmers at my level. It won't be difficult for me to find an interesting job. To be quite honest," he added, surprised by his own words, "I don't care."

"What do you mean?"

"In the past," he explained, "I used to think that work means everything in your life. I felt I was being measured by my professional achievements and that I would be a lesser person if I let myself slip back from the forefront of professional development. Now I realize that many things, such as freedom, equality, and pride, are much more important than work. After you test D-positive, you treat all those things as axiomatic until you discover they are not within your reach."

Dana took the last sip of her coffee, patted her lips lightly with her napkin, and put it on the table. Then she gave John a long, reflective look.

"You said 'no more talking about the past,'" Dana said severely. "If you've finished your coffee, there is something that I'd like to show you."

"What?"

"Something nice."

"Is it far?"

"Why? Do you have other plans for the evening?"

"Actually, I don't."

"Let's go then," she said, rising from her chair.

They left the restaurant and walked long, deserted corridors until they reached a part of the ship unfamiliar to John. They climbed winding stairs at the end of one corridor leading to another short passageway ending at a door. A sign on the door said, "This door must be locked during take-off and landing and when the bridge faces the sun."

"What is this?"

"You'll see. I don't want to spoil the surprise."

Dana opened the door, and an intense light turned on automatically. They walked into a strange, long, narrow room with arched walls. Along the wall at the door's right, John saw a low seat made of square cushions that could have accommodated eight or ten people. Dana sat on it and motioned him to sit beside her. The distance between them and the wall in front of them, in their seated position, was no more than six feet.

"What is this place?" John asked with curiosity.

"You'll see in a moment. Close your eyes now—no cheating! I'll turn off the lights and tell you when to open them. Are you ready?"

"Yes, yes," answered John.

"No peeking ... now you can open your eyes," said Dana after a few seconds.

John opened his eyes and was astonished by what he saw. The room was in total darkness, but the wall before them had turned transparent, and a million stars shone through it. It was a spectacular view, like he had only seen in movies. But unlike the movies, John felt the stars' presence as if he were floating in them. He held tightly onto his seat in an attempt to overcome the sensation of hovering that had taken hold of his senses. It felt like he was about to detach from his seat and fly toward the stars.

"What's that?" he asked with open amazement. "Is it a window?"

"Sort of, but not exactly," Dana said cryptically. Her voice betrayed the satisfaction that she derived from her successful surprise. "The wall you saw coming in is a screen wall that gives a representation of what the area in space would look like if we were moving at regular speed through real space – don't ask me more because that's all I know," she added, laughing at John's puzzled expression.

"It's amazing," said John, without attempting to disguise his excitement at the view.

"Yes, it's something special. I come here a lot after my shift and could sit here forever, watching the stars appear and disappear before my eyes. But being here all by yourself is not as fun."

John sat, relaxed, and looked around. What a spectacular

vision! His heart beat heavily as if trying to push out all his burdens to make space for the stars. His left hand met with Dana's. Perhaps it was an accidental touch, or maybe he had subconsciously extended his hand toward her. He didn't care how it had happened ... her hand felt good; it was a warm spot in the cold room, and he held on to it. They sat together, looking at the screen, hypnotized. Time lost its meaning, and John kept still, praying in his heart for this moment, never to end.

"I'm cold," Dana whispered.

"Come closer," answered John, "you'll feel warmer."

"Thanks," she said, and he felt the warmth of her body against his. Her free hand held his elbow.

"Why are we whispering?" John asked. "There's nobody here."

"I don't know," she whispered back, "but it seems unnatural to speak loudly here. Maybe it's the stars."

He pressed her hand gently and didn't answer. Instead, he kept gazing straight ahead at the stars.

"John ..." she began.

"Yes?"

"Mmm ... nothing."

"No, what did you want to say?"

"Doesn't matter ... Hey, look," she added excitedly, pointing at a comet that left a long fire tail streaking across a corner of the screen.

"Amazing!" said John.

"Amazing," Dana agreed.

They sat again in silence. John's senses were split between the inebriating view of the stars flying before his eyes, the soft touch of Dana's body, and the faint scent of her perfume.

"Dana ..."

"Yes?"

"Thank you. For all this."

"I'm only doing my job, sir," said Dana. The smile at the corner of her lips showed her pleasure.

"I'll say that you're very committed to your work, then," John kidded back and then became silent again.

"Why don't you look at me?" Dana asked after a while.

"I'm looking at the stars," said John defensively. He suddenly felt a great tension and an uncontrollable fear of his unexpected proximity to Dana.

"Look at me," she ordered.

Slowly, almost painfully, John turned his head, looked at her face, and then into her eyes. In slow motion but with apparent inevitability, John felt his head get closer and closer to Dana's until their lips met. In a split second, the stars were forgotten. They became the center of the universe, and everything else ceased to matter.

The touch of Dana's lips was electrifying, soft, and gentle, all at the same time. *She's not like Maya;* the thought popped into John's head when his mind resumed some level of functioning. *She's something else. She's ... real.*

John managed to detach himself a little from Dana by a strong exercise of will. "This is not a good idea, you know," he whispered desperately.

"It's a great idea," she retorted, keeping her eyes shut. "Don't stop."

"I don't think that we should develop a relationship. It wouldn't be fair on my part, I am positive, and I have no right to barge into your life like this."

"I'm not marrying you tomorrow morning. We have a whole week before us; a week is an eternity. Stop overthinking."

"I'm not like that. What will you think of me? I'm staying in New Australia, and you're returning to Earth. I don't want you to think I'm taking advantage of you or that ..."

"John!" she interrupted the flow of words, pulling him toward her.

"Yes?"

"You talk too much."

"I ..."

"Are you going to kiss me or not?"

John knew that any attempt to resist was doomed to failure. He didn't want to resist. For the first time in ages, he felt genuine and unreserved warmth from this young woman. Tomorrow is another day, he thought. Tomorrow, he'd think what to do. Meanwhile, time was precious and shouldn't be wasted ... at least, not the little time the future held for them.

The last days of the flight felt like a dream to John. He spent every free moment with Dana, and their bond grew strong. He allowed himself, against his better judgment, to become involved in a close relationship with her—much closer than he had ever experienced with Maya, the only serious girlfriend he had ever had back on Earth.

Dana was funny but knew how to be serious when he felt like baring his soul to her about some burden emerging from the past. She radiated warmth but did not choke him, and every time they parted, even if only for a short time, he counted the minutes to their next meeting.

But eventually, the flight came to an end. The passengers were asked to make their final arrangements eight hours before landing. John and Dana sat together for the last time in the star view room, which would soon be locked for the landing.

"So, what now?" John asked after a long silence.

"Now we get ready for landing," she answered simply.

"No, I mean ... what about us?"

"We talked about it. I have two weeks' leave in New Australia before the ship returns to Earth. Why should we worry about the future now? Two weeks is an eternity."

"For you, everything is an eternity," John complained.

"And rightly so. Look at us—it seems like we've known each

other forever, and we've been together only one week. After my two weeks in Andania, we'll talk and decide what we should do. Maybe you'll be fed up with me and counting the hours before I leave by then."

"More likely that you'll be tired of me."

"You men are not reliable. You know, here on the ship, it's something else. You are alone, bored, and without friends, and I look like a good thing to you. Later, on the ground, you may have different ideas."

"That's who you think I am?" John asked, astonished at the idea that Dana could suspect him of being a person like that.

Dana snuggled a little closer to him.

"No, but I can't be sure, can I? I haven't known you long enough and don't know what to expect. If my feminine instinct got it right, you're not the kind of man who will run away when you no longer need a relationship that could complicate your life."

"I'm certainly not like that!" John said emphatically. "But I'm the one who is complicating your life, not the other way around."

"Have I complained?"

"Not yet. But I know that the carefree days are behind us."

"Do you always worry so much?"

"Only when I care, and I care about you."

"Mm ... 'care about you' sounds like a prelude to the proposal 'let's remain good friends.' Is that what you're going to tell me? That you feel like a 'friend' to me?"

"No, certainly not!" John answered with sudden panic. Could Dana not have fathomed the depth of his feelings toward her?

"Then tell me what you feel?"

"I ..." John started and stopped.

"Yes?" she prompted him.

"You know ..." he answered with embarrassment.

"No, I don't. I need you to tell me."

John held her waist tighter and gazed into her eyes.

"I'm sure that after one week, you know exactly how I feel."

"Do you know what I feel?" Dana eyed him, inscrutable as she pushed him a little away from her.

"I think you feel like I do."

"You know, I believe the eight hours we have left won't be enough for you to tell me you love me. Why is it so hard?"

"It's not hard at all. It isn't hard to love you."

"Then tell me."

"I just did."

"No. Tell me, 'I love you.'"

John looked again into her eyes.

"I-love-you-Dana," he finally said in one breath and almost in a whisper.

"All right then. That wasn't so hard, right?"

John didn't answer. Instead, he kept looking at her and asked, "And you? What do you feel?"

"I feel that I've met the best person I could ever dream of meeting and that I'll never love somebody else as much as I love you. You only have one serious flaw."

"That I'm D-positive?" John asked sadly.

"No, that you talk too much."

"We'll fix that right away," John answered, smiling, and pulled her gently toward him.

CHAPTER 5

The sun was high in the sky, and the cargo area around the ship reflected blinding light, much stronger than what John ever saw on Earth, but maybe that was only a subjective feeling caused by the extended stay within the enclosed walls of the ship. John stood at the first-class compartment exit door leading into a small building through a long plastic sleeve. He contemplated the area through its transparent top and sidewalls. The small size of the spaceport surprised him—the one on Earth was huge. The ship waited at the end of one of many large structures connected directly to the main terminal, and to John, the place looked unreal. He had not imagined that the Andanian counterpart of the airport would look so shabby.

Far away, above the building's roof, he saw a distant chain of mountains, or perhaps only high hills, partly hidden by clouds. A pleasant spring breeze played with his hair, and he enjoyed its refreshing touch after the stuffy air he had breathed inside the ship. The feeling was one of rebirth, like seeing the world for the first time.

The tourist-class passengers were already streaming out through a lower passageway. For the first time, John realized how many people had been on the ship–certainly hundreds–although he neither saw nor felt their presence throughout the trip. Dana stood beside him, looking excited.

"I must go back inside," she said at last. "Before we can disembark, the crew must take care of procedures that will take a few hours."

"How are we going to meet, then?"

"I'll be at the Andania City Towers Hotel, where the crew will stay. When you're through with immigration procedures, come over to the hotel and look for me there, or if you get there early, wait for me."

"Okay," John agreed. "I guess it'll take time before I'm done with all the bureaucracy anyway."

"Do you know where you'll be staying?" Dana asked.

"No," said John. "The Andanian representatives, back on Earth, told me everything has been taken care of and that all matters will be handled from here. It's so convenient that I don't have to worry about anything."

"See you soon, then?" Dana asked.

"As soon as possible," John answered.

She took a step toward the ship, and he watched her. It was hard for him to part from Dana, even for a few hours, without softening the separation with a close touch that would keep him going until their next meeting. But this time, too many people were around. Dana never told him about her limitations as a crew member, but John assumed that her superiors would frown at her romantic involvement with a passenger. He took a quick look around and noticed some crew members in the vicinity, so he resigned himself to parting from Dana with a wave of his hand. Then, he turned around and stepped into the plastic sleeve that led to the terminal.

Inside the building, John stood patiently beside a massive pile of luggage until he recognized his bags and received a slip of paper with an identifying number. This having been taken care of, he was allowed to pass into a large hall where a long line of passengers waited before entering a room. Surprisingly, almost everybody in the queue was young—most of them in their twenties. Although most passengers were men, he also saw quite a few women.

John looked at the line in despair ... at least two hundred people queued up ahead of him, but soon, the line grew longer behind him, which made him feel a little better. After a few minutes, the man who stood before John turned back. He was more or less John's age but thinner and at least a head and a half taller than him. His trimmed hair was a bright red.

"My name is Barak," he volunteered, "and what is your name?"

"I'm John Hektor."

"Please to meet you, John," said Barak, extending a hand for him to shake.

John took it and shook it. He felt a great relief realizing that, in his new land, one could make the acquaintance of a stranger without having to worry lest he might turn out to be a pure one who looks down at you, knowing that you are positive. He had never felt so free as in that moment.

"Likewise," he said, smiling.

"Long queue, isn't it?" Barak commented.

"Very long, but it can't be helped," said John resignedly.

"Are you here all by yourself?" Barak asked.

"Yes, although I have a girlfriend in the ship's crew."

"Is she going to stay in Andania?"

"We don't know yet. We'll see," John said wistfully.

They fell into silence, having exhausted all the conversation topics available to strangers who had just met, and Barak turned back. No more than twenty people waited ahead of them now, and John watched how each stood, in turn, before a clerk who sat behind a counter asked him a brief question; then, he walked to one of the rooms—apparently the one that fitted the answer they gave. Barak's turn came quickly, and he disappeared into the room at the right of the counter. Finally, John's turn came.

"Name?" asked the clerk.

"John Hektor," he answered.

"Passport," said the clerk, and John handed it to him.

"Room number two," said the clerk, giving his passport back to him without lifting his head from the papers on his desk. John could have sworn that he had not looked at him even once.

Room number two was the same one Barak had been sent to, and John approached it quickly. In the room, he saw several desks manned by other clerks. Barak sat in front of a desk next to an exit door, beside which stood a man in uniform whom John took to be an airport policeman. When John entered the room, the policeman pointed with his finger at one of the desks without speaking. John seated himself before a clerk immersed in a pile of documents. He saw blocks of blank forms to the clerk's right and a pile of filled-out ones to his left. Each form had a passport attached to it, and John assumed that he had to hand his to the clerk, which he did.

After a few seconds, the clerk glanced at John. He looked no older than twenty and seemed tired.

"Welcome to Andania," he said, but his voice lacked the ring of genuine pleasure.

"Thank you," said John. He was taken aback by the clerks' behavior in the terminal–he had been looking forward to a much warmer welcome. Throughout his flight, he had been trying to picture his arrival at his new homeland and had always imagined a ceremonial welcome, perhaps with the participation of a local personality. Andania's representatives on Earth had stressed John's importance to them, given his special professional skills. They had repeatedly told him how lucky Andania was to be able to count him among its sons.

The clerk took the passport that John had handed to him, tore a set of forms from the pile on his right, and started to fill them in. Now and then, he would stop and ask mechanically for additional information without looking at John.

"Chronic diseases?" he asked.

"None," said John.

"Have you ever undergone any surgery?"

"No," John answered.

The clerk continued filling in the forms, extracting additional details from his passport and a list he held before him. Five minutes later, he pushed the set of documents toward John. "Sign here and here, please ... and here on the back also," he added after John signed as requested.

The clerk stapled John's passport to the forms and threw them atop the pile to his left. A few clicks on his keyboard produced a small, green booklet from a printer under the desk. John was surprised to see his picture on the booklet's first page.

"This is your ID from now on. Don't lose it because there is little you can do without it, and obtaining a replacement takes time. Your passport goes to the Ministry of the Interior. You'll be issued an Andanian one instead, should you have to travel to the New Nations territories. Questions?"

"Yes, look here, I have some questions ..."

"I suggest that you keep them for some other time," interrupted the clerk, who fixed his gaze on the screen on his desk. "I see that the next transport is almost full and is leaving right now. If you move quickly, you may catch it."

John had many questions to ask but also wanted to get to the city as quickly as possible to get himself organized and meet with Dana. The temptation to go quickly overcame the need to ask questions, and he got up fast.

"Thanks for the tip," he told the clerk. "Where should I go?"

"Go out through the red door there," said the clerk, pointing at the door at the edge of the room. "Quick!"

"Thank you very much," John threw at him and ran toward the door that bore the sign "Exit."

The red door opened into a backyard where John saw a truck with its engine running, beside which stood another policeman. On the truck, about thirty young men sat in two rows facing each other. Next to the back door sat his newly made friend, Barak, who waved at him.

"Get on quickly, boy," said the policeman.

"What about my baggage?" John asked, worried.

"Don't worry," the policeman said, "it's being taken care of. Nothing will be lost, but be careful not to lose the receipt they gave you. Now get up on the truck quickly 'cause it's moving."

John handed Barak the little bag where he kept his documents and the small money he had left. Barak put it on the seat beside him, then extended a hand to John and pulled him into the truck. He barely got seated when the policeman closed the truck's back door and shouted something to the driver. The truck moved immediately with a jerk that almost caused John to fall onto Barak. By the time he managed to sit correctly, they had already left the terminal area and were running along a narrow road.

The truck was bare, mustard-colored, and covered only with a coarse fabric of the same color; its edges flapped vigorously in the wind, making a deafening noise. John had a good view of the area behind them from where he sat but couldn't see where they were heading. The terminal looked like an isolated building in the middle of a dusty plane, almost a desert, placed at the end of the straight, bumpy road on which the truck traveled recklessly.

"Where are we going?" John yelled to Barak, trying to overcome the engine's loud noise, the flapping fabric, and the wind.

"They said we're going to receive basic training," Barak shouted.

"What's that?" John asked, his voice barely audible over the noise.

"I asked," Barak answered, "but they said we'll be told when we get there."

"How long is the trip?"

"About an hour and a half," said Barak.

"An hour and a half?" John was amazed. "The city can't be that far from the airport. Are you sure?"

"That's what they said. Let's wait and see," said Barak philosophically. "Meanwhile, I'll catch a nap. I'm wasted."

John watched enviously how Barak curled up, his head resting on his backpack, and in seconds fell asleep. He, in contrast, was too excited to even think about sleeping. This was a new, different world, and he knew a long time would pass before getting used to his adoptive home. He sat straight and drank in with his eyes every detail, near or far, that he managed to glean. Not for the first time, he felt like a character in a movie.

The truck came to a sudden halt, and John woke up in a panic. The day's excitement and fatigue had taken their toll, and he had fallen heavily asleep like most of his fellow travelers. It was almost completely dark outside, and John wondered what the local time was. He didn't know enough about New Australia to be able to estimate the time by the light. He knew the day lasted twenty-six Earth hours, making working synchronously with the New Nations a little challenging. The local people had undoubtedly found ways to deal with this difference.

The driver cut the engine, and a sudden silence ensued. Someone outside approached the truck's back door and removed the stoppers that held it up so that it turned on its hinges and fell with a loud thud.

"Jump down everybody, quickly!" a voice shouted from outside.

John picked up his bag and looked at Barak, who blinked, trying to wake up.

"They are not polite," John commented. "I plan to have a few words about it when I meet the person responsible for our reception."

The truck stood almost empty now, and Barak urged John to speed up. "Come on, let's get moving," he said. "It's never a good idea to be last." He jumped down from the truck and waited for John, who ostentatiously descended very slowly.

"Everybody! Form groups of three here before me," yelled the unknown voice. "Come on! You're not old ladies. Start moving!"

"Who do they think they are?" said John, outraged. "I don't understand why they think they can talk to us like that."

"What did you expect?" Barak asked. "I've never been in the army before, but I'm sure we'll have to get used to the discipline."

"The army?" John asked. "What does this have to do with the army? Does the army run the immigration procedure?"

"You really don't know?" Barak asked with surprise.

"What don't I know?"

"Did you read the papers you signed in that room at the terminal?"

"I assumed that those were immigration papers. Why?"

"Because those were draft papers," Barak said simply. "Welcome to the army of Andania. Now, let's go and follow orders before we get into trouble."

John followed Barak as if in a dream. The army? He didn't mean to join the military. It was a mistake. He would have to explain it to them.

They reached the others, who stood in three groups, and Barak pulled John into the ranks. "Listen," he whispered, "until we understand where we are and learn the rules, it's better not to stand at the ends of the lines or in the first line, where you get noticed. It's the golden rule with a street cat like me—never make yourself conspicuous." John didn't answer. He was in too great a shock to say anything.

They had formed ranks on a concrete surface located between two low buildings. Before them stood a lean officer who wore an unfamiliar uniform.

"My name is Captain Eton," he said in an authoritative low voice. "I am the commander of this company, and you owe total loyalty to me. My soldiers are required to carry out my orders precisely and without questions."

He spoke as he walked along the first row, gazing into the faces of his new soldiers, scanning them as if to learn their features by heart.

"You are not soldiers. Not yet," he continued. "You are nothing! You aren't worth anything. But I'll make soldiers out of you. The best possible soldiers. This base–this army–has many laws and rules. I don't expect you to learn all of them immediately, so let's start with a few simple ones."

A tense silence fell on the ranks. The young men, already confused by finding themselves standing in a lighted yard immersed in the darkness around, listened tensely, worried lest any slight lack of attention might make them miss some vital piece of information. Captain Eton walked from right to left and left to right, never stopping. His high, shiny boots hit the concrete rhythmically, making a loud thud at each step. Despite the cold air of the desert night, his sleeves were neatly rolled up. John stood motionless, cold and weary, waiting impatiently for the tirade to end.

"Law number one," yelled Captain Eton after a brief pause. "You never speak to an officer unless first addressed. If you wish to speak, you raise your hand and wait for permission to be granted. Understood?"

A choir of "yes" came from the ranks.

"Here you say 'yes, sir,' and you all answer together, not in installments," said Captain Eton, sounding angry. "Understood?"

This time, the answer, "Yes, sir!" came clearly and loudly, and the captain nodded in approval.

"Law number two," he continued. "When an officer speaks to you, you stand at attention at three paces from him. Clear?"

"Yes, sir," the ranks answered.

"Good. Now, here's what's going to happen today," explained the captain. At last, he stopped his menacing walk, stood before them, and looked at them. "Behind you is the building of the supply unit. When we are through here, you'll receive basic equipment there. Afterward, you'll be shown your sleeping quarters. You have exactly two hours from now," he looked at his watch, "to organize. In two hours–dinner. You have twenty minutes to eat. After dinner, I'll start interviewing you in alphabetical order. You," said the captain, addressing a soldier in the first row, "what's your name?"

"Albert," answered the youth.

"I didn't hear you," said the captain.

"Albert," repeated the young man, louder.

"I can't hear you," the captain almost yelled.

Albert looked at the captain, disoriented. "Albert, sir," someone whispered from the ranks.

"Albert, sir," Albert repeated.

"Now I heard you," said the captain. "You'll be the cadet on duty of the company and will make a list of names of everybody. I want the list ready before I start with the interviews. Clear?"

"Yes, sir," answered the scared Albert.

"Good. Dismissed," said the captain as he turned on his heels and left.

The young men walked quickly toward the supply building. John turned to Barak.

"It's a nightmare," he said, "I'm not supposed to be here. I must get to the city. I'll go and talk to the captain."

"I don't recommend it," said Barak curtly. "He made himself very clear about what we are and are not allowed to do. And besides, later tonight, you'll have an interview with him and the opportunity to explain everything."

"You're right. It's a real scandal, the way they misled me. I'll explain to him that this was purely an administrative error, and it'll all come out right in the end," said John.

"Sure," Barak reassured him, "but I suggest you behave like everybody else and avoid getting into trouble. Let's go and get some basic equipment and find a decent room. With a little luck, we'll find adjacent beds and stay together."

John followed Barak willingly. In the short time since they had met, he had learned to like this practical young man. Even if it was only for this one night, he thought staying with him was better as long as they were together in the base. Being alone in that place wasn't pleasant, and making new friends when he was about to leave seemed pointless.

John walked beside Barak toward the supply unit with renewed optimism. The mistake they made at the terminal would undoubtedly waste him a full day, but tomorrow, he would be back in town. Dana was certainly asking herself what had become of him, he worried. He had to find a way to call her.

CHAPTER 6

John was cold. He was cold inside his uniform and his body. The cold was all he was able to think about. The world revolved around his frozen cheek, wet shirt and pants, and stiff boots that hurt his feet. But more than the pain, it was the loss of feeling at his fingertips that worried him.

The soldier before him stood in front of a fuming pot heated by a field heater that spat a blue gas flame. John stood silently—nobody raised his voice in the big tent, filled with frozen faces. He let the hot gases coming from the bottom of the pot flow around his body with almost sensual pleasure for a moment before floating away.

The clock said it was early morning, but the darkness inspired a deep night feeling. It had taken John's company almost two hours to erect the tent, laboring under incessant showers rendered harder by a freezing wind. At last, the tent stood on a slope next to the company's camp. The hilly ground was the only place in sight that hadn't been flooded and where a semi-dry spot was to be found.

Bivouacked in a tiny scout's tent, John had awakened from the cold in the middle of the night despite his exhaustion. Barak, his tentmate, wept quietly in his sleep, like a child lying scared in the dark.

"Barak!" John called. He was still confused by the unusual awakening.

"Ha ... who? What?" Barak mumbled.

"Wake up quickly!" John shook him. "You're soaking wet. Get up, get up!"

John lay on his side on the thin, soaked mattress, trying to light his pocket lamp, which was too wet to function. Heavy rain hit the tent with a loud sound. Outside, voices called out, and light illuminated the rows of tents. John tried to lift his backpack, which held all his precious belongings, but he soon realized that it was impregnated with water and had become too heavy. Resigned, he left it lying in a puddle of water.

"What's going on?" Barak asked in a panic. He sat up quickly and looked around him. "The place is flooded!" he announced as if noticing it for the first time.

"Thank you for letting me know," said John bitterly. "I'm wet from head to feet."

"So am I. It's bloody cold here."

Voices sounded close from the line of tents, and a familiar voice shouted, "Everybody out. Form groups of three." John recognized Sigmund's voice, the platoon sergeant. John crawled out of the low tent, feet first, and stood beside it. Barak came out after him, and they both hastened to reach the gathering around the sergeant. On his way, John checked his weapon, from which he never parted, even for a second. The gun was an automatic rifle made of stainless metal, and the rain couldn't damage it. John stood straight in the open without trying to hide from the rain. Since he was thoroughly wet, seeking cover wasn't much point.

"Quickly!" Sergeant Sigmund ordered without wasting time. "Go to the truck and unload the central tent. We'll set it up on this slope here. You three," he added, pointing to John and two other soldiers standing next to him, "take the pegs and start making supports for the corners. The rest come with me."

John welcomed the opportunity to move his body and find relief from the damp cold. He worked quickly, paying no attention to the fact that he kept hurting his frozen hands that barely managed to hold the pegs. The strong wind made things worse, and the central pole fell on them twice, dragging the heavy tent onto their heads. However, after a long struggle, they finally erected the tent, and John and the others found cover from the wind and rain. John was mildly surprised to discover how patiently he stood in line before the lifesaving pot of hot porridge. Still, he worried that this could mean the cold had finally induced in him a dangerous apathy.

The soldier in line before him moved aside at last, and John approached the pot to fill a bowl with the porridge. It was a tasteless paste except for the generously added sugar, which he would never have touched in his previous life. His previous life ... seemed so remote, even though it had all happened only three months before.

The porridge heated John's body quickly and forcefully. It traced a clear and burning path toward his stomach, and every inch by which it progressed brought a revival to his senses. John could have sworn that he felt his body thawing and life returning to his frozen limbs as he seated himself on a large rock that had become a convenient seat in the tent. He kept his face close to the bowl to avoid wasting even a little of the heat it gave off.

He knew that thinking about the cold was wrong—a kind of self-pity. In a few weeks, his world had been turned upside down three times. John had been forged into a resilient and fatalistic person. Strangely, he found some satisfaction in this fatalistic masochism that fed on his ability to withstand the blows that fate liked to deal him. How changed I am now, he thought, from the confused youth who had been unwillingly drafted into a foreign army. He remembered how naïve he was on that first day ...

John stood outside the little room where the captain interviewed his new soldiers. He wore a uniform made of coarse fabric that irritated his groin and made his whole body uncomfortable. The new boots bulged in all the wrong places, and, in general, he felt that nothing, including himself, was in the right place. He consoled himself that the nightmare would be over after the captain listened to his explanation. Everything would be behind him tomorrow, and he would laugh about it with Dana.

Other conscripts stood near him in groups of two or three and spoke in undertones. Some looked familiar and must have been on the same truck that had brought him to the base, but others had surely come on different trucks. Barak had already been interviewed and gone to their room to organize his equipment.

At last came John's turn, and he walked impatiently into the captain's office. The captain was seated behind a small desk, writing in a large notebook.

"Name?" the captain asked without looking up.

"My name is John Hektor," answered John, pointedly refraining from ending his sentence with the required "sir." He had decided beforehand that addressing the captain in that fashion would be inappropriate for someone who, like himself, was not supposed to be there, and John believed that the point was best made right away.

The captain stared at John, who stood negligently with his hands in his pockets.

"Attention!" ordered the captain in a dangerously low voice.

"But, I want to explain ..." John started to say, but a shout from the captain silenced him.

"Attention, I said!"

The captain's voice sounded so authoritative that John stood at attention without another word.

"What's your name, you said?"

"John Hektor, sir," John answered this time.

"You may sit down," said the captain, pointing his pen at the chair before his desk.

John sat straight, feeling embarrassed.

"Welcome to the company, John. I reviewed your file, and I must say it's very impressive. Not all my new soldiers are well-educated; we need high-quality soldiers to join us. I hope you will succeed here with us," he continued. John shifted uneasily in his seat. "Do you have any particular problem or question?"

"Yes, sir," said John, glad that he, at last, was getting to explain his situation. "I'm simply not supposed to be here. It's all a mistake, and I would like to sort it out so I can return to the city and move on."

"I don't understand," said the captain with surprise. He pushed toward John the form that he had signed. "Isn't this your signature?"

"Yes, absolutely," John answered heatedly, "but I didn't know I was signing enrollment papers. I was misled into believing that those were immigration forms, and that's why I didn't bother reading them. I'm here by mistake, you see?" He looked into the expressionless face before him and went on explaining. "I agreed with the Andanian representatives to the New Nations that I'd get a job in my field of expertise, which is important to Andania. It's inconceivable that I'm wasting my time here while I'm expected by those who require my services. So, can we arrange to give me a lift back to the city early tomorrow morning?" John concluded.

"I'm afraid that that's not so easy, boy," the captain answered with a softer note. "Didn't the representatives tell you that in Andania, service in the army is compulsory?"

"Yes, they told me there is such a service, but I'm not a child, and I have completed my studies, so I understand that it does not apply to me."

"Not exactly. Not exactly," said the captain, shaking his head. "Every Andanian citizen must go through basic training regardless of his age. We are a nation that lives in a dangerous neighborhood. We are pioneers; if you don't know the basics of self-defense, you become a burden on society. Therefore, there is a minimum of three months of basic training that everybody must get unless you are impaired."

A sudden panic got hold of John. "But ... but the representatives promised me that someone would be waiting for me and would take care of giving me a job immediately on arrival."

"That's one way of doing it," the captain agreed, "in which case you would have been called for basic training after six months at work. The two options have no big difference because you must spend the same time here in both cases. On the other hand, the option you have signed for allows you, if you want to and if we want you, to remain in the army after the three months of basic training. If you aren't willing to stay on, you'll be free to leave and work in your profession as planned. So you see, you aren't missing anything."

"But now ..." John started to say, "I can't. I've got something ... I must get back to the city."

"Waste no more words, boy. It's impossible, and it's not in my power either. Tomorrow morning, we leave for the training camp up in the mountains, and there's no way out for those who are here. I'm sorry," he added. He looked compassionately at John, who had slumped in his chair as if the ceiling had fallen on him. "But at least you should know that you have come to the best company, and your comrades are high-level people. You'll enjoy being here."

"Sir," John said with a trembling voice, "I've got a girlfriend who's waiting for me in the city and doesn't know what has become of me. She's certain to think that I have run away from her or that something terrible must have happened to me. She's returning to the New Nations with the ship that brought me here, and I must get in touch with her and explain what happened. I have to!"

The captain regarded John for a few seconds. When he spoke, it was clear that he understood his predicament.

"Listen, soldier," he said, "what I'm going to do is against all rules and laws, not to mention my specific instructions. Conscripts are not allowed to use the communication lines of this base. I'll deviate from my orders, but only this once," he warned him. "Come here tomorrow morning, after the line-up, when the platoon sergeant orders everybody to stand by the trucks. I'll be here and arrange a communication line into the city from this room."

"I'm deeply grateful, sir," said John with feeling, "I am truly grateful. Really."

"You'll have a chance to prove it yet," said the captain simply. "Tell me what number you need to call so we won't waste time in the morning."

"I need to call the Andania City Tower Hotel, sir," said John.

"All right. Go now. I've got a lot more work," said the captain. John turned and walked toward the door, and then the captain called him. "John!"

"Yes, sir?"

"In this army, you salute when you come in and when you leave."

"Sorry, sir," John apologized. He saluted clumsily, and the captain answered, bringing two fingers negligently to his head.

"Tell the next one to come in," he ordered.

The captain's head was already immersed in his notebook, and John left silently.

The following day, John woke up with difficulty from a surprisingly deep sleep. The room where he slept contained ten beds, side by side. It was a bare concrete building with a window next to the door located at each end. Barak, who had magically organized his bed and equipment in the brief time John had been gone, welcomed him with a smile and heard the news.

"I'm glad that you're not leaving. I mean," he added quickly, "of course, I'm sorry that you can't go back to the city, but I'm glad you are staying with me. I think that, together, we'll have a better time here."

"And what do you plan to do after the three months of training?" asked John.

"Oh, I don't know. I may want to stay in the army, but it's too early to think about it now. Let's wait and see."

The lights went off, and John had to get acquainted with his military equipment in the dark with the help of the little light that came in through the windows. He did so slowly and as silently as possible, trying not to wake his comrades, who were all already fast asleep. Once he completed his initial arrangements, he decided that the wisest move would be to get into bed right away. He didn't know how many hours of sleep they would get but did not expect to be allowed a long rest ... which was fortunate because he wasn't. When a ruthless hand suddenly switched the lights on again, it was still dark outside. The voice of the platoon sergeant boomed into the room without any regard for the sleeping men.

"Up, everybody! Get up!" he yelled. "Morning call here in twenty minutes. Everybody shaven, with clean teeth and boots. Get on with it!"

The morning roll call passed without problems. Each soldier identified himself to the sergeant, who nodded as if to say his face had been cataloged and filed away. The sergeant explained what gear they needed for their two-week training course and what had to be left in the rooms. Afterward, he sent them off to the dining room, with half an hour allowed for breakfast. Then, another roll call, this time outside, to check the equipment before leaving for the training camp.

The departure review was long and tiresome, and a few soldiers got sent back to their rooms to fix flaws in the gear or how it had been packed. Eventually, the sergeant ordered them to go and stand by the trucks in the parking lot.

"You coming?" asked Barak when John started walking toward the captain's office.

"Yes," he said, "in a moment. Keep me a spot next to you." He walked swiftly away, and Barak didn't get to ask more questions.

The captain was waiting for him in the office, and John stood at attention in the doorway and saluted.

"No need to salute while we're performing an illegal operation," said the captain with a smile. "Here, I'm dialing the hotel. Be quick with your conversation and run to the parking lot. Meanwhile, I'll delay the departure. Move," he ordered in haste, cutting short a further attempt on John's part to thank him.

At the other end of the line, a woman's voice said, "Andania City Hotel, how can I help you?"

"Please put me through to Dana Dorf," said John.

"Is she a guest?" the voice asked. "I don't see her name on the guest list."

"Yes, yes. She's a crew member on the ship that arrived yesterday."

"Ah, I see. They order rooms for the whole crew, not on a name basis. I have here a list of the names of the guests in those rooms ... wait a second," she said, and John waited, following tensely the noises of paper being shuffled around at the other end. "No," she said at last, "I can't find it right now. Call again later, please."

"I can't. I must talk to her now."

"But that's not possible. I don't know which room she's in. It's early morning, and the morning manager is not here yet. I'm the night receptionist and don't have the list."

"But ... still ... please," said John in despair. "I won't be able to call later," he pleaded. The noise of the truck engines being warmed made it clear to him that his time had run out. "Just take a message for her, please ..." he started to say, but the receptionist cut him short.

"I have another call. Try again later. Sorry," she said, and the line went dead.

John replaced the receiver on the table and turned toward the door, a heavy weight, much greater than his gear, burdening his shoulders. He stumbled toward the trucks and his unclear future.

But now was the present—a different one. John looked around the tent. He felt detached from the sense of cold and the frustration that the weather had induced in his comrades. As he had promised himself on the ship, he taught himself to avoid self-pity and not to accuse anybody else of the responsibility for his misfortune. He knew he was guilty of stupidity for signing papers without reading them and not asking Dana for her address. It was only his fault that they had separated and that he hadn't found a way to contact her once the ship had returned to Earth.

After a week of despair, a sudden idea gave John renewed hope. He had written a long and detailed letter to Dana, telling her how he had found himself away from her and in the army, and mailed it to her care of the shipping company. A month later, his name was called during mail time at the morning roll call. His heart missed a beat and then started pounding ... nobody except Dana knew where he was. His disappointment was abyssal when he saw the letter the platoon sergeant held in his hand—his letter with a large stamp said, "Unknown–Return to Sender."

After this experience, John had simply given up trying. Not

because he had forgotten Dana–on the contrary, he thought about her every free moment. During the long hours he kept guard at the camp's perimeter, he had long, imaginary conversations with her. He used some of his conversations to explain the reason for his forced disappearance and seek her forgiveness; in others, he imagined they were being reunited. John was a realist, and he knew that only a miracle would bring them back together. He knew the laws of probability and could have calculated a figure for the likelihood that a soldier in New Australia would be able to get in touch with a woman who spent part of her time at an unknown address on Earth, light years away from him, and the rest on a commercial ship; the flight plan of which he didn't know. He chose not to make the calculation.

"Listen up, everybody!" one of the officers called. He stood in the middle of the tent, completely wet. John admired how his company's officers kept up behavior that inspired calm and strength. This particular officer was certainly as frozen as he was, but he stood straight, giving no sign of discomfort as if standing in the freezing cold with his uniform soaking wet was a matter of course for him.

"The field training was supposed to end two days from now," he announced when all present stood around him, "but the captain has decided to shorten our stay because the weather conditions won't allow us to carry out the training as planned. We leave for the base in twenty minutes. I need five volunteers to stay with me to dismantle this tent and to pick up the company equipment."

John was surprised to notice that he had raised his hand and volunteered. He stood at attention with four other soldiers before the officer who issued detailed instructions.

What happened to me? Why am I volunteering for these jobs? I never wished to call attention to myself. But, on the other hand, I have no reason to hurry back to the base. He was stuck there for a long time anyway, and the best he could do was learn to go along. Without overthinking. Without remembering too much. Like a machine. *Yes, this way, it's easier. Mechanically ... don't think, don't look forward to anything, and don't miss anybody.*

John started hammering pegs out of the hard soil with a broad smile. He no longer felt the cold and ignored the rain that hit his already-soaked uniform. Yes, he felt convinced; it was good this way.

CHAPTER 7

Life at the base wasn't too hard on John once he got used to his low new-recruit status. Once he accepted that virtually every other soldier on the base had the power to give him orders and stopped considering every order a personal offense, his life became easier.

The training was tough, but he often derived some intellectual pleasure from it. Physical activity, weapon training, night watches, field training, more night watches, equipment-operation class, kitchen duty, cleaning duty–the days were never the same. On evenings and during weekends, when they did not train, John had sufficient time to rest, read, and have some semblance of social life within his platoon.

The technical classes were the ones he really liked because he had an easy command of electronic apparatus–radio and night-vision equipment–and the more sophisticated systems allowed him to lay his fingers on a computer keyboard.

During these classes, John learned to respect the sophistication of the Andanian defense system. Andania's border with the Newists' territories was very long and, mostly, ran along the natural obstacle of a chain of high hills and low mountains. Several narrow, winding passages led into Andania, making moving forces and equipment through them challenging. The passages were well guarded by the army, which successfully foiled the Newists' attempts to infiltrate the Andanian territory. However, five passages were broad and easily negotiable by heavy vehicles. Guarding those five passages only with soldiers would have required an effort well beyond the small Andanian army's power. That's why FOS–Andania's Frontier Obstacle System–had been developed to guard the passages. Each passage had walls of armored concrete with embedded laser guns and motion sensors. The passages were two to three kilometers long, and anybody wishing to pass through them into Andania had to spend a long time within those walls. When the motion sensors detected movement in a passage, they activated the laser guns automatically. The laser guns fired at random to save energy, but because of the length of the passages and the large number of guns, almost anything moving through a passage was sure to be hit. It was an ingenious and effective system that protected those passages almost perfectly. It required only a small number of well-trained soldiers to operate. John enjoyed learning about it and other advanced techniques the Andanians developed.

On the other hand, the social life at the base was poor. The instructors spent their free time in the nearby town, a sleepy settlement that had been given the grandiose name of "New Eden." The training base had been named "Eden Base" after it. However, the trainees were not allowed outside the base, and female company was out of the question. The three female soldiers who served at the base had no interest in the recruits and were off-limits.

It was rumored that the tea served on every occasion and virtually the only hot drink available contained a chemical additive used to suppress sexual desires. John never longed for a woman, but he attributed it to the hard training that left him with little energy for anything else and to his longing for Dana. He wasn't worried about the rumors of an additive in the tea; he thought that, given his limited options, he was better off repressing his instincts.

His friendship with Barak, which grew stronger with time, helped him immensely. Barak was an incurable optimist, chronically happy and finding the bright side in every situation. He had the instinct of an alley cat, able to walk tight lines and catch opportunities quickly before John even noticed them. When a tasty dish was served on a festive occasion, Barak always managed to get more portions and distribute them among his friends. His uniform was always perfectly ironed, and he was always the first to be issued new equipment from the supply unit, but he never forgot to get one for John as well. His ability to be liked by his superiors was amazing and permitted him to do and say things that left his friends speechless. Now and then, he would turn up in the middle of the night with a rich meal and always managed to obtain permission to skip training in favor of imaginary "base organization duties."

Sometimes, John would get depressed, usually during resting periods, when he had no way to keep his mind busy. One day, on such an occasion, he was allowed a glimpse of Barak's inner world. It was a free evening, and the soldiers watched an old movie in the small mess hall that doubled as a club. After a while, his comrades' laughter bothered John so much that he couldn't stand it anymore. He quietly left the club and seated himself on a small mound at the edge of the base. He had been sitting there for perhaps half an hour, gazing into the darkness and trying to calculate how long he still had to wear the uniform —the time had become confused in his mind because of his accumulated fatigue and his unwillingness to look ahead to the unclear future.

A figure seated itself silently beside him–Barak.

"Lousy movie, ah?" he said after a while.

"Don't know, I didn't watch," answered John in a low voice.

"So what's the deal? Feel like coming to the kitchen with me?

The cook on duty is a friend of mine, and he'll let us make a proper omelet."

"I'm not hungry," John answered testily. "You go. I'll stay here for a while."

"Are you planning to stay here and sink in self-pity?"

"No, it's not that. You won't understand because you've never screwed yourself up with your own hands. You're too quick and clever."

"Is that what you think?" said Barak, sounding amused. "Then be it known, sir, that nobody ever screwed himself worse than I did. That's how I learned not to be a smart ass, but the tuition fee was too high."

John jerked his head up in surprise. "What's the story?" he asked.

"I was in fifth grade when our school decided, as a service to the community, to run D-tests for a whole month for those who wished to fulfill their duty early. All the young teachers who hadn't taken the test signed the D-test form, and two tested positive. One of the two was a math teacher I hated, and I was mighty glad she couldn't bear the shame and left the school. But the other one was a young history teacher I liked very much. I don't know what happened to him, but one day, a different teacher walked into the room and introduced himself as the new teacher. That's it. That evening, I cried because I felt that, perhaps, I got a deserved punishment for my happiness that the math teacher had to leave."

Barak paused for a minute and threw into the darkness a few stones he had been playing with. Then he continued in a monotonous voice.

"Children were not allowed to take the test without their parents' permission. I decided to show everybody how pure I was, so I went to my father with the form and asked him to sign it. He simply said 'out of the question,' which ended the discussion. I turned to my mother, hoping she'd convince my father, but she didn't want to listen. I pleaded with her and explained how important that was to my social status in the school because those who tested negative became instantly popular with the kids who didn't dare to take the test. But all my pleas were of no avail.

"Now I know they knew something more than I did and were trying to protect me. But at the time, I thought they were simply not ready to listen and didn't care if it was important to me. So I faked my parents' signatures on the form and took the test." Barak laughed a bitter laugh and kept talking into the darkness before him.

"Can you imagine," he continued, "how I felt when my parents were summoned to the school and told that I had tested positive? I never considered the possibility because my whole family was pure, including my two elder sisters. They no longer lived with us and had taken the test long before. And you know what the worst part was? My parents weren't mad at me. They never yelled at me. They only looked at me sadly and shook their heads in disbelief."

"That sounds familiar," said John. Suddenly, he saw his friend in a different light. "You feel guilty as if you could have prevented it, as if it were your fault. That's a terrible feeling."

Barak nodded and continued to look straight ahead as if to find the words for his tale in the darkness.

"During the first week, I refused to go to school, but then the vice-principal came to our house and talked to me. He explained that the test results are secret until you turn eighteen and that the other kids would never know unless I told anybody, and I'd be able to go on as usual. He convinced me, and I went back to school. I told everybody that I had been sick at home with stomach flu. That helped me through the awkwardness of the day–until I got home.

"At home, a surprise waited for me. All my belongings had been packed in two bags, and an old lady was waiting for me in the living room. My parents weren't there. The woman explained to me that she had come to take me to a special institute where I would learn together with kids 'like me,' meaning homeless D-positive kids. She gave me a letter from my parents. It explained that they were acting in my best interest and that, even though parting from me was difficult, they did it for my sake. They also said that it would be best if we never met again."

"How could they explain such a thing?" John asked indignantly.

"It doesn't matter. You don't want to know. I finished reading the letter, picked up my bags, and left the house without looking back."

"It must have been terrible for you," murmured John. He felt a lump in his throat as his own memories surged in his mind.

"It was pretty bad, but that's not all," Barak said pensively. "I lived at the institute for almost one year and read my parents' letter every day. I tried to understand it, but I couldn't. One day, after a last read, I burned it and ran away from the institute.

"During the years after my escape, I lived mostly in the streets. I joined gangs of young people, many of them D-positives like me, and I learned how to make the most of my day."

Barak stood up for a moment, then sat down again and kept silent, drawing geometrical shapes in the sand with his shoe.

"So when did you decide to come to Andania?" asked John. "I understand that, after all, you were managing okay."

"I did until I read my name in the paper."

"Your name in the paper? Why?"

"It seems that my running away from the institute provoked a quiet and complicated investigation of my family, which took years. The results of the investigation astounded the authorities. My father was a talented microbiologist who worked in a govern-mental research institute. It turns out that he was D-positive, but he had developed a method that made it possible to foil the genetic test, which many people had used to pass the test and be consid-ered D-negative. My sisters were positive like me, but my father taught them how to pass the test and gave them the materials needed.

"Only then did I understand that with my stupidity, I had brought a disaster not only upon myself but also upon my family and God knows how many other people my father had saved from a life of inferiority."

"What happened to your family?"

"They were all arrested and tried. They were all found guilty of different grades of crimes against humanity, and they will all spend the rest of their lives in jail."

John gazed into Barak's face. It was blank and didn't betray the emotions affecting him.

"You shouldn't feel guilty," he tried to console him. "You didn't know."

"No, I didn't know, and I don't feel guilty. Only then I understood that my parents had sacrificed me in an attempt to save the rest of the family from ruin. They had to show a credible repulsion for a son who had tested D-positive to fend off suspicion. Pity it didn't work. It perhaps was the logical thing to do, but I never forgave them for giving me up so easily and not trusting me enough to explain the truth to me. I stayed in town all those years, hoping things would change and they might want me back. Silly of me, wasn't it?"

"Not at all. I understand it completely."

"But after they arrested my family, I had nothing to look forward to on Earth, and that's when I decided to come over here. The Andanian representatives gave me fake documents that got me on the ship and helped me buy the ticket, so here I am."

"I'm sorry ..." John didn't know what to say but felt he had to say something.

"Don't be. The old Barak doesn't exist anymore. I've put everything behind me, and you'll be wise to do the same and to stop thinking about the troubles of the past."

"I don't ..."

"We both know what you're going through. No point in denying."

"But, really ..."

"Cut the bullshit," Barak interrupted him. "What about getting a girl?"

"What do you mean? There are no girls here."

"Right. No girls here, but lots of them in New Eden."

"But we can't get there. And besides, it's not allowed. We can get in trouble."

"Have I ever got you into any trouble?" Barak rebuked him. "Don't worry. Everybody does it, and the officers look the other way. A truck is leaving for New Eden in a few minutes. If we hurry, we can catch it and won't have to walk."

The way to New Eden, less than four kilometers, passed in a flash, and the truck stopped at the town's outskirts. Barak and John jumped down, and Barak approached the cabin window to thank the driver, a soldier who worked in the supply unit with whom Barak had made friends since the first day.

"What do we do now?" John asked.

"Let's go in there," Barak said, pointing to a door from which music and colored lights emerged. "We must be back here in two hours; otherwise, the truck won't wait for us, and we'll have to walk back to the base."

The bar's music was so loud that conversation was next to impossible. The room was full of civilians, and only a few uniforms could be seen. John was relieved to note that in the confusion, nobody paid any attention to them. Barak approached the bar and ordered two beers. No alcohol was allowed on the base, and it had been a long time since John had drunk a beer. It tasted wonderful.

They stood with their backs to the bar and watched the crowd.

Young men and women gyrated on the dance floor to the rhythm of a modern song. John enjoyed looking around. He hadn't been to such a place for ages.

"Wait for me here," said Barak, disappearing into the crowd. A few minutes later, he reappeared with two young women in tow.

"John," he shouted above the music, "this is Cindy, and this is Hanna."

"Nice to meet you," said John. The girls smiled and nodded.

"Hanna and I are going to dance a bit. You keep Cindy company. I'll see you here in an hour and a half. Don't be late," he admonished him and left with Hanna.

John didn't know what she expected of him. Cindy was a good-looking young woman, although her body was a little too plump for his taste. She looked childish with her round face and long, blonde pigtails. Her dress was made of a light fabric that inflated at her every move and hid her body well.

"How are you?" John asked after an awkward silence.

"Okay. Do you want to dance a little?"

"Yes, if you'd like to."

"Let's dance, then. Tell me a little about yourself. Your friend didn't tell me anything."

"Oh, there isn't much to tell. I came from Earth a little while ago and am in the army. What about you?"

"I'm learning to become a trained nurse."

"How old are you?"

"I'll be nineteen next month."

"Do you come here often?"

"Yes, this is a nice place, and I like to meet new people, particularly soldiers. Let's dance," she added, pulling him toward the dance floor. The song that was playing had been a hit in the New Nations two years before and sounded familiar to John. The dance was a slow, and Cindy moved naturally to press her body against John's.

"Where are Barak and Hanna?" John asked after a while.

"Who cares?" said Cindy. "They're gone. Want to go, too?"

"I think I'll better wait for Barak here."

"As you wish," she said quietly, and they kept dancing.

After the next dance, they returned to the bar, and John ordered drinks. He didn't know what to do with her. He tried to make conversation but without success. They stood silently for almost half an hour, and then Cindy placed her glass on the bar and looked at John.

"I need to go for a moment," she said, walking away.

John waited for her by the bar, drinking one beer after the other, until Barak showed up and motioned to him to come.

"Quickly," he ordered, "the truck should be here any moment now."

They stood outside for less than a minute when the truck stopped before them, and they climbed in the back.

"Wow," said Barak, "that Hanna is something. How did it go with Cindy?"

"We danced a little, and then she had to go. It was nice."

"It was nice? It was nice! But ... but didn't you go with her? Didn't she invite you?"

"Actually, she asked me if I wanted to go, but I was afraid that I would miss you, and besides, it was nice in the bar, and it didn't sound like a good idea to leave."

Barak lifted his eyes to heaven in disbelief and then looked at John as if to check if he was pulling his leg.

"You're unbelievable. She invited you because she meant something. And you want to tell me that you refused? Tell me, from what planet are you–don't answer that; I know the answer. I tie myself in knots to get you a girl that will let you unwind a little, and you sit with her like a geek at the bar? I don't believe it!"

"I don't think she meant anything special," said John defensively. "She just wanted to dance."

"Oh," said Barak, "you are more stupid than I thought. Those girls want only one thing. When I pointed at you, she said you were cute and asked if you were free. I told her, 'Of course,' and we decided who was going with whom. What were you thinking?"

"I'm sorry," said John, "I didn't understand, I didn't think ..."

"Listen to me, my dear friend. Life is short, and you can't go on dreaming about Dana and behaving as if you were living in a monastery. This way, you'll never get over it."

"It's not that," said John defensively. "That's not what got in the way. It's just that I wasn't in the right state of mind. Perhaps it's true that they're putting chemicals in our tea. It simply didn't cross my mind."

"Believe me, the way I functioned, they put nothing in our tea. And I drink more tea than you do."

The truck entered the base through the main gate, and John and Barak kept their heads down to avoid recognition by the guard at the gate. The truck stopped near the supply unit, and they jumped down quickly to join the crowd leaving the club after the movie.

That night, John couldn't find sleep. Barak's words kept coming back to him. To forget Dana? It might be possible, but he didn't want to forget her. He wondered if she had forgotten him. Somehow, he was sure she had not, but surely she thought he had run away from her. Perhaps she hated him for it. And maybe she understood and was waiting for him ...

He fell asleep with her face in his mind, like every night.

CHAPTER 8

"John!"

Captain Eton's voice caused John to snap into a state of full attention, a reflex he had acquired after months of hard training. He stood in a long line for the uninviting paste that passed for food, which a cook dispensed from a large pot. After a morning of field training, though, he would have eaten almost anything.

"Yes, sir?" said John. He didn't manage to keep a tone of surprise out of his voice. Having his almighty commander seek him out personally was more than unusual.

"I have orders to return to the base," said the captain, "and I can't say that I regret it, with the bloody heat we've had these days. But the reason for our return is not the weather," he explained. "Tomorrow, a civil screening committee will interview soldiers who seek job offers after basic training. We have four specific requests for soldiers that the committee wants to interview. Your name is on the list."

"What's the screening committee, sir?" asked John.

"It's a governmental committee that locates candidates for key jobs. It seems that your profession is in great demand."

"What will happen at the interview?"

"They'll ask you questions, and if they find you suitable for their needs, they'll offer you a job."

"And what if I don't like the job?"

"You are not obliged to take it. You can talk to the absorption representative who has you under his jurisdiction to hear alternative job proposals. You can also decide to stay in the army if you want to. But I guess this is not an option for you, right?"

Captain Eton spoke the last sentence without looking at John. Instead, he stooped, picked up an empty bowl, and poured himself water from a nearby jug.

"I ... don't think I'll want to stay on, sir," said John. "I don't think I'd make a good career soldier."

"I thought that would be your position," the captain sighed. "But you'd fit all right. You're a fine soldier who uses his head and could contribute much. I'll be sorry to lose you, but I knew that from the first day."

"I ..." John started, but his commander stopped him.

"Don't apologize. I understand. We'll have roll call in a short while, and then we'll be heading back," he said before he turned on his heel and left.

The soldiers stood in silence and waited for their commander. Roll calls occurred several times a day during training and were part of the daily routine. Each soldier had his equipment packed beside him, and every team that used shared equipment had it organized and ready for leaving. At the order, everything would be loaded onto the vehicles within two minutes.

The soldiers waited. They didn't mind waiting; that's an integral part of life in the army; if you can't wait patiently, you're not a good soldier.

At last, Captain Eton approached the ranks, walking that purposeful walk of his that always conveyed strength. He stood before them, contemplating them at length.

"Soldiers," he shouted so everybody would hear him, "I just

received combat orders. We're not going back to the base because there's been a development in our sector. Agricultural Unit seventy-three has been attacked and destroyed by Newist militias that infiltrated through one of the secondary passages not covered by FOS. The unit that guarded that section of the border was too small and was destroyed. There is concern for the fate of AU72 and AU74. Everyone must learn his map on the way and get acquainted with the area. Platoons A and B, under my command, will move toward AU72. Platoons C and D, under the command of my deputy, Lieutenant Miller, will deal with AU74."

John felt a shiver running down his spine. This wasn't training anymore; it was the real thing. He was surprised to discover that he wasn't scared. He'd be scared soon enough, though, he guessed.

"You're no longer rookies," Captain Eton continued. "You are good and trained soldiers, and I'm sure that we'll be proud of you. Good luck to everybody. All aboard!" he concluded.

The company spread out quickly, following the drill. As if in a dream, John found himself seated beside Barak in his platoon's armored vehicle, which bore the sign "Platoon A." He noted with surprise that Barak was smiling broadly as he watched the other soldiers climbing quickly into their vehicles. Each platoon–twenty-five soldiers, five sergeants, and an officer–carried a lot of equipment, ammunition, and weapons. Everybody got in his vehicle, and the captain gave the order to move.

"You seem in a good mood," John commented to Barak. "Aren't you scared?"

"I'm scared to death," Barak admitted, "and you?"

"It's strange, but I feel no fear. Maybe something's wrong with my head."

"Don't worry, you'll pee in your pants yet," Barak reassured him jokingly.

It took them two hours to reach the observation point above Agricultural Unit seventy-two. By the time they arrived, the sun had cast long afternoon shadows. The vehicles stopped behind a hill chosen as the observation point, and the teams climbed to the top on foot, crawling for the last few meters. From the top of the hill, the buildings and fields of AU72 were clearly visible.

"Wait here," said Sergeant Sigmund to John's team, which he commanded. "I'll go to the captain."

He crawled quickly backward and ran sideways to where Captain Eton was lying. The two platoon commanders and the rest of the sergeants joined them. John scanned the valley below him with his eyes. The buildings of AU72 stood visible, about seven hundred meters away, and so were its fields. It was a tiny agricultural unit. John counted fifteen individual houses and two large buildings. Farther away stood other buildings that looked like animal shelters and barns.

It was quiet; nobody moved outside. Smoke curled lazily from the central structure's chimney, which John assumed served as a communal building–perhaps the mess hall. The structure farthest away from the observation point seemed damaged as if its back wall had collapsed, and a little smoke rose from it. Because of their position, it wasn't possible to see precisely what was happening on that side of the building.

John listened, trying to hear whether any noise was coming from the inside, but heard nothing. The strong back wind that blew over the hill's top made listening to sounds coming from the valley impossible. He strained his eyes, trying to see farther away, toward the green fields, but nothing moved there either. The area seemed empty of Newist forces, and nobody else was in sight. It looked as if the place had been deserted without a fight.

Sergeant Sigmund crawled back to them, bearing orders. "Listen up," he whispered. "First, we must not make any noise because the wind is at our backs and will carry every little sound toward the unit. Secondly, our heat detectors show the presence of people inside the buildings. We don't know who they are but must assume they are Newists."

"And what if they are the settlers?" somebody asked.

"Well, we can't ask them, can we? Besides, why would the settlers hide within the buildings?"

"Maybe they are scared that they may be attacked," hazarded John.

"Maybe, but we can take no chances. Our working assumption is that what awaits us inside the building is Newists in ambush. They may have hostages, and we must consider that when we go in. Clear so far?"

The sergeant looked around and ensured that everybody nodded in assent, then continued.

"It'll be dark soon. The captain will go in with Platoon B. Our platoon will check the buildings at the edge of the agricultural area and cover the flank of Platoon B. Our team will go first into the southern building that stands at the edge of the fields—anybody needs help to identify it?" A few seconds of silence confirmed that nobody did. "Good," said the sergeant, "after we check that the building is clear, we move an additional hundred meters to the edge of the constructed area and take a position there to cover that section in case of fire. Night vision glasses and weapons ready, everybody, from the moment we move. Clear?"

Everyone nodded again without shifting their gaze from the settlement.

"We'll make a long detour behind the small green hills before those two trees. See? Good, then go check your equipment and get ready. Take only the essential gear. All the rest will wait for you in the vehicle. Be ready for a last check and orders in fifteen minutes. Questions? No? Then take five more minutes now to learn the area by heart and climb down."

John inspected the area below him at length and tried to memorize every characteristic point. He carefully scanned the planned approach route, trying to locate points that would later help him know his position. When he felt confident that he had learned every possible detail, he signaled Barak that he was going and crawled back until he reached a point where it was safe to stand without being seen from the valley below.

Slowly, mechanically, according to the drill, John emptied his pockets of all unnecessary items, blackened his face with the paste provided by the army, and jumped up and down to make sure that he wasn't carrying any rustling items that might give away his position. Afterward, he checked his weapon, ammunition, and nightglasses. When his review was completed and gone over twice, he seated himself by the vehicle and waited for the order to leave. Now that everything was in order, he could allow himself to feel scared.

John's team formed a column that moved in absolute silence. Stooping, they took position near the building they had been ordered to check. Third in line after the sergeant, John watched as he operated the heat detector. The detector's screen remained black while the sergeant scanned the building repeatedly, signifying the absence of any living body in or around it. The sergeant turned back to whisper to John and the soldier beside him, "The building looks clean. You two come with me. The rest remain here. Pass the order."

John whispered the order to the soldier standing beside him and got up to follow the sergeant. The three of them walked cautiously, with their weapons ready to shoot, toward the building's open door, showing a vast hall inside. From where they stood, they could see agricultural tools lying around while a body lay on the floor at the far edge of the hall. The sergeant pointed the heat detector at the body, but the screen remained black.

"John, watch the entrance. I don't want any surprises," he ordered, then turned to the other soldier. "You come with me. Let's see what's in there."

John took his position near the door, his weapon pointing outside, trying to keep a low profile and avoid making noise. Now and then, he glanced inside to see what the others were doing. A deafening explosion made him turn. He barely had time to see the sergeant and the soldier flying in the air like rag dolls before the blast threw him toward the thick bushes that surrounded the building. His last thought, before he lost his senses, was that the body had been booby-trapped. Then, his world became enveloped in darkness.

When he came to, John was surprised to discover he was still alive. He was sure nobody could have escaped that ambush, but perhaps the enemy had thought him dead already, so he had been spared. But what had happened to the others? The surroundings were quiet, and he heard no shots. He tried his night-vision glasses, but they were broken. Luckily, the night was clear, and the light was sufficient to see what was happening around him. As he slowly, carefully crawled toward the other buildings, he passed near one of his comrades' bodies but didn't try to identify him.

A low whimpering sound came from one of the structures—a woman's voice or maybe a child's. John crawled toward the building from which it came, using the cover offered by the bushes around him. He reached a position from which he could see the central area and, to his astonishment, saw Captain Eton's familiar figure running before the main building and leaning against the wall. John hoped that it meant that the others, too, had survived the ambush. The captain stood there, listening to the sounds from the building and debating what to do.

John saw two figures appear behind the captain. Without thinking, he aimed his gun and squeezed the trigger. The first figure fell face forward, and the captain turned around quickly and started shooting at the other. A few seconds later, the two of them lay lifeless on the ground.

"Sir," John shouted, "it's John. What should I do?"

"Come over here," ordered the captain.

John dashed toward his commander and leaned on the wall beside him.

"Good job, John," said the captain, nodding appreciatively. "I think you just saved my ass."

The captain was breathing heavily, and John allowed himself to take deep and quick breaths.

"I was hurt in the explosion, sir. I was out for a while and don't know what happened."

"We had a tough battle, and we have quite a few casualties, but I think the two we handled just now were the last ones. We have gone through all the other buildings. Let's go in."

"Sir," said John, "I think someone is inside. Do you hear?"

"Of course I do. I'll go in, and you wait for me to call before you come after me."

John watched his commander go into the building and felt lonely again. After a long minute, he heard the captain's voice. "John, you can come in, but be prepared for a hard sight."

John went into the building, his heart pounding. A frightful sight awaited him. Forty or fifty bodies of men, women, and children lay scattered around. The Newists had assembled all the settlers in that room and then shot them at close range. The whimpering they had heard from outside came from a woman who was lying on the floor in a pool of blood. John gaped at her, helpless, while her body twitched forcefully. She tried to sit up and then fell back, lifeless. Complete silence fell on the semi-dark room as John ran outside, driven by a need to vomit.

A minute later, the captain joined him and put a comforting hand on his shoulder. John's body shook uncontrollably, and he propped his gun against the wall. He simply wasn't able to control a loud cry from his throat, and he kicked the wall with all his strength until his foot hurt.

"It's okay, boy. It's all right," whispered the captain in his ear.

"I ... I," John tried to say, but he only managed to weep again.

"Take this," said the captain, handing him a liquor flask. John gulped it down even though it burned his throat. He coughed and then took another long gulp. He felt a little more in control of himself; his body no longer shook, and he managed to stop crying.

"Hey," said the captain, putting out his hand for the flask, "don't finish all of it. I need some, too."

Captain Eton swallowed a good measure, lifted his radio, and spoke shortly. "End of mission. The last building is clean. All bodies not on guard positions come to me."

As if by magic, the whole area suddenly bustled with activity. Tired, sooty, and dirty soldiers who had been hiding behind buildings and shrubbery stood up, filled the square, and formed ranks before their commander. The company's vehicles stormed in, and with them came the supporting units that started to care for the wounded. The Newist militia had consisted of more than fifty fighters, and they had all been killed.

Barak hadn't been seriously wounded, but his hair had almost entirely disappeared in the blast that had killed the sergeant. He ran to John and hugged him with all his strength.

"I thought you were dead," he shouted. "I saw this huge blast, and the building you searched went up in flames. I didn't dream that you might have survived. How did you do it?"

"I was lucky, simply lucky," said John. "I was in position near the door, and the blast threw me into the bushes. That's how I wasn't seriously injured. You look like a plucked chicken, you know."

"We need to get you a mirror, boy. You aren't so hot either; you look like something out of the trash can. Anyway," he added, "I must go and get checked by the doctor. My head is exploding, and my belly hurts as if someone kicked me with spiked boots. See you later."

John looked at his good friend, and, for the first time, he understood how short the distance between life and death was.

It was now time for the sad task of identifying and burying the settlers. Everybody had to participate in the hard job, explained the captain, which would be performed under his deputy's command. John walked heavily toward the main building with bowed head and shoulders, but the captain's voice stopped him.

"Come here, John," he ordered.

John turned around and stood at attention at the regulation distance from his commander.

"At ease, John. You're not going there; you've seen and done enough for one day. I want you to come with me and help me prepare a report of the casualties."

"Thank you, sir," said John, overwhelmed by relief.

"I'm the one who should thank you today," said Captain Eton briefly, and without another word, he walked toward the command vehicle.

John watched his commander walk confidently away, and not for the first time, he did so with admiration. After a few seconds, he hurried after him.

BOOK TWO

All service ranks the same with God –
With God, whose puppets, best and worst,
Are we: there is no last nor first.

Robert Browning–Pippa Passes (1841) epilogue

CHAPTER 9

The secretary smiled at the young officer, gazing at the shining gold bars that adorned his shoulders. "You can go in, Lieutenant," she said to John and nodded toward the door.

John rose heavily from the soft armchair in which he had been sinking. The last few days had been hard work for him, with little sleep, and he had allowed himself to doze off in the comfortable seat.

The room to which the secretary had directed him was spacious, with large windows that did nothing to keep out the day's bright light. A skinny, red-haired young man stood by a functional desk. As John opened the door, he hurried toward him, shook his hand briefly, and hugged him.

"Hi!" he yelled. "Come in, boy."

"Hi, Barak," John answered with a shy smile. "Good to see you."

"Good to see you after all this time. How long has it been?"

"Almost five years."

"Wow! And look at you ... if we don't do anything to stop you, you'll turn into a general."

"You know, I always thought that you would become a general and I would leave the army after basic training. See how you managed to trick me?"

"Come here," said Barak. He motioned him toward one of the two armchairs before his desk and sat in the other. They looked at one another, John trying to find his friend from the old days in the impeccably dressed Barak who sat there, facing him.

"Well," Barak asked, "how did they manage to keep you in the army for so long?"

"After you left, I decided to stay 'for a while,' but I never found a good reason to leave. And you," he went on, "after you were taken to the hospital from the battle of AU72, I thought I'd see you back in the company in no time. Only a month later, I heard you had been discharged and were not coming back."

"Yes," said Barak, turning serious. "As you know, I went to the doctor after the battle. I felt more or less okay and thought the worst damage had been done to my hair, which had been burnt away a little. But when the doctor checked me, he suspected internal bleeding, apparently due to the blast, and shipped me off to the nearest hospital. And thank God for that because, on the way, I lost consciousness and barely made it there alive. But you," inquired Barak, swiftly changing the subject, "why did you stay on? I thought you hated the army."

John looked at his shiny boots, shifted uncomfortably on his seat, and answered without looking at his friend.

"After the carnage at AU72, everything changed. When I saw what the Newists did to those peaceful civilian settlers, I understood that I couldn't stand aside and go to Andania City to play with my computers. That's why I remained in the army."

"All right. I agree with you that the Newists are barbarians. But, in their defense, we must say that we took from them those good, agricultural lands they claim to be their own. You, too, in their place, would have counted that as an act of war."

John lifted his gaze from his boots and looked at his friend with amazement.

"You justify them? They are not human beings," he said vehemently. "No human being could have done that to women and children ..."

"No, no. Of course, I don't justify them. I'm only saying that you could have expected that ... but let's not talk about that now. This is no time for arguments."

John was happy to change the subject. The images of the carnage of AU72 had left a deep scar in him, which would never disappear. Sometimes, he dreamed about it and woke in the middle of the night, reliving the last moments of the woman he saw returning her soul to God.

It must have been tough on Barak, too. He looked at him and tried to bridge the gap of years that lay wide open between them. But then Barak smiled at him, a warm smile, and for a moment, he turned back into the boy that John had met in the immigration line. "You look good, John," he said appreciatively. "How's everything?"

"I'm all right, but look at you–assistant to the Minister of Commerce. You've made it!"

"Don't get carried away," said Barak with modesty, "I'm only the assistant to the Deputy Minister of Commerce."

"What's his name?"

"Deputy Minister Yabalan. He's bound to rise to great heights. Minister Sarpash holds him in great esteem and takes his advice on virtually everything. He's a brilliant man–you'll see."

"Which brings me to the point. Why am I here?"

"You're here because you're my friend," said Barak, "and because you're talented, with the required technical skills, and an officer in the army. You fit the bill exactly."

"Which bill?"

"The Deputy Minister needs a military secretary. We prepared a profile of the required characteristics and ran it through the central computer, which printed out a short list of five names. Yours was the second name on the list. The moment I saw it, I knew you were our man."

"But I'm in the army ..."

"No problem. The government has precedence on army matters, and the army will lend you to us for as long as we need you. Think of the fun–we'll be working together all the time, like in the good old days." Barak winked at John.

"Hmm ... I don't know," John started to say. Before that moment, he had never thought of working for the government. He liked his army job as a platoon commander in the company he had trained in, and leaving his command was not in his plans.

"I thought you might struggle over this," Barak stopped him mid-sentence, "and therefore, I made convenient arrangements for you. You are on leave from the army for three months, effective immediately. During this period, you'll have a chance to learn your job and decide whether you like it. If you don't, you can stop working here, enjoy the rest of your paid leave, and return to your platoon. What do you say?"

"Well ... it sounds like an offer that can't be turned down."

"It can't. I made sure of that," said Barak with a self-satisfied smirk.

"So, what now?" John asked.

"Where are you staying?" asked Barak instead of answering John's question.

"My stuff is outside in the waiting room. I haven't checked in at the hotel yet."

"Good. Then my driver will take you to the apartment we've rented for you. It's not big," he said apologetically, "but it's within a convenient distance from our offices here, and I think it'll be very comfortable for you."

"I see that you thought of everything," said John appreciatively.

Barak got up and walked to the communication panel on his desk.

"You know me," he said. "I don't leave anything to the hand of fate." He pushed a button on the panel. "The driver will be waiting for you outside," he added.

"Okay. I'll get organized at the apartment, and then what? Should I come back here?"

"No. Today is your first day, and I suggest you rest and get organized. Come in at around half-past nine tomorrow morning, and I'll give you some details about your job. Meanwhile, you should use the time to get acquainted with your surroundings. I would have liked to go out with you to some bar," he added apologetically, "but I have to get a zillion documents ready for my boss."

"I understand, don't worry."

"Unfortunately, it's not like in the past, you know," Barak interrupted him. "Now I have great responsibilities, and I'm no longer master of my time. It's annoying that I can't spend time with you today, but we'll have fun together soon."

"Sure. I'm counting on it."

"You know, this is an amazing city. There's nothing like it on New Australia and perhaps even on Earth. You can find opportunities that won't come your way elsewhere."

"That'll probably make it more difficult for me to fit in," joked John, faking concern. "After all, I'm only a simple provincial soldier."

"We'll look after you," Barak reassured him earnestly. "I'm sure that after a few weeks, you won't even think about returning to your former simplistic life. Here, you'll find all the intellectuals and the powerful people. This place is something else—the city has character and presents unlimited opportunities for those who know how to move around. You'll see what I mean soon enough."

Barak walked toward the door, his hand on John's back pushing lightly. He opened the door and shook his hand. "It's good to see you here, John. Welcome," he said warmly.

"It's good to see you," said John, "thanks for everything."

"Don't mention it. See you tomorrow."

John turned around and walked to the gate where Barak's driver waited. Everything was well organized, as he would have expected of his old friend.

The apartment turned out to be small–a tiny sleeping room with an adjoining bathroom and shower and a small sitting room next to a tiny kitchen, which also doubled as a dining room with a round table that seated three. To John, who was used to military life, the place seemed very elegant. He immediately organized his belongings, hanging his spare uniforms and civilian clothes in the small cupboard near the bed. During his time in the army, he had come to realize how important it was to treat every place where you stayed, even for a brief interval of time, as "home." The alternative was to live without a home, and human beings need a corner to call their own.

John walked around his apartment. He felt great, particularly since, for the first time in years, he was relieved of the heavy responsibility of command. His deputy had the command now, and John knew he could rely on him to do a proper job. He had no reason to be worried, but he felt uncomfortable thinking he hadn't properly passed the torch. The summons to Andania City had come unexpectedly without any details, except that he had been chosen to go on a special mission. When he had addressed his soldiers for the last time, he believed he would see them again in a few days.

He decided that his new and unexpected carefree feeling was worth enjoying as long as the burden of a new position wasn't yet on his shoulders. He poured a drink from the cooler that a kind hand had filled with various supplies and sat in an armchair facing the large screen of the home computer. He zapped through the channels and learned the options until he got bored and left the apartment. It was almost seven p.m., and he had begun to feel hungry.

He wore civilian clothes and was about to leave for a restaurant that Barak's driver had recommended when a loud ring had him rushing to the communication board. He saw Barak's secretary's face on the screen and opened the communication channel that let her see and hear him.

"Good evening, Lieutenant. This is Eva, Barak's secretary."

"Good evening, Eva," answered John politely.

"I just wanted to tell you–in case you asked yourself what the arrangements with the apartment are–that we have arranged for a cleaning woman to come and clean. She'll also ensure you're always stocked with basic supplies, but you'll have to buy anything special beyond that. She has a key, and you don't have to worry. Everything has been taken care of."

"Thank you very much, Eva. You're spoiling me." He had other questions that he needed to ask: what time the cleaner would come, how many times a week, and so on, but he didn't feel like prolonging the conversation.

"Don't worry, Lieutenant. Every employee of your level has the same privileges. We aren't doing anything special for you; these services come with the job. But if you need anything special, don't hesitate to call me. I have instructions from Barak to help you with your every need. And the truth is," she added with a broad smile, "that even without instructions, I'd be happy to help you."

"Thank you, Eva. I appreciate it," said John, trying to hide his embarrassment. "You're very kind."

"My pleasure, Lieutenant. Maybe," she added after a brief pause, "one of these evenings, after work, I could take you for a tour of the city and show you a few places ..."

"Thanks, really," said John. He wanted to end the conversation, which threatened to become too tight for comfort. "I appreciate your offer."

"We'll talk about it, then?"

"Yes," said John resignedly.

"Meanwhile, good night, Lieutenant," she concluded, and her image disappeared from the screen.

John strolled through the neighborhood, carefully looking around and studying his surroundings as if they were a potential battle-field. He had visited Andania City many times during the last few years, but always for brief visits of a few hours, and now he had to learn to live there.

He had a lot to think about. He began to sense that Andania City was a different place from the others he had known. The ways of the people there were unlike anything else he knew. He wasn't a bigot, and since joining the professional army, he had met several women. But man-woman relationships in Andania were something special.

On the one hand, family values were cherished and religiously adhered to, but on the other, young unmarried women were open to casual relationships. The feeling that "maybe there's no tomor-row" made young people want to enjoy every piece of Life. Once they built a family, the party was over; they did everything to strengthen it, causing yesterday's wild youths to become serious and settled couples. Despite his years in Andania, John still didn't understand all the nuances of the Andanian society.

Even though he had opened himself toward women in recent years, never before had any woman come on to him so openly as Eva after speaking only a few words to him. He felt embarrassed and curious simultaneously but decided to put off dealing with her. He needed to learn more about this place and its customs first. Now, he wanted to concentrate on good food. After a long stretch during which he had only eaten army rations, he became enrap-tured by the new tastes on his plate. John knew how to become single-minded and focused when he wanted to, and right now, nothing else seemed worthy of his attention.

CHAPTER 10

J ohn's head had never hurt so severely... its back pulsated strongly, and each pulsation seemed to push a spike into his brain. It took him a great effort to open one eye to look at the clock beside his bed. It said seven in the morning, but he felt as if he hadn't slept at all.

The wine he had drunk with his delicious dinner wasn't particularly strong, but it contained sufficient alcohol to make John want more. He had ordered a sweet drink named "Geem," then something colorless and tasteless that burned his throat. From that moment on, his memory was kind of fuzzy. He remembered a few kind faces belonging to people who had sat and drunk with him, but he had no idea when–and for that matter, how–he had returned home.

With great care, trying to keep his head from making sudden movements, he painstakingly got himself seated on the bed and extended a searching hand toward a bag on a small table next to it, from which he took two capsules that he swallowed without water. He sat motionless on the bed for ten minutes, breathing slowly until the pain became bearable, and he felt that standing was again an option. Then he got up and walked the short distance to the shower.

He stood for a long time under the jet of hot water, shaking away the mists of sleep until he felt that his head had cleared enough. On a shelf in the shower, he saw clean towels of all sizes, but, from habit, he picked up a small one that looked like the army towel he had been using for the last few years. He stood before the mirror and carefully dried himself, still uncertain of his balance. He was drying his short hair when the bathroom door opened unexpectedly, and he saw an unknown young woman standing in the doorway. She scrutinized him, smiling an amused smile without showing any sign of embarrassment.

"Hi," she said, "you must be John."

John lowered the towel that seemed to have shrunk and become tiny, trying to cover himself with it. But, for some reason, he felt more embarrassed by his pathetic attempt to do so. He stood with the towel hanging downwards, hoping it covered at least part of his body. He didn't dare to look down to find out.

"And who would you be?" he asked with surprise.

"I'm the cleaning woman," she said.

"The cleaning woman?" he echoed in amazement. He had expected an older woman, someone who had been doing cleaning jobs all her life, not a young woman like the one staring at him openly and without a sign of embarrassment.

"Yes, the cleaning woman. But I can also make coffee," she said, smiling broadly at John. "I'll go to the kitchen to brew some. You look like you might need it."

She left, closing the door after her, and John dried himself quickly and dressed in his uniform. He had yet to get over the surprise of her presence and wasn't sure how to behave.

In the kitchen, a steaming pot of coffee waited for him on the table, with two cups standing beside it. She dropped the kitchen towel she held and went straight to John.

"My name is Tasha," she said, holding a hand for him to shake. "It's short for Natasha," she explained.

"And I'm John." He had difficulty shifting his gaze from her face but didn't want to stare into her eyes. "As you guessed," he added, smiling an embarrassed smile.

He looked at her until he started to feel that his study of her was taking too long for comfort, and then pointed at the table and said, "Let's sit down and have coffee. I apologize for my manners. I woke up with a terrible headache this morning, and I'm not focused."

They sat at the table, and Tasha poured coffee. John added milk and sweetener and drank silently, his eyes fixed on the table-cloth. After a while, the silence became oppressive, and he felt that he had to say something.

"So what do you do? Do you clean apartments for a living?"

"Well, that's not my main thing," she answered thoughtfully. "I study geology but work part-time as a cleaning woman to pay for my studies. To tell you the truth," she added conspiratorially, "this is my first job. I hope you'll be patient with me if it takes me a while to get used to the needs of your apartment." John started to nod vehemently in agreement but had to stop when a sharp pain in his head reminded him of last night's escapade.

"Don't worry," he reassured her, "I'm used to doing everything for myself, and any help I get, I'll feel pampered."

She looked at him gratefully and then raised her hand to touch the corner of his right eye.

"What's that scar?" she asked.

"This? Oh, nothing. It's a little scar that I bought myself in the army."

In reality, the scar was the result of his foolish attempt to dismantle a weapon in contravention of the instructions, which resulted in a strong spring jumping off it and hitting him near the eye. He had cursed himself, but that was nothing compared with how much his commander had cursed him for almost blinding himself because of his lack of discipline. The stitches that the army medic had given him hadn't been made masterfully, so he wound up with a little crescent-shaped scar.

"It must've hurt terribly," she said, opening her eyes wide like a little girl seeing something new and unique.

Tasha had big, dark eyes. Her black hair was cut short around her neck, as was fashionable with young people in Andania City. Her skin was white, almost translucent, highlighting a light, reddish tan—proof of the hours she spent in the open. Her shapely body was lean but rounded in all the right places. John couldn't find any flaw in her. Her presence threw him back for a moment to another time and encounter on the ship that had brought him to New Australia. The same primeval feeling—one special to a meeting with a girl who still displayed the untamed spontaneity of youth—lingered in his mind.

This thought brought him an immediate feeling of guilt. Was he betraying Dana in his mind? But Dana was no longer a part of his reality. She hadn't been real to him for years, and still, not one day passed without John thinking of her. He had spent time with other women, but they had never been to him anything more than momentary partners for a pleasant time. Now, he became aware of a strange feeling, as if his glances at Tasha were too inquisitive.

John shook his head, trying to free himself of the strange, indefinable sensation. It must be the alcohol, he concluded. The peculiar excitement was attributable to the hangover and nothing else. The way to dispel those feelings was to talk. He had to babble fast and about neutral topics.

"How old are you?" he asked and immediately cursed himself for it. A neutral topic is 'the percentage of fat in Andanian milk' or 'the price of bread,' not personal stuff.

"I'm twenty-three. Do you believe me?"

"If you say so," answered John, surprised by how the question had been put.

"If so, you're a sucker. I'm not yet twenty. Do I look that old to you?"

"No, really," John answered apologetically, "twenty or twenty-three are both very young."

"How d'you like my fingernails?" she asked as if John hadn't spoken. She put her right hand on John's left hand and drummed on its back with her long fingernails.

"I don't know, I'm not an expert," mumbled John. Her jumpy style of conversation was making his head spin.

"So, when d'you want me to come 'n clean in the evening?" Tasha asked.

"I don't know. Whenever it is convenient for you. You're coming twice a day?"

"Yes. Those are my instructions. At least twice a day. Any time you need me more, it can be arranged."

"All right. Now I must go, okay?"

"No problem. I've got a key," she said. She stood and picked up the coffee cups, then became engulfed in her kitchen chores, ignoring John's presence and barely answering goodbye when he left the apartment.

John left earlier than he had to and walked to work. He needed to use the time to put some order in his thoughts and in the strange feelings that were bothering him. Perhaps it was the long time he had spent in the army, away from regular life, he concluded, that had displaced him from everyday social life. Now, he'd have to make an extra effort to fit back in.

CHAPTER 11

John's first week at his new job passed without any noticeable incident. On the first day, Eva had accompanied him to his office–a small room located at the end of a faraway corridor on the third floor of the Ministry of Commerce building. John realized that he had been assigned the farthest possible room from Barak's office, which was illogical, but he knew better than to look for logic where bureaucrats reigned. He wasn't sorry about his location, which also meant being far away from Eva's oppressive attention.

Eva had handed the keys to the office to John. "Pity we're so far from one another," she had said sorrowfully, "but don't you hesitate to call me if you need anything. Anything," she added invitingly.

"Thanks," John had said without any show of enthusiasm.

"Promise?" she had pressed.

"Absolutely," John had lied. He had forgotten Eva immediately and turned his attention to the computer keyboard on his desk.

In the army, John never had much time to spend on computers, but he jumped at every opportunity to exercise his working skills and keep up to date as much as possible. After all, he expected the day would come when he would return to his civilian occupation as a programmer.

John got acquainted with his computer tools the whole morning of that first day. He soon discovered that many files were password-protected and inaccessible to him. Nevertheless, he enjoyed every minute of his work. He sank deep into his new toy until his rumbling stomach reminded him that it was time to look for something to eat.

He had been so eager to get rid of Eva that he had omitted to ask her about the lunch arrangements. He was so hungry that he almost called her, although the result would almost inevitably be an invitation to join her. A knock on the door checked him before he pushed the button of the communication board.

"Come in," he called.

The door opened, and a woman, about thirty years old, walked in. Her short hair was blonde, and she wore black pants made of imitation leather fabric and a red-knitted, short-sleeved shirt appropriate for the day's heat.

"Hi," said John with open surprise, getting up quickly.

"Hi," echoed his visitor, smiling broadly at him. "It's been long since I saw a man stand up to greet a lady. All the self-centered machos here can learn from you."

"Oh," said John, "it's an instinct–I didn't think ..."

"That's what I was talking about," she said, still smiling. "You must be John."

"Yes, I'm John. And who are you?"

"I'm Samantha from the computation center. But everybody calls me Sammy."

"Sammy. All right. And whose secretary are you?"

Sammy lifted her chin and glanced at him.

"How appropriate of a chauvinist soldier to ask such a question," she said. "Sit down for a moment–you may need to," she added jokingly.

"Why?"

"Because I manage the Computer Center of the Ministry of Commerce. I hold a Ph.D. in advanced mathematical methods and am responsible for every piece of information and all the hardware in this building, including the one on your desk."

"Then you ..."

"Yes. Technically, I'm your boss for professional matters, anyway. You report to Barak, who carries out the policy of Deputy Minister Yabalan. But as far as the rest is concerned ..."

"I'm sorry," said John with embarrassment. He felt that he was blushing. "I didn't mean to be a chauvinist or to insinuate ... I didn't mean to insult you ..."

"No offense taken, don't worry. I'm used to this kind of reaction. Forget it, and let's get down to business. I came to see how you're doing. Have you been to lunch yet?"

"Truth is, I don't know where it is."

"Good. I haven't eaten either, and I'm starving. Let's go, and I'll fill you in on the way."

They left, locking the door after them. John reprogrammed the lock with his personal access code and wasn't worried about leaving his bag and belongings behind.

The coffee shop was on the ground floor of the building, a two-minute walk. As Sammy led him toward it, she pointed at various office doors along the way, naming the persons who occupied them and the positions they held. At the coffee shop entrance, they stood before a large machine with buttons to be pressed to order a meal. John had never seen such a device before, but after watching Sammy order her meal, he immediately understood how to order for himself.

The tables scattered around the room were bare and functional, and the place was crowded. Sammy chose to sit at a small, empty table rather than join others at a larger one.

The coffee shop atmosphere was pleasant enough despite the loud noise that made it difficult to have a real conversation. The walls were also bare, and little or no thought had been spent on the coffee shop's appearance.

"So, what did you manage to see today?"

"Not much. I played a little with my terminal to see what the system could do. I think the reaction time is good, but it's very slow in elliptical procedures. It's not a system as advanced as the ones I worked with on Earth."

"Yes, I know. We can't reach their level because they don't let us buy the most advanced processors they have. They always make sure that they maintain a qualitative advantage over us. Their capabilities are astonishing. I'd die to lay my hand on a system like the New Nations Organization uses," she added dreamily.

"Still, we can do a lot with what we have here. For instance, one of the tricks I tried was ..."

They sank deep into a technical discussion that resembled a dance. John led with one step in one direction, and Sammy immediately sidetracked him to a related topic she was more interested in. As the conversation continued, each learned more about the other and became better prepared for the next step. After a few minutes, their conversation resembled the movements of professional dancers who go on stage after long and tiresome rehearsals.

"You're a pro," Sammy said at last, appreciatively. "They told me so, but I thought they were exaggerating."

"You're not so bad yourself," John retorted. "You know," he added wistfully, "I haven't had a professional conversation like this for years. I forgot how much I missed it until now."

"Well, now you'll have every opportunity. I'm always happy to exchange views with someone who knows what he's talking about. But now it's time to go back."

They got up, placed their trays on the moving belt of a machine that swallowed them, and walked back to John's office. When they reached it, John said, "Come in for a moment, please. I want to show you the problems I've been experiencing with the system. Here," he added, checking the list he had prepared that morning, "all the files in the folder 'deployment plans' and those here, as well, you see? I couldn't get into any of those."

"Yes," said Sammy, nodding. "You need a special access code to get into those files. We've generated a code for you, written here." She handed him a folded piece of paper, which he unfolded. He glanced at it and saw a lengthy access code and, beside it, the statement "not for YYBZ files."

"What's a YYBZ file?"

"Those are secret files to which only the Deputy Minister has access. Even I can't get in—so don't try."

"But I'm his military secretary and have the highest security clearance. I may have to use them."

"No chance. I told you that only the Deputy Minister can access this part of the system. We built it according to his specific instructions so that even our experts couldn't crack the code and get in. He's the only person in the world who can."

"It doesn't make sense to me," said John. "You always need to have someone else who knows. What if something happens to the Deputy Minister? Or if he forgets what the access code is? Certainly the Minister also knows?"

"The Minister?" said Sammy, a tone of contempt ringing in her voice. "That puppet knows nothing at all. Can you see Yabalan trusting him with a secret access code?"

John was astonished by Sammy's words. He had heard much about Minister Sarpash and his dedication to Andania, and he couldn't understand Sammy's scorn for him.

"I don't understand what you mean," he said. "As far as I know, Minister Sarpash is a great man who did a lot for Andania, and we owe him a great debt of gratitude."

"Yeah, yeah," said Sammy cynically, "that's exactly the way he wants us to think about him, but, at least theoretically, he's my boss, and I don't want to talk about him. I've said too much already. You'll learn with time. Now I've got to run to a meeting. Welcome, and I'll see you around," she added quickly.

She waved her hand and left, leaving John deep in thought. This city held many surprises for him. It didn't resemble any other place he knew in Andania, and the people spoke and behaved differently from those he had met before.

The afternoon went by amazingly quickly for John. Nobody knocked on his door, and no calls came over the communication board. Around five p.m., he began to hear sounds of people leaving–doors slamming and quick steps loudly heard in the corridor–and he realized he had no idea what his working hours were supposed to be. He hadn't thought about it before because, in the military, his working hours included the whole day.

Pushing the " Barak " button on his communication board connected him instantaneously to Eva.

"You've caught me just leaving, Lieutenant," her face told him from the screen. "What can I do for you?"

"I wanted to ask about my working hours," he apologized.

Barak's face appeared on the screen next to Eva's.

"Is that you, John?" he asked. "Sorry I couldn't see you today. Did you manage okay?" Without waiting for an answer, he said, "You were asking about working hours? Well, officially, we work nine to five, but we expect some flexibility from you that is compatible with the Deputy Minister's needs, pretty much like I do. Right now, I'm going to a meeting with him, and God knows when it'll end. Anyway, you can leave every day at five unless we have other plans."

"You know, Barak, I still have no idea what my job is. I'd like to hear a little about ..."

"You'll pick it up. You'll soon learn," Barak interrupted him impatiently. "Okay, I must rush now. Talk to you tomorrow."

The screen went black, and John sat there, staring at it. His new employer behaved strangely–nobody seemed genuinely interested in John, but maybe they were merely giving him time to adjust. John knew every new place was different, and new rules had to be learned. Patiently. And if his job here was less of a strain than he was used to, it was all for the best.

He put his few belongings—a pen, a notepad, and wallet—into his little bag, turned off the light, shut the door behind him, and walked pensively home.

A pleasant surprise was in store for John when he reached his apartment—an inviting hot meal waited on the table set for him.

"I didn't know what you prefer to eat," said Tasha seriously, "and I hope you'll like what I've made. I've made vegetable pie and soy steak."

"Wow, what a surprise! I wasn't expecting it. I was told you would come to clean, not cook."

"Right. But I like to cook. Besides, this is my first job, and I want to make a good impression," she said candidly.

John smiled secretly at Tasha's simple openness. She seemed unable to hide her thoughts and shared them readily with him.

"I'm impressed. Thanks. And I'm sure I'll like the food. I'm easy to satisfy ... I didn't mean it like that," he added quickly when Tasha's expression showed that he had hurt her feelings. Her face was amazingly expressive, like a mirror of her thoughts, and it changed continuously. Looking at her was like watching a pantomime show.

"Oh, all right," she said. "I think the pie is good; it usually is. But tell me the truth, please."

"Promise. But where's your plate? Why did you put only one plate on the table?"

"No, thanks. I'm only the cleaning woman, don't forget. I'm supposed to serve you."

"Nonsense. Bring another plate and sit down to eat."

"No, really," Tasha said shyly, "you eat ..."

"Out of the question! If you don't sit with me, I won't eat either."

That settled the argument, and they sat down to eat Tasha's pie, which tasted good and split the soy steak, which was "hard but nourishing," as John's mother used to tell him.

That made him think of his parents, whom he hadn't spoken to for a long time. He had only spoken with them via video link twice. The last time was when he had graduated from the army academy. With the new rank on his shoulders, he had felt the urge to share his pride in his achievement with someone who cared. He had blown a month's worth of pay on a conversation that had turned out to be unsatisfactory and hadn't provided the warmth he longed for. On the other hand, his first call had lasted less than one minute and had been paid for by the army. It allowed for nothing more than a brief exchange of information–" I'm all right, Mom, Dad. Are you okay? How's everybody? I'm glad to hear that you're doing well. Yes, I'm fine," he had managed to say again before the line had gone out and the next soldier in line had approached the communication panel.

Now, for the first time, he felt a real need to call and hear his parents' voices. It was perhaps because he had suddenly found himself again living in a normal apartment instead of an army camp. He thought that, after all, we need a few stable things in our lives, even when we are mature adults.

"You haven't heard a word I've said!" Tasha complained.

"No, no. I heard. You were talking about your studies. I was listening. But I've just remembered that there's something I need to do."

"Okay. I need to leave anyway. Here you go, everything's in order," she added after the last plate went into the kitchen organizer that also kept the dishes clean.

John got up and escorted her to the door. He couldn't get used to treating her like a cleaning lady, but he knew he had to try to give her the feeling that she was doing a proper job. She looked very fragile to him, and the last thing he wanted was to hurt her feelings.

"Thanks for the meal," said Tasha, turning around on the doormat.

"Thank you," said John. "It was all delicious."

"I'm glad. I'll be here tomorrow morning, as usual," she said and left.

As usual? What a strange statement from someone who had just started working that day. But Tasha was out of the ordinary in almost every aspect. John was charmed by this strange young woman because of her weirdness, winning innocence, and spontaneity.

With an effort, he turned his thoughts to the upcoming conversation with his parents. The Ministry of Commerce paid for the communication system in his apartment, and calls to Earth were not blocked. He decided that this meant his employers didn't object to him using it. He approached the keyboard and ordered the call, seeing that it was almost seven p.m. in his parents' time zone. By the scheduled time of the call, about one hour later, his parents would be in the living room resting after dinner. He sat in an armchair, waiting for the call to come through, and, for the first time since his departure from Earth, he looked forward to talking to them.

John was startled awake by the ring of the communication system ... the fatigue of the last few days, combined with the excellent dinner, had caused him to doze off in his armchair. His army life had taught him to jump instantly from a state of heavy sleep into complete awareness, and in a matter of seconds, he got up, seated himself on the chair in front of the communication system, and pushed the "accept" button. His mother's familiar features appeared on the screen; she looked completely different from what John remembered. She seemed much older, and her face was sad.

"Mother ..." said John, but his voice broke. He felt helpless, not knowing what to say or how to bridge the distance of time and space.

"Johnny, honey," said his mother, "you look so good, so strong and handsome. And what is that rank? Are you a colonel?"

"No, Mom," John smiled at her. "Not yet a colonel, only a lieutenant. You look good too, Mom," he lied.

"So you got my letter?" she asked.

"Letter? No, what letter? I haven't received any letter. Where's Dad?"

"I wrote to you more than two weeks ago, to the last address you gave me. I thought that was why you were calling."

"No, Mom. It takes more than one month for a letter to get to Andania. I haven't received any letter; I just missed you and Dad and decided to call. I have a new job in the city, so now it's easier for me."

Something unfamiliar in his mother's expression stopped him. The slight delay in the screen response, because of the distance, made the conversation seem unreal; nevertheless, he sensed something strange in his mother's behavior.

"Then, you don't know about your father ..."

"What is it that I don't know?" John asked in sudden panic.

"Your father passed away a month ago, Johnny. I'm sorry. I had no way to tell you other than writing you a letter."

John felt suddenly emptied of all his strength and sat there, staring at his mother without speaking. He fought back the tears that surged at the corners of his eyes, lowered his head, and asked quietly, "How did it happen?"

"It was old age, Johnny. He was brokenhearted because of our world and the people in it. He simply found no more interest in life. He said to me, 'I'm fed up. I'm going. I've nothing to look forward to here,' and he faded away before my eyes until, one morning, he didn't wake up, just like that. He didn't suffer. He only went away, just like he said he'd do."

"And how are you holding on, Mom? Do you manage all right?"

"Your brothers help a little. They come sometimes, and that helps some. I'm coping. But ... oh, I miss him so much, Johnny," she said, bursting into tears.

This proud woman–always so cold and far away–could no longer hold her tears back, and John felt powerless to help. He wanted to go to touch and comfort her, but all he could do was sit there, murmuring useless words of comfort.

"I want to go with him," she wept, "I don't want to remain here alone, without him. I want to go too ..."

She became silent, then wiped her tears with a handkerchief that appeared in her hand as if by magic and forced a smile.

"I'm sorry. We shouldn't be wasting the short time we have. Tell me about you. What's new with you? I'm sure you're doing well."

From that moment on, they continued a surrealistic conversation in which they both tried to strengthen the other without success. John ended the call with a promise to call again soon and often.

John sat in his chair for a long time after his mother's wrinkled face disappeared from the screen, searching for the inner strength he needed to get up and go on. He tried to remember his father as he had always seen him: quiet and authoritative, with enough strength to give to everybody. Still, John found it hard to accept the fact that his father, of all people, had willfully surrendered his life. He recalled the good times with his father as tears ran uncontrollably down his cheeks. But now that nobody was watching, he no longer fought them.

When his tears finally dried, he knew one thing for sure: he wanted to drink and to get drunk, to stop the flow of images that chased the pictures from his childhood around in his head. He left the apartment without turning off the lights and walked quickly toward the bar where he had spent the previous evening. That was the only way he knew to exorcise all his demons and shut out his thoughts from his head.

CHAPTER 12

Barak stood by his desk, briefing the people in the room. Besides John, two others were present. One of them, Rakkash, later introduced himself to John as the "Public Relations Manager." The other, whose name John hadn't caught, held the title of "Director of Documentation," which meant he was responsible for taking the Deputy Minister's picture wherever he went.

"Please pay attention," Rakkash told the Director of Documentation when John entered the room. "You must catch the Deputy Minister at an angle that will make him look taller than the Minister. It is also important that you concentrate on having him as much as possible in the picture, together with the ambassador of the New Nations."

"I made sure that the ambassador's seat is next to that of the Deputy Minister," added Barak. "You shouldn't have any problem with that. Hi, John," he said when he noticed he had joined them. "Take a chair. I'll be with you in a moment. Just finishing something."

John sat silently and listened to the instructions that Barak gave the others. All that talk about camera angles and protocol made little sense to him, and he let his mind wander to a computer problem on which he had stumbled the day before.

A few minutes later, the Director of Documentation and Rakkash left, and John focused on Barak.

"Oof ..." Barak complained. "Why must I waste my time explaining such simple matters? Well, we are ready, more or less."

"You know, I don't have a clue what you're talking about," John pointed out.

"True, true. You're right. I'll explain." He sat behind his desk, raised a glass with a pink liquid, took a couple of sips, and started to explain. "Today is the Council of Commerce opening assembly, which marks a new business year. To celebrate it, we have a special meeting this afternoon in the People's Council Hall. Yan-Nibar, the People's Council head, will open the ceremony. Afterward, as protocol requires, he'll hand the conduction of the ceremony to the Minister of Commerce, Sarpash. The importance of the event is that it is broadcast to the whole of Andania and the New Nations, and that's the reason for all the detailed preparations."

Yan-Nibar! The Head of the People's Council, the operative arm of the Andanian government, was a mythological figure on account of his long fight for the unification of all the various factions that ruled different parts of Andania—unification that had brought about the creation of the People's Council, which he had been repeatedly elected to head ever since. The people admired him, mainly because of all the economic advantages the unification brought about, strengthening Andania's position vis-à-vis the New Nations Organization. John had never imagined that the day would come when he would find himself in the same room with Yan-Nibar.

"Am I supposed to be there?" he asked, hoping he was.

"Of course. All the staff has to be there. In a moment, I'll get you into the Deputy Minister's office as soon as he's free."

"At last," John commented. He had started to feel superfluous after an entire week on the job, during which he hadn't yet made his boss' acquaintance.

"He wants to meet you," said Barak.

"You know, I've never seen Yan-Nibar in person. This is an important event for me."

"You'll see him today. But don't be fooled by his soft talk and his appearance. He's not all that people think."

"What d'you mean?"

"He's the façade of our government. He talks like a ruler and looks like one, and because of him, we can pass many decisions and laws that somebody else wouldn't have a chance of getting accepted by the People's Council. But, in reality, he's a spineless weakling."

"Who's running the show, then?" asked John.

"That's a complex question. Let's say that you and I are very close to the nerve center of Andania. The strong man in our government—which is no secret to those who understand a little about our politics—is the Minister of Commerce, Sarpash."

"Now you've got me confused," said John. "The rumors I heard about Sarpash are that he's not something ..."

"Aha!" Barak laughed, "I see that the toddler is learning to walk already. You're right. He's a stuffed shirt, but he doesn't know that. He thinks he's the real thing."

"So, what are you saying?"

"I'm saying that Sarpash thinks he's the strong man, and he thinks he's running the show. The one who's really in charge is the one who makes Sarpash tick, or, in other words, our boss Yabalan. That's why, my friend, he who influences Deputy Minister Yabalan—meaning your humble servant—greatly influences every-thing that goes on in Andania. You see now?"

Barak's extraordinary explanation had been given with a smug smile, and John didn't know whether to take Barak's words as a joke or the truth. But before he had time to ask more, a voice came from the communication panel on Barak's desk. "The Deputy Minister will see you now," said Eva.

"Come on, John," said Barak. He got up quickly and walked to the door without looking back to see if John was following.

Deputy Minister Yabalan's office was located near Barak's. It was a spacious and elegant office filled with expensive furniture. In the ante-office sat two secretaries who didn't even dignify John with a glance when he walked by them. Barak knocked lightly on the door, then walked in without waiting for an invitation. The Deputy Minister was sitting on a couch in one of the corners of his office. Two men, unknown to John, were seated in the armchairs facing him. Barak stood by the door, and John stood at attention beside him by force of habit.

"At ease, soldier," Barak whispered with open mockery.

John blushed and slightly released his body's tension but didn't assume a full "at ease" position. John sized up the Deputy Minister as the two unknown persons took their leave with elaborate parting words. He looked for signs of the strength Barak had hinted at but couldn't find any. The man was small and round, with salon-blown hair which, at the same time, seemed to stick to his scalp. He was soft-spoken and never looked his interlocutor in the eyes. If asked to define him in one word, John would have called him 'oily.'

The guests left, and the Deputy Minister turned his attention to Barak and John.

"Come over here, please," he said, pointing at his large desk. Apparently, the protocol did not allow simple employees in the guests' corner.

Nevertheless, he shook John's hand. John was surprised to be met by a sweaty and limp handshake, not in tune with the "strong man" image of Yabalan that he had pictured.

"Welcome, Lieutenant," Yabalan greeted him. "I've heard a lot about you, and I'm sure your contribution to our plans for

Andania will be great. I'm certain that you understand the importance of our plans," he added conspiratorially.

"Ahem ..." Barak intervened in what sounded like a reproachful tone. "The lieutenant hasn't yet had the time to learn all the background material needed for his job. But I'm briefing him with the appropriate speed. Nothing to worry about, sir."

"All right, all right," said Yabalan dismissively. You'll obviously attend today's ceremony," he stated.

"Those are my orders, sir," John said formally.

"Good. Then, take into account that after the official ceremony, the Ministry of Commerce holds an annual cocktail party in honor of all the companies that do business with Andania and of the ambassador of the New Nations. All the high society of Andania will be there. That will be a good opportunity to get acquainted with many important people. Now I've got to deal with other matters," he said, looking at Barak. "I'll see you later."

John almost saluted, but the Deputy Minister had already turned his attention to the papers on his desk. It seemed that, as far as he was concerned, his employees were no longer in the room. Barak walked out without another word, and John followed suit.

"So now what?" he asked. "Do you have any special instructions for me?"

"No. Go and get organized, and I'll see you at six for the ceremony. Eva will explain how to get there."

John was left alone in the corridor. He stood there for a minute outside the door of Yabalan's office. After the meeting, he still didn't know what his job was or the plans of which the Deputy Minister had spoken.

Back in his office, John tried to concentrate on computer exercises but with little success. He was happy to hear the light knock on the door that he had learned to recognize as Sammy's.

"You're going to the ceremony?" she asked, standing at the door.

"Yes, I've been asked to. And you?"

"I pass. Doesn't appeal to me. I just wanted to give you a word of warning …"

John lifted an eyebrow but didn't speak, so she went on.

"It may be … there is a good likelihood that Yabalan will invite you to a private party after the cocktails. You must find a polite way to refuse if you're not like that."

"Like what?"

"You know …" Sammy looked embarrassed.

"No, I don't. Like what?"

"Like Yabalan. One who likes men."

"Are you saying that Yabalan is gay?"

"Of course. Didn't you know that?"

"How should I know? Anyway, I'm not."

"I guessed that much. But everybody knows about Yabalan and his preferences. We just don't talk about them, and nobody cares about them."

"I don't care either; why should I? But why do you think that he'll invite me?"

"I can't be sure, but he might. You're a beautiful guy, and I won't be surprised if they'll come on to you … that way, he'll be able to find out if you have "inclinations." If you don't refuse to go, you're in trouble because he'll take that as an interest on your part, and if he finds out later on that you're not into it, it may cause him embarrassment with his friends."

"But if … *when* I refuse, won't that offend him all the same?" asked John.

"Not if you do it gently. He'll simply understand that you're not interested and will leave you alone. You only need a good excuse. A headache or something."

John mused on what Sammy had just told him. It showed him how little he knew about his new environment and its strange rules. He smiled an embarrassed smile.

"You just saved me. I don't think I would've caught on to it alone. I owe you."

"You're welcome," she said, smiling back. "I'll be happy to save you any time."

"Funny that Barak didn't warn me. He must have known that I might end up embarrassing myself," John thought aloud.

"Welcome to Andania City," said Sammy. She waved at him and left.

The ceremonial hall was packed. John estimated that more than a thousand people sat there, with the first three rows filled with all the important people who had their reserved seats. He stood by himself next to the third row. He preferred to stand there rather than sit in one of the last rows, where it would have been difficult to see what was happening on stage. Barak was seated at the back of the stage, behind Yabalan, with the aides and other staff members, but John chose not to inquire whether he had a seat reserved for him there. He felt more comfortable in the cozy anonymity of his dark corner.

Yan-Nibar was already seated by the table on stage, wearing a white suit tailored to look like an army uniform. Sarpash sat beside him on one side and Yabalan on the other. Silence fell upon the hall as Yan-Nibar stood up and approached the podium to begin his speech. He had a deep voice, and he enunciated each word with care as if a word not carefully spoken might break up before reaching his lips. Despite all the effort he put into his speech, he swallowed the endings of many words, creating a slurred effect similar to the manner of a drunkard trying to sound sober. The result sounded peculiar, and to follow his words, one had to focus all his attention on their meaning.

"Honorable friends," he began his address pompously, "I am glad to be here today to open this wonderful evening. My friend and partner, Minister Sarpash, will talk more about the many exciting projects planned by the Ministry of Commerce."

"He can't stop babbling, can he?" a voice whispered near John's ear. John turned and saw Rakkash standing beside him, smiling and nodding. "Let's hope he'll be brief this time for a change," he added.

"Mmm," John mumbled noncommittally without shifting his gaze from the stage. The contempt expressed by his colleagues against what John viewed as the almost mystical symbols of the government of Andania, Yan-Nibar, and Sarpash left him astonished. He had never been interested in politics; he had been sure that everybody admired the two statesmen, as he had heard from his first day in Andania. Making fun of them simply didn't seem right to him.

After a while, Rakkash, obviously discouraged by John's cold shoulder, moved away and positioned himself near the first row. Photographers and other people, looking very busy, approached him occasionally and got instructions.

The speeches went on and on. Sarpash spoke after Yan-Nibar, and then came the turn of other apparently important people. Deep in thought, John paid no attention to the speeches until, after a final loud round of applause, the audience got up and streamed through a large door into the adjacent hall, where refreshments were being served. He stood there, uncertain what was expected of him, until he saw Barak approaching him. He signaled him with his hand, and Barak stopped.

"Why didn't you come on stage?" Barak asked with open anger. "It's bad for the Deputy Minister if not all his aides sit behind him during public appearances."

"Nobody told me that I should sit there," said John apologetically, "I stood here because I wasn't sure ..."

"Never mind," Barak interrupted. Then, as an afterthought, he went on rebuking him. "It's obvious that the size of his entourage evidences the importance of every politician–and I worked so hard the whole week to ensure everybody had a seat on stage. Well," he added impatiently, "I must rush. Try at least now to correct the bad impression."

"But what am I supposed to do?" John asked, feeling lost. However, Barak was already on his way to the cocktail hall and didn't hear his question, or if he did, he chose to ignore it.

A few hundred guests walked around the cocktail hall and conversed in groups and couples, creating a loud noise. Waiters moved dexterously in the crowd, handing out a constant supply of snacks and drinks. John didn't see a familiar face in the crowd and felt lost. He took a position near the door and tried to find someone he knew with whom to exchange at least a few words, but with no success. He felt relieved when a young man approached him.

"Lieutenant," he addressed him unceremoniously, "I see you're not mixing with the guests."

"I'm new here and don't know anybody," John answered.

"Allow me to introduce myself," said the young man. "My name is Jay Miner, and I am the son of the president of 'AIM–Andanian Intelligent Metals.' Perhaps you have heard of us?" he asked, holding a hand for John to shake.

AIM was not unknown to John. As the largest industrial concern in New Australia, it drew its power from the natural resources of the mines it controlled.

"Of course," said John, shaking the young man's hand. "Pleased to meet you."

"My pleasure, entirely, Lieutenant," Jay said graciously. "It's a shame that a talented soldier like you stands here, all by himself, instead of using the time to get acquainted with the nightlife of Andania City. I'll tell you what," he said, brightening up. "My good friend, Deputy Minister Yabalan, is throwing a private party as soon as this cocktail hour is over, and he agreed with me that it would be very nice if you would care to join us–it's not a formal occasion," he added quickly when John, who was now really scared, started shaking his head. "You don't have to worry that this is your boss' party. It will be an intimate occasion–just a few friends and good food."

"I'm grateful to you for your invitation–and to the Deputy Minister, of course," said John, Sammy's warning ringing vividly in his ears, "but I feel unwell. As soon as my official role in the function ends, I'll run home and get into bed until morning."

Jay gave him a slanted look and nodded, the disappointment apparent on his face.

"Oh. All right, if that's how you feel ..." he said.

"Yes,..." John left his answer hanging in the air.

"See you some other time, then," concluded Jay.

"Absolutely," said John, but Jay had already turned his back to him, and the answer got lost in the room's noise.

John walked around for a few more minutes, hiding behind a glass of an unfamiliar-tasting drink until he felt sure nobody was paying any attention to him. Then he put his glass on the table near the door and left.

Despite his instructions to stay and participate in the cocktail party, he felt that he'd had enough, and, for the first time since he joined the army, he decided to act against his orders. Let them fire me, he said to himself while his anger mounted. He wasn't sure that the place was right for him anyway.

CHAPTER 13

The days after the ceremony were uneventful. Barak never again mentioned his friend's departure from the protocol. John decided not to mention Yabalan's indirect invitation and move on. Toward the end of the week, Barak summoned him for a briefing.

"Next week, we are going to have a critical meeting with the representatives of the New Nations," he said. "This is an unprecedented meeting at which we'll be talking about important issues, and it'll take place at the New Nation's base."

"What's the 'New Nation's base'?" John asked, having never heard of it.

"It's the new seat of the NNO's representatives, which is located in no man's land, between us and the Newists. That's where the NNO delegation works."

"I thought they were located in Andania City," said John with surprise.

"No," Barak explained, "here they only keep a small office that works with us on daily matters. Their base has been positioned outside Andanian territory to avoid hurting the feelings of the Newists."

"As if those barbarians had feelings," John spat bitterly.

"You'd be surprised," said Barak quietly. "Don't think that we have a monopoly on feelings. They, too, feel hurt from our actions, and the sooner we realize that, the better for us."

"Maybe ..." John said, looking unconvinced.

"Anyway, we'll be there for three days. We leave in four days. By then," he said in a peremptory tone, "you must have full command of all the maps of the border between the Newists and us, of the metal mines, the agricultural units, and the deployment of our forces."

"What does that have to do with commercial talks?" John inquired with open surprise.

"It does, it does," Barak answered impatiently. "You're the military secretary of the Deputy Minister, and one can never tell when he'll need answers to all kinds of questions. You, in any case, must have them ready."

John was a good soldier and knew better than to argue with orders, even those that didn't make sense, so he returned to his office and started to get ready. He made working copies of all the required maps and data, most of which he was already familiar with from past activities. A review of the current deployment of the army at the border was readily available on his computer. By the day's end, he felt he already knew all the relevant information. He spent the rest of the week making arrangements with the units on the field according to the travel plan that Barak had given him.

The trip to the NNO base took about two hours. Deputy Minister Yabalan rode in the vehicle immediately after John's. The rest of the delegation was distributed among the various vehicles that followed. The first and last vehicles were part of the military escort joining them at the checkpoint before they entered no man's land.

It was almost dark when John finally saw the NNO base with

its buildings scattered against the side of a green hill. A few words with the gatekeeper gained them access to the perimeter, and the escort turned back toward the checkpoint. The NNO representatives escorted Yabalan with much ceremony to the ambassador's house, where a richly furnished suite awaited him. The delegation's remaining members were directed to much more spartan quarters, which consisted of a row of prefabricated units that reminded John of a toy train he had played with as a child. John's room was small but comfortable, and he organized his belongings in it quickly.

A light rap on the door got his attention as a voice came from outside. "Dinner will be served in half an hour in the main building, sir. Thank you, sir," the voice added over the footsteps moving away on the wooden porch. The rap and the announcement repeated themselves at the door next to John's room and eventually faded away, presumably toward the next building.

John changed from his fatigues into his best uniform and, half an hour later, joined the crowd that waited outside the main building. About fifty people had gathered before the door leading into the dining room, about twenty of them employees of the Ministry of Commerce whom John knew at least superficially. They whispered as John stood aside, watching. Then, a hand gently took hold of his arm.

"Hi," said Sammy, who had joined him. "What are we waiting for?"

"I've no idea," John answered. "I just got here."

Sammy stood beside him silently, holding his arm naturally, as though she had always done that. After a while, someone opened the door, and the crowd started to file in.

"Let's go in," Sammy said, pulling him toward the door.

The dining room was large and filled with long tables. Someone had distributed knives and forks on the red tablecloths, but John saw no sign that special care had been taken to decorate the room for the guests. They sat at the first free places they found, and Sammy started talking with her neighbor, who was obviously a local employee. At John's right sat two people he didn't recognize, who conducted a heated discussion and ignored his presence altogether. Overall, John felt relieved when the dinner ended, and, seeing that Sammy had disappeared, he walked quickly back to his room. The next day's plans left little room for rest, and he wanted to call it a day.

Each prefabricated building had three rooms and a shower with hot running water, and John rushed to take possession of the one in his building before anyone else had the same idea. He enjoyed standing under the hot water, letting it wash away the day's fatigue. A few minutes later, walking back, he was surprised to see the light on in his room. He was sure he had turned it off on his way to the shower, and he didn't like the idea of an intruder in his room.

He walked swiftly to the door and banged it open. Sammy was reclining on his bed.

"You scared me!" she complained. "Do you always open doors that way?"

"Only when I suspect a burglary," John answered, smiling. "What can I do for you?"

"You can start by shutting the door. I'm freezing."

John dropped his kit and towel on the bag he had left in one corner of the room and walked up to the bed, waiting for Sammy to speak.

"This bathrobe suits you, soldier, do you know that?"

"I'm sure you haven't come here just to compliment me on my bathrobe."

"No," said Sammy. She took John's hand and pulled lightly. "Why don't you sit down beside me for a moment?"

"I think it may be better for me to stand," John said quietly.

"God! You're going to make this difficult for me, right?"

John pulled Sammy's hand, and she got up from the bed. She

stood beside him, so close that John felt her rhythmic breath on his face.

"I don't know what you mean ..." he started to say but stopped when Sammy raised her hand to caress his cheek.

"I don't think you're a dolt–and if you aren't, you know that I ... how shall I put it ... I'm interested in you."

"You're drunk!" John uttered. There was no room for mistake; the smell of alcohol coming from her mouth was too strong.

"I may have had a little drink after dinner," she conceded, "but only to gather the courage to come here. I'm not drunk."

"Sit down on the bed," John ordered. "You're so drunk that in a moment, you'll drop on the floor."

"You know what," Sammy said with sudden anger, "Tell me I don't interest you. Tell me that you find me repulsive, and I'll go. At least be a man and tell me the truth."

"I find you very attractive," John said softly, "but I also know that you are my boss and that we shouldn't get involved as long as we work together. Besides, I stay away from drunken women who don't know what they're doing."

"Bullshit," Sammy giggled. "At the Ministry of Commerce, everybody gets involved with everybody else. This is the norm here. I mean,... except for myself. I've always kept my distance... until now. I don't believe you're such a nerd ..." she added with a sigh.

She tried to approach the door, but her feet betrayed her, and she stumbled. John moved quickly and caught her before she fell. He lifted her and held her tight while she regained her equilibrium. Sammy opened her eyes, blinked, and gawked drunkenly at him.

"After all, you're hugging me ..." she murmured.

"I'm not hugging you. I'm holding you to keep you from falling. Come on," he said, "I'll walk you to your room."

Sammy's room was nearby, and she walked silently, supporting herself against his side. She hadn't locked her door, which opened when John touched it. He felt the wall until his hand reached the light switch and turned it on, then he walked her in and closed the door.

"Do you think you can manage by yourself?" he asked.

Sammy nodded in assent and lay down on the bed, her eyes shut.

"John," she whispered.

"Yes?"

"Turn off the light on your way out."

"All right. Good night," he said softly.

"John!" she called again, opening her eyes. "I know what I'm doing. Maybe I was stupid to drink a little too much today, but next time, I won't need the booze to come to you." She closed her eyes-and seemed to have fallen asleep, but she opened them again and gazed at him. "Please tell me if we have a chance," she whispered weakly.

John stooped over the bed, took her hand, and kissed her brow.

"We'll talk about it when you are sober ... if you still like the idea."

"John, you talk too much," she commented, then turned on her side and fell asleep.

A shiver ran along John's spine. Dana had told him that he was talking too much, and Sammy's words were so evocative of Dana that a rush of memories surged in his head.

Sammy was sleeping peacefully. John covered her with a thin sheet, then turned off the light and stood by the door. He looked at her figure on the bed, barely discernible in the little light from the few lampposts scattered around the compound. For a moment, he imagined that she was his Dana. Sammy's words resounded in his head, "You talk too much ...." The last beautiful hours spent with Dana, right before their landing on New Australia, came back to him as if they had happened the day before. With an effort, he took his eyes off the bed, closed the door, and walked heavily back to his room.

The morning air was pure and cold, and John didn't mind the need to wait outside the dining room. Through the windows, he watched as the waiters prepared the long tables for breakfast. John had gotten up early, as he used to do every day. When he reached the central building, only a handful of local employees waited to be let into the dining room.

At last, the door opened, and John sat at the edge of the first table. The plastic tableware was simple and not so clean, but the strong smell of coffee from the coffee pot on the table attracted all his attention. He poured himself a cup, drank quickly, and then poured a second. As the hot liquid infused new purposefulness into his body, he turned to the central table on which various dishes were displayed. Types of cheese that John hadn't seen in a long time adorned the table, along with bread, vegetables, and fruits. He ate with appetite, stimulated by the fresh morning air coming in through the wide-open windows.

By the time John finished his breakfast, only a few other people had come to the dining room. It was still early, with the first meeting more than one hour away, and John decided to use that time to tour the base. As his first random target, he chose a group of one-story buildings opposite the Andanian sleeping quarters. He strolled, listening to the morning sounds coming from the rooms he passed. Suddenly, the door of a room in front of him opened without warning, and, to John's surprise, Barak's figure appeared in the doorway. He was taking his leave from a man and, after a few words, turned around and left toward the Andanian quarters. Instinctively, John hid in the shadow of the building near him and continued to watch. His surprise increased when he got a good view of the man who had been talking to his friend. The man's identity was unknown to him, but he had no trouble guessing his origin by his clothes, the unkempt beard, and the way he tied his long hair. Undoubtedly, the man was a Newist. But what was a Newist doing at the base of the New Nations? And what business did Barak have talking with him?

John approached the window of the room into which the Newist had disappeared, looking for a place from which he might see what was inside, but he couldn't find a safe place hidden from the sight of the people within. Still, from the little he saw, it was clear to him that at least three Newists were present and that they had weapons. The presence of armed Newists at the base while an Andanian delegation was there was a grave and puzzling matter. John walked quickly away, then almost ran to the sleeping quarters of the Andanian delegation. He reached Barak's room, knocked briefly on the door, and turned the handle. Barak was standing in the middle of the room, organizing his bag. He looked with surprise at John, who had closed the door behind him and stood without speaking.

"Yes, you may come in," said Barak. John, however, was unimpressed by his cynicism.

"What were you doing there?" John demanded threateningly.

"There? Where? What are you talking about?"

"You know very well what I'm talking about," John retorted angrily. "There. With the Newists. With the enemy. With my and your enemy that strolls around here armed to the teeth. What is this?" John continued heatedly but tried to keep his voice low. "Is this a trap?"

Barak's expression grew serious. He dropped a pair of socks from his hand and spoke in a low, quiet voice.

"Sit down, John," he ordered, pointing the finger at the straw armchair near a small desk.

"I'd rather stand," John said, acting stubborn.

"Sit down, I said!" Barak ordered again. This time, his voice was authoritative and carried no trace of friendship. John sat in the armchair and, without moving his gaze, waited for Barak to speak.

Barak dragged a chair from another corner of the room and sat facing John.

"What you saw this morning is part of the purpose of this trip. You were supposed to hear about it from Yabalan later today, but I'll explain briefly since you already discovered that the Newists are here."

John moved restlessly in his seat but refrained from asking questions, waiting patiently for the explanation.

"The New Nations' representatives are acting as brokers between us and the Newists," Barak explained. "Minister Sarpash has been holding secret negotiations with the Newists for months now, using Yabalan, at his instigation, to reach a breakthrough in our relations with them. We are progressing well, but the talks have reached a critical point. The NNO helps us, and the commercial talks are, in fact, a cover-up for the secret negotiations with the Newists. Do you understand now why we keep everything hush-hush? If the fact that negotiations are taking place leaks at such a delicate stage, the whole thing may blow up in our faces."

"So what's going to happen now?" asked John.

"In fifteen minutes, we have the plenary session of the commercial talks. At this meeting, we split the participants into working teams, and all teams–Andanians and NNO people–will adjourn to separate meeting rooms for detailed discussions ... everybody except the two of us and the Deputy Minister. We will meet with Yabalan for a briefing, after which we will talk with the Newists."

"What is the level of the Newist delegation?"

"Ah, it's the highest level!" said Barak enthusiastically. "We are going to meet with the president of the Newist people, Tafa-Aru Sed, and three of his closest advisors–the head of the military forces, Tibargo; Sed's deputy, Nazameb; and his foreign minister, Takira. This is indeed a team with which we can do business."

"But ... but can we trust those barbarians to honor their under-takings?"

"You'll be surprised," said Barak, smiling forgivingly. They are very practical people, and it is much easier to reach an agreement with them than with some of our people. Don't stick to precon- ceived ideas."

"Mmm ..." John said doubtfully. "I'll believe it when I see it happening with my own eyes. I know the murderous bastards ..."

"I know them too," Barak interrupted him. "Don't forget that I was wounded in battle against them. Nevertheless, Yabalan believes—and I am with him—that reaching peace and under- standing with them is possible. I see that you're not convinced," he added when John's expression left no doubt about that, "but that doesn't matter now. We follow our boss's instructions. Let's get moving before we're late for the plenary session."

The plenary session turned out to be primarily a ceremonial event, kicked off by greetings from the head of the Trade Committee of the New Nations Organization, followed by a similar speech from Yabalan. Both avoided any mention of the Newists.

The session ended with the NNO representative announcing the names of the participants in the various committees; then, everybody went to their prescribed meeting rooms. Barak and John waited for all participants, including Yabalan, to leave and then stepped into a small meeting room adjacent to the audito- rium. Yabalan was waiting for them in an elegant armchair and didn't bother to get up or acknowledge that his aides had arrived. It was no secret within the Ministry of Commerce that Yabalan was an egomaniac and made it a point to remind his subordinates of their place at every opportunity.

"Come in, boys," he said, speaking condescendingly. John and Barak took two small chairs placed before the deputy minister.

Yabalan turned to Barak. "Have you brought John up to speed?" he asked.

"I did. Actually, I had no choice after John discovered the pres- ence of the Newists here at the camp and attached the wrong inter- pretation to it."

"Good," said Yabalan, and John wasn't sure whether he was

showing pleasure or anger, perhaps because he had been deprived of the opportunity to break the news to John himself. "Then we can cut to the chase," he said. "First of all–and there should be no need for me to tell you this–I want to impress upon you that our talks here, including the fact that they are taking place ... everything–and I mean everything–is top secret. Nobody except the three of us can know anything about them."

"And Minister Sarpash, of course," John corrected.

"Mmm ... yes and no. Sarpash, of course, knows about our contacts, but he has entrusted me with the details, and it wouldn't be right to feed him bits and pieces of information. When something worth reporting crystallizes, I'll report to him."

"Mister Deputy Minister, sir," said John, a sudden thought occurring to him. "If the talks are so secret that even the minister doesn't know what's going on, perhaps it isn't safe to discuss them here, in a room that may be bugged."

"Nothing to worry about," explained Yabalan. "I have asked my NNO friends a direct question about this, and they have assured me that there is nothing to be concerned about. They're dealing with that."

"Yes, but they might ..."

"Let's waste no more time!" Yabalan cut him short. "I tell you that this is a non-issue. We can move on. What's the schedule?" he asked, turning to Barak.

Barak pulled a piece of paper from his inner pocket and consulted it. "We're meeting at their quarters in half an hour," he said. "We have three hours until lunch break; then we'll have lunch in the mess hall so that our people see us and assume that we're participating in the trade talks. After lunch, we have time until dinner. Our NNO friends will keep our delegation busy throughout the afternoon, and the Newists will leave in the middle of the night to avoid being seen."

"May I ask a stupid question?" said John.

"Please," said Yabalan, "but be quick," he added with an evident lack of patience.

"If we want to be so secretive about it all, why the trade talks cover-up? Couldn't we simply, the three of us, come over here for two days and work freely without hiding from our people?"

Yabalan rolled his eyes to the ceiling. "Explain, Barak," he ordered.

"We can't simply disappear into nowhere for two days. If we are missing for that long, people will gossip, and the secrecy of the talks will go down the drain."

"Oh, all right," John murmured. "I'm not used to that kind of thing yet."

"You'll learn," Yabalan simply stated. "Now, let's talk about what's going to happen today. Sed wants to know which agricultural settlements we will hand over to him when we sign the non-aggression agreement. This is a major point of disagreement right now. All other issues have been solved. Regarding the mines, we have already agreed to a co-management with our recognition of Newist ownership."

"I don't understand, Mister Deputy Minister," John intervened. "Are we going to hand over ownership of all mines to the Newists?"

"Well, not all the mines. Not this one, near Andania City," explained Yabalan, indicating a point on the map that covered the small table between them, "which remains officially owned by us."

"But I don't understand. I always thought that the economy of Andania was dependent on those mines. If we give the Newists ninety percent of them, how will we support our economy?"

"You don't understand how bright the agreement we have conceived is," Yabalan explained patiently as if speaking to a small child. "We are not handing the mines over to them. We only recognize that they own them. This is only a moral victory for the Newists–a recognition of the rights they feel have been usurped by us–but this has no practical result. The mines remain in our hands with a lease of two hundred years. We will build peaceful relations with the Newists during that period, and everything will look different."

"But ... I beg your pardon for asking, sir, but what happens if, after we recognize that they own the mines, the Newists decide that they want to exploit them by themselves and kick us out? How are we going to stop them? We won't be able to take them back by force with all the NNO representatives working there and acting as a human shield."

"The question is legitimate, John, but don't worry. Tafa-Aru Sed is a reliable man who seeks peace, and I trust his word. Besides, the New Nations Organization is aware of all the nuances of the agreement."

John listened attentively to the explanation that Yabalan was delivering with a strength that comes from inner conviction. When he asked no more, the deputy minister continued.

"Let's talk about the agricultural settlements. Here, we must be cautious. We currently have one hundred and twenty operational settlements covering all the cultivatable areas around Andania. The Newists demand that we hand over thirty of them. This is a problem because our projections show that ninety settlements are the minimum needed to meet the demand of the Andanian population at its expected level twenty-five years from now."

"Fifteen years," Barak corrected.

"I've seen your figures, Barak. But my experts tell me that twenty-five years is a more realistic estimate. Anyway, we'll get there at some point. That's why we need to include in the agreement an undertaking of the Newists to sell us produce from these agricultural settlements, as needed."

"Sir," John intervened, taking advantage of a brief pause in the conversation, from which he felt left out. "Why do they need our agricultural settlements? They have the entire surface of New Australia to themselves. We are only a tiny spot on the map. They can grow vegetables wherever they want."

"That's why we have statesmen, thank God, who understand what they do, and we have soldiers who follow orders," said Yabalan in a scornful tone that brought a flush to John's cheeks. "The problem's parameters are that the Newists have claims on those settlements, not because they need them to grow vegetables, but because they feel that we took them away from them. And the truth is that there will be no peace and no agreement between the Newists and us unless we give those settlements back."

Yabalan got up from his armchair and started to pace the room in excitement, his voice rising to a high pitch. "The material with which true statesmen work is made of what can be done, not what we want to do. In this case, we must give up a few measly settlements for the real goal. But the reward ... ah, the reward is worth it."

"And what will the reward be?" John asked quietly.

"But of course, it will be the recognition of Andania by the New Nations Organization as an equal partner in the family of nations. And then ..."

"What will happen afterward?"

"Afterwards," Barak intervened, "is the greatest part of the plan that the Deputy Minister has devised. Even though we are not supposed to praise a man in his hearing, there is no doubt that the plan is sheer genius."

Barak's face shone with enthusiasm. Yabalan, on his part, had seated himself in his armchair and kept his eyes shut, a smile of satisfaction on his lips.

"So, what's going to happen afterward?" John insisted.

"Afterwards," said Yabalan with conviction, "we will develop trade relations with them, living in good neighborhoods with the Newists, and they'll understand that they have much more to gain when they live in peace with us. Time works for us. We don't have to agree beforehand on matters in which agreement is hard to reach, such as the exact nature of our relationship. Time will naturally settle these things. Getting into a state of non-belligerence is the achievement that will make all that possible."

"But we will reap the fruit of the agreement right away," Barak added. "The NNO has sided with the Newists all along, probably because they assumed that, in the long run, the Newists will be the ones to prevail. The NNO cannot get into a situation where they lose their easy access to the mines, which are essential to their economy. But if we reach an agreement with the Newists, we will immediately enjoy all the diplomatic advantages deriving from the fact that the NNO can develop much closer relations with us."

"All right," said Yabalan, rising from his seat. "Time to go. Remember, gentlemen, this is a critical meeting. Andania's fate is in our hands, although she doesn't know it. This is a weighty responsibility. Very heavy indeed."

They filed out of the room, with Yabalan leading the way and John coming last. We walk like ducks, John thought. I hope we're not sitting ducks.

CHAPTER 14

I t was dark when John entered his apartment and dropped his bag on the floor. The last two days had been unusually exhausting, perhaps because of the weight of the responsibility that learning of Yabalan's plans had put on his shoulders.

As far as John was concerned, the meeting with the Newists had taken place in a surrealistic atmosphere. He had unexpectedly found himself face-to-face with the cruel enemy, and his boss and his friend Barak treated them like old friends. They shook hands warmly and laughed at the expense of Yan-Nibar and Sarpash. John was particularly disturbed when the Newist leader, Sed, commented jokingly that Sarpash's hairstyle was a better fit for a fashion show than for a statesman. Instead of answering coolly, defending the minister's honor, Yabalan had joined in the joke and had explained that Sarpash hated the hairdo but was willing to suffer from it because it was the style worn by NNO officials, "and everybody knows that the only thing that matters to Sarpash is to have Earth people suck up to him and honor him." John had distanced himself from the small talk, standing at a corner of the room and keeping a severe countenance, but except for Barak, nobody had paid any attention to him.

On the other hand, Barak had walked up to him and whispered in his ear, "Lighten up, John. We are working hard to keep a friendly atmosphere." However, John didn't feel like joining in the laughter and remained standing in his corner.

The talks had proceeded in a laid-back atmosphere, with the participants eating incessantly from various foods placed on a central table. Most of the time, Yabalan and Sed consulted the map and spoke quietly. Nobody took minutes of the discussions, and John had wondered how anybody would remember what had been said in a few days. Perhaps they were recording all this, he hoped.

John had been called on a few times to explain one point or another on the map, but most of the time, Yabalan seemed familiar with the details and managed without help.

The lengthy discussion had taken place almost exclusively between Yabalan and Sed, although occasionally, an aide commented on or helped his side. After nearly three hours, Yabalan had raised his head from the map and had addressed the people in the room.

"Friends," he had said, "it is always a pleasure to do business with Tafa-Aru Sed. Today, we made big progress, and now it's time for us to sit alone and clear up a few remaining points. I appreciate your help so far. I'd like all of you to go to your rooms ... except for you, Barak," he added.

If "everybody" but one must leave out of a group of two, John had mused, doesn't that mean that there is only one they want to get rid of? But an order is an order, and John had left without arguing.

He had never seen the Newists again since they had left during the night. The following day, he found John wasting time at a dull plenary session devoted to reviewing the work of the various groups. Sammy only showed up briefly and didn't try to talk to him. After lunch, John was glad to have the opportunity to slip away with the excuse that he had to organize the vehicles that would take them back to Andania City.

The trip had been uneventful, although John had felt extremely tense throughout it, perhaps due to his face-to-face meeting with the Newists. He had also felt nervous about the late departure time imposed on him by Yabalan, who wanted to sum up the delegation's work "carefully."

His tiny apartment seemed now to John to be a safe haven in which Yabalan and Barak couldn't bother him—a familiar place where no surprises had to be feared, or so he thought.

By the little light that filtered through the blinds, he noticed a body lying in a fetal position on the soft cushions of the sofa. It was Tasha, he soon realized, who was sleeping peacefully. John approached the couch and watched her in silence. The smile pasted on her sleeping face made him smile, too. In her sleep, Tasha looked half child, half woman, and something about her made John want to protect her even though there was nothing to protect her from.

Tasha was wearing "fatigues," which meant a short, canary-yellow shirt and tight shorts of matching color to her. They did a poor job of hiding her shapely body. John watched her sleep, enthralled by her simple, natural beauty. As if sensing his presence, she opened her eyes and stared at him.

"Hi," she said softly.

"Hi," John echoed. "Taking a nap?"

"I'm sorry," said Tasha, sitting straight on the sofa. I didn't mean to fall asleep, but I waited for you and dozed off. You said you'd be back in the afternoon," she pointed out, speaking accusingly.

"That was the plan, but all plans are open to changes where I work. You shouldn't have waited up for me."

"But I wanted to serve you dinner," said Tasha simply. "I've cooked something special 'cause I knew you'd be tired and hungry."

"You shouldn't have. Really. That's much more than is expected of you."

"I don't care! I wanted to cook for you, and I did. But now," she added with dismay, "everything's cold 'cause you're late. You know what? Go and shower; meanwhile, I'll heat everything up again."

The suggestion appealed to John. He was starving and longed for a jet of hot water to wash away the day's sweat and the road's dust. He showered quickly and dressed in a T-shirt and shorts. An inviting scent from the dishes on the table welcomed him to the kitchen.

"I've got a little problem," said Tasha when John sat at the table. He lifted his eyes from the plate, and she continued. "At this time of night, there is no public transportation, and I live too far away to walk home. I was thinking ... if it's no trouble ... if it's okay with you, perhaps I could sleep on the couch?"

"Oh, but of course. Certainly," John said quickly to avoid giving the impression that he had any reservations. "I wouldn't dream of letting you go home alone at this time of night. But I can take the couch. You sleep in the bed."

"No, no. I got used to the couch. I'm comfortable. I'm small, and it's not a problem for me to sleep there. The night is warm, and I only need a sheet. You're too big for this tiny sofa; besides, it's your apartment."

"All right," John said, resignedly. Tasha's arguments made sense, and he saw no point in arguing. "Let's eat now," he said.

"I've eaten already," said Tasha, "and I'm falling off my feet. If you don't mind, I'll go back to sleep. Okay?"

"No problem. Good night."

"Good night," said Tasha and walked away from the table. When she reached the kitchen door, she stopped and turned toward him as if in an afterthought. "You're cute," she said, "thanks," and then the darkness of the living room swallowed her.

The feeling was strange–familiar but unidentified–and John tried to understand it through the barrier of semi-consciousness. As he awakened, he fought to capture this pleasant feeling before it disappeared, as pleasant sensations often do, eluding your senses the moment you wake up. He tried to define it; it was nice ... yes, definitely nice ... and soft. John wanted to linger in that nirvanic state, to savor it more and more, but after a while, he gave up and allowed himself to emerge from the confusion that accompanies the state of semi-deep sleep. The sensation didn't disappear while he slowly shook away the mists of sleep; it had to be real.

Tasha!

He opened his eyes and, without moving his body, slowly turned his head to the right. Tasha lay next to him, deep in sleep, the smile of satisfaction still on her lips. Her right hand touched John's right shoulder lightly, and her face rested on the pillow so close to his that he could feel her sweet breath on his eyelashes. She opened her eyes drowsily as if John's gaze had been enough to wake her up, and her smile deepened.

"You were right," she announced, "the couch is bumpy." Her hand briefly touched John's cheek and then went back to rest on his shoulder. "Lucky you told me to come here to sleep," she mumbled, then shut her eyes again.

John wasn't sure whether she had fallen asleep again but decided not to respond. He knew he hadn't meant to invite her into his bed, but deep inside, he was grateful for the misunderstanding. With the back of the fingers of his left hand, he caressed her cheek lightly, but Tasha, perhaps instinctively, took his hand and moved it away.

John lay motionless, watching her sleep, fearful that even a tiny movement might awaken her and send her back to the couch. During the rest of his sleepless night, he learned all her sleeping habits. She moved from her side with her knees and shoulder pressed hard against his body. She went through various intermediate positions, winding up lying on her other side and almost falling off the bed.

Despite his tiredness, sleep didn't come back to John quickly. At first, his efforts to chase away impure thoughts about Tasha kept him awake, but finally, when he realized that his efforts to ignore her presence had failed miserably, he gave up his fruitless struggle and let himself become wrapped in his senses. When he fell asleep, his exhaustion got the better of his thirst for the feel of Tasha's presence.

The sound of running water in the shower filtered through John's awareness, and he fought to open his eyes. Tasha's delicate scent filled the air next to him, and the night sensations returned to him in a flash, still confused by his slow awakening from a deep sleep state. Something bothered him, though, and he couldn't put his finger on it. He was sure he had behaved like a perfect gentleman and hadn't taken advantage of Tasha's trust. Still ... could it be that in his state of semi-consciousness, he had done something that he should regret? And if he hadn't, why had the notion popped up in his head that he may be trying to repress a memory?

He lay motionless, trying to recapture the feel, but couldn't remember anything more. He allowed himself to sink again into the twilight zone of sleep. He concluded that if anything happened, Tasha's behavior would have to reflect it, which would tell him.

The sound of running water ceased and was replaced by the pattering of wet feet. John closed his eyes, feigning sleep, and waited. As Tasha entered the bedroom, John peeped at her from behind his eyelids. Her body was wrapped in a small towel, her short hair was wet and shiny, and she stood, with her back to John, before a chair where she had laid her clothes. Slowly and naturally, she dropped the towel and picked up her T-shirt. John watched, hypnotized, unable to move his gaze away from her shapely body and smooth skin. She stood so close to him that he felt the wave of heat she had carried with her from the shower.

Tasha dressed quickly and then approached the bed. "John," she called quietly.

John faked a complex awakening, hoping to supply a convincing imitation that would leave no doubt in Tasha's mind that he hadn't seen anything of what had happened in the room before. Tasha's smile seemed amused ... did that have a meaning, or was it perhaps John's unclean conscience playing tricks on him? Was it possible that she had known all along that he was awake and decided to play games with him, dressing in that irresistible way? Or maybe the smile was the outcome of something that had happened that night, the memory of which eluded him? The questions kept bouncing around inside John's head without answers.

"Good morning," he answered, yawning heavily. "What time is it?"

"It's almost nine," she said. "Why don't you get ready while I fix your breakfast?"

"Fine," said John, getting up quickly without looking at her. Being near her affected him, as no other woman had been able to influence his senses before; he needed to get away from her and stifle his desire before things got out of control.

He brushed his teeth, shaved, and got into the shower. Tasha's perfumed scent was strong in the confined space and overcame the smell of his soap, or maybe his brain was playing tricks on him. John turned the water temperature to almost painfully cold and stood under the stream for a long minute, attempting to chase his thoughts away. When the cold water failed him, he had to admit that Tasha's presence had been acting as a magic potion, increasing his lust for her in a matter of hours. So, "why not?" he asked himself. There was nothing wrong with her being the cleaning woman. Cleaning women, he argued, aren't barred from social life. And, strictly speaking (he realized, brightening up), John wasn't

Tasha's employer. On the contrary, they were both employees of the Ministry of Commerce–equals, consenting adults who were free to enter into a personal relationship if they wished.

The question remained of whether Tasha was interested in becoming involved with John. On the one hand, John's logic told him that a cleaning woman doesn't steal into her employer's bed in the middle of the night for no purpose. On the other hand, however, Tasha behaved so naturally and with such a lack of inhibition that, perhaps, no second meaning should be attached to it beyond the simple truth that she was more comfortable there than on the couch. Without additional clues, John concluded that no conclusion could be reached.

He dressed quickly in light shorts and a short-sleeved shirt, sprinkled too much aftershave lotion on his face, and hurried to the kitchen where Tasha waited with a heavenly-smelling breakfast. He sat at the table and started on it with a wolfish appetite. Tasha sat facing him and ate slowly, shooting an occasional glance at him with what John thought were mocking eyes.

"You are hungry!" she said, smiling with overt pleasure.

"Oh, yes," said John, speaking with a full mouth. The food they served me during the last few days wasn't particularly good–in any case, it was nowhere near the stuff you cook."

"Thank you kindly, sir," Tasha laughed, managing to curtsy without getting up. "I see you're not in uniform. Don't you have to go to work?"

"Nope!" John answered, smiling. "We've been given a long weekend in recognition of our hard work these last few days, although I haven't had time yet to plan how to use it."

"Why don't you come with us to the lake?" she asked immediately.

"Which lake? And who's 'us'?"

John kept his head down as he spoke, hoping that his heart, which thumped noisily in his chest, wouldn't betray his excitement at the invitation.

"Oh, right. I should've explained. One of our friends, Dor–his father has a very nice cabin near a small lake in the middle of Oaktree Forest. It's not far, a two-hour drive at most. Anyway, Dor invited a few friends over for the weekend, and I planned to go this morning. Why don't you come with me?"

"Oh, I don't know," John hesitated. " I can't come uninvited."

"Oh, please, lighten up, will you?" she interrupted him. "It's no big deal. Everybody brings friends without a formal invitation. We take sleeping bags anyway–bring yours, okay? One more mouth to feed won't make any difference; they always bring an awful lot of food. So what d'you say?"

"Are you sure that it won't bother them?" John asked again, but only half-heartedly. He had already decided that a weekend on the lake with Tasha was worth a little embarrassment with her friends.

"A hundred percent! It's decided, then," she concluded. "I'll call Dor. He was supposed to drive me there and must be wondering where I am. He'll have to pick us up from here."

"Why don't we go separately?" John asked.

"Do you have a car?"

"I can get one from the Ministry of Commerce. I have a right to one for the weekend. I'll call them right away."

"Good idea," Tasha agreed. "This way, there's no rush to leave, and we won't hold them up. I'll tell Dor."

John sat back in his chair and sipped his coffee with absolute pleasure. The weekend was shaping up to be the best since he came to Andania.

The drive to the lake took only two hours, but John and Tasha didn't hit the road until late afternoon and only reached the cabin toward evening. The information that John received when he started his work at the Ministry of Commerce didn't take into account the transportation manager's personality.

"Too late," the manager had said to John. "At this time of the day, I don't have anybody who can get a vehicle ready for you."

"But it's not ten o'clock yet," John pointed out.

"I know what time it is," the Transportation Manager answered ungraciously, "but I have my work plan, and you're not in it. We started to prepare the vehicles early this morning. It's a shame that you left it to the last minute. Good day," he added mockingly and hung up.

It was Eva who eventually managed to talk the vehicle's manager into stretching the rules and assigning a car to John, who, in the process, had to beg, admit that he was being granted a great favor, and suffer miscellaneous insults from the manager and his assistants.

On the way to the cabin, they also had to stop at Tasha's apartment, where she picked up a bag with a few things to take with her. When they reached her apartment building, Tasha jumped out of the car and asked John to wait a few minutes. John was disappointed that she hadn't invited him up–he had looked forward to seeing her apartment and learning a little more about her, and waiting outside was a blow to the intimacy he had hoped to achieve. Those "few minutes" stretched into more than half an hour while John waited patiently in the car, repressing the impulse to walk up to her apartment to see what was taking her so long. At last, Tasha returned and, without so much as a word of apology for keeping him waiting, jumped into the car and said, "Let's get moving, John."

It was almost dark when John stopped the car next to a picturesque cabin near a small lake that looked little more than a pool. A young man got up from the rocking chair near the door and approached them. He and Tasha hugged, and then he turned to John.

"I'm Dor," he said, smiling warmly. "You must be John.

Welcome."

"Thanks," said John, smiling back. "It's beautiful here."

"Yeah. Can't complain. Come in and get organized. Chow'll be ready in a moment," he added, pointing at a young couple who tended to a small campfire by a wooden table a short distance from the cabin.

John and Tasha took their bags and rucksacks into the cabin. The building was built of wood and stone, and the inside matched its rugged outside. Furniture was scarce–a rough-cut wooden table and matching cupboard, a few chairs, and some rugs were all the cabin had to offer. They picked an empty corner to drop their equipment.

"I need to go to the bathroom," Tasha announced. "If you need to, go out behind the cabin in the little wood. We don't have regular toilets here," she added, shrugging her shoulders, "but the shower is great. There," she said, pointing at the only door inside the cabin. She then took something from her bag and left.

John looked around him. A young couple sat hugging on the floor at the other end of the cabin. They were the only occupants of the room and sat in silence, staring straight ahead. John felt that ignoring them would be impolite and walked up to where they sat.

"Hey, guys," he said, smiling. "My name is John, and I'm here with Tasha."

The boy kept staring as if John hadn't spoken, but the girl lifted her eyes and gave him a long look. Then she smiled and spoke.

"You a student?" she asked.

"No. I'm a soldier."

"A soldier," she echoed. She nodded in comprehension. "What d'you do, soldier?"

"I work at the Ministry of Commerce," John answered, feeling uncomfortable. Something about the girl's behavior was weird, not to mention the boy who kept ignoring the conversation.

"Want some?" she asked and handed John what looked like a

piece of mushroom.

John looked at it without understanding what she was driving at. "What's this?" he finally asked.

"What are you, a dork?" asked the girl. Then she burst into high-pitched, hysterical laughter.

"John," a voice came from behind him, and a hand tapped his shoulder. Tasha had returned. "Leave her alone," she said, "she's stoned."

"What do you mean? What's the matter with her?"

"She's eaten mescal. It's a mushroom that contains a drug similar to mescaline. They grow around here, and anyone can pick them. Unless you're used to it, I wouldn't try it if I were you. It might be pretty dangerous if it turns out that you're allergic to the thing."

"So, what are they? Drugged?" John's face betrayed the disgust that he had always felt toward junkies.

"Really ... is this the first time you've seen something like this?" Tasha asked nonchalantly.

"No, but ..." a scary thought crossed his mind. "You take it too?"

"Not really. But I've tried it in the past. Potent shit, that is."

"Tasha," John implored her, "don't touch that thing! It's not for you."

Tasha glanced at him strangely–almost angrily. "You're not my father," she said, "and I can take care of myself."

Then she turned away from him and left the cabin.

John sat by the lake, looking for movement in the still water. Dinner had been a simple, quiet function. The couple of junkies had not joined them. Besides them, only the couple who had tended the fire, Dor, Tasha, and himself, were staying at the cabin. Spirits were high at dinner, and Tasha and her friend had chatted noisily. In contrast, John had felt excluded from the conversation, which revolved around people he had never met.

After dinner, they sat around the fire, singing and laughing. John did his best to fit in but with little success. Tasha got up when the fire almost died out, and the night turned cold. "I'm tired, and I'm going to sleep," she announced. "Good night, everybody."

The others remained by the fire, but conversation languished. A few minutes later, Dor poured a bucket of water on the cinders, and everybody went inside.

The cabin was dark, but when John's eyes grew used to it, he saw that Tasha had dragged her sleeping bag to a far corner of the room. He opened his sleeping bag next to his stuff, undressed down to his underwear, and lay down to sleep. Sleep eluded him, and he tossed from side to side. He had been trying to sleep for quite some time when he sensed a presence and came to a sitting position with a jerk. Tasha was kneeling beside him in her eternal shorts and T-shirt.

"I didn't want us to go to bed feeling angry at each other," she whispered. "No, listen to me!" she urged, putting a finger to his lips when John tried to explain that he wasn't mad at her. "I misbehaved. I apologize. I got mad at you because I thought you were patronizing me, but I shouldn't have reacted as I did."

"I was only worried about you," John whispered back. "I didn't mean to overstep my boundaries."

"I know. But you shouldn't worry. No reason."

"You're not taking that shit?" John asked again.

"Ah-ah," said Tasha, shaking her head.

"You never did?" he insisted.

"Once or twice," she answered impatiently. "Don't start again, okay?"

"No, no. All right. Now that I know that you don't do drugs, I'm not worried."

"Good. Friends again?"

"All the time," John said, smiling.

"Goodnight," said Tasha, smiling back at him, returning to her sleeping bag.

John's instincts also worked when he slept. He sat up quickly and silently and scanned the room, searching for the origin of the noise that had awakened him. The noise consisted of strange moans, and it took him a second to find where they were coming from–Tasha's sleeping bag. Worried, John jumped to his feet and stole to Tasha's corner. The sight he saw there hit him like a hammer. Dor and Tasha shared the sleeping bag, and the movements and noises left no doubt about what was happening there. John tiptoed back and got silently into his sleeping bag, hoping Tasha hadn't noticed him.

Lying in his sleeping bag, he closed his ears to the sounds around him and, by some miracle, fell asleep again.

"Do you have to?"

"Yes, Tasha. I'm sorry. I just realized that I have to do something urgent at work."

"But John," she pressed, putting her hand on his arm as if to stop him, "we're going back tomorrow morning anyway. You deserve some rest, right?"

"Sorry. I can't," John answered dryly, pulling his arm away from Tasha's grip.

"Oh, okay," she said moodily, "if you must ..."

John stared at her thoughtfully. She looked like a little girl with her toy taken from her. He climbed into his vehicle, turned the ignition, and drove away. Looking back, he hoped to see Tasha standing there, watching him drive away, but she had already gone inside the cabin. And perhaps she had already forgotten that he existed, he thought bitterly.

CHAPTER 15

The door opened abruptly, and the four men in the room jumped to their feet at the sight of the man who had stomped in.

"Yan-Nibar," Sarpash exclaimed with surprise. Yan-Nibar storming all alone and unexpectedly into a room was, indeed, an unusual sight. John had never seen him in the building before.

Sarpash's spacious room seemed suddenly small, so much did Yan-Nibar fill it with his personality. Yabalan bowed slightly in Yan-Nibar's direction, an act that was foreign to Andanian customs. "Sir," he mumbled, but Yan-Nibar ignored him altogether. Barak stood silently, gazing at his shoes, and John chose to imitate him.

"This time, you've gone too far!" Yan-Nibar yelled at Sarpash.

"What would seem to be the problem, Yan-Nibar?" Sarpash inquired in an innocent tone.

"What's the problem? What's the problem, you ask? That you're undermining my government and acting without my permission and behind my back, that's the problem," Yan-Nibar shouted, his face redder than usual.

"Really! I don't know what you're talking about, but maybe we should go into my private office and talk without ..."

"No! We're going to talk it out here before this scumbag," he added, pointing at Yabalan, "who undertakes important diplomatic talks about which I, the Head of the People's Council, do not know. And I need to hear about them secondhand?" Yan-Nibar shouted. He was boiling with rage and barely managed to control himself.

"I ..." Yabalan started to say, but Yan-Nibar's raised hand checked him. "You'll shut up!" he ordered.

"Yan-Nibar," said Sarpash in a calm, quiet tone. His embarrassment was ill-concealed, but he managed to keep his voice low. "I don't think it is desirable to let this discussion deteriorate. It won't do either of us any good."

Yan-Nibar calmed down a little and shot a sideways glance at Sarpash. "Is it true that you planned to fly to Earth and sign an agreement with the Newists? Answer me!" he ordered when Sarpash hesitated.

"Well ... yes and no," said Sarpash, but Yan-Nibar stopped him again.

"And when were you planning to tell me about it? After everybody in Andania but me gets informed?"

"Of course not. I was planning to bring the matter of the trip before you today. This was the purpose of the meeting that you interrupted here, and that's why these gentlemen have been summoned," he explained, sweeping the room and its people.

"Since when do you need an entourage to speak with me? And besides, why didn't you ask for my permission to have talks with the Newists before you started them?"

"It's a sensitive matter ..." Sarpash mumbled.

"You don't say!" Yan-Nibar mocked him. "So sensitive that I am not permitted to know about it?"

Silence fell in the room. It was apparent that everybody felt embarrassed by the argument. Without warning, Yan-Nibar turned to John. "Who are you?" he asked.

John jumped to attention and answered, "I am Lieutenant John Hektor, sir, at your service."

"Why are you here?"

"I am the military secretary of the Deputy Minister, Mr. Yabalan, sir."

"So," Yan-Nibar said dangerously, turning again to Sarpash, "am I to understand that I'm less important than the military secretary of that sucking-up boy of yours? Or perhaps I cannot be trusted as much with 'sensitive' information?"

Sarpash's face, which had turned severe initially, now assumed a determined expression.

"If you want to go on talking to me, you'll have to do it privately. I'll be in my office," he said, walking to the door.

"Wait a second," ordered Yan-Nibar, but Sarpash made a dismissive motion with his hand and, without turning back, disappeared into his private office.

"I'll show you," mumbled Yan-Nibar, but followed him into the room.

"Maybe we should postpone the conference," suggested Barak in an undertone.

"We can't leave Sarpash here alone," commented Yabalan, "in case he should need anything. But I don't feel like meeting Yan-Nibar again after the degrading performance he just gave us here. I'll be in my office. You wait here for orders from Sarpash."

Yabalan left the room, keeping a straight back, but he had clearly been badly hurt by Yan-Nibar's words, and his embarrassment was evident. John wouldn't have been surprised to see him burst into tears then and there. Barak sadly watched Yabalan's departure, then said to John, "He's badly hurt. I don't think he should be left alone right now. I'll go after him. If Sarpash needs anything, give me a call."

Barak ran after Yabalan, and John was left alone in the room—

sounds of shouting filtered through from Sarpash's office. John took a position near the door, which Yan-Nibar hadn't shut, and listened to the exchanges between the two strongest politicians of Andania.

"You're a crook, a liar, and a traitor," Yan-Nibar yelled.

"I don't need to take any of this from you," Sarpash retorted heatedly.

"But you do need to take instructions and approval from me— and I'm telling you that you can dream of flying to Earth, or anywhere else for that matter, and you're not signing any agreements either. Is that clear to you?"

"Yan-Nibar," said Sarpash, clearly trying to check the anger in his voice, "the agreement is the result of many months of unbelievable effort. We've reached the best agreement we can ever dream of, and I won't let you ruin it. You'll give your blessing to it, thank me publicly for all my efforts, and praise me for the results I obtained for Andania so that I will receive well-earned recognition for my historical achievement. Understood?"

"You're dreaming," Yan-Nibar answered incredulously, "and you're sick in the head. Fame is all that matters to you, isn't it? For the sake of your public image, you are willing to sign stupid agreements that will put Andania's basic needs in jeopardy in a matter of years. I will play no part in it."

"You have no choice, my friend," said Sarpash in a mellow voice. "Unless you play ball, I'll regretfully have to disclose to the public that little problem you have with drugs."

Silence fell on the other side of the door for so long that John started to worry that something may have happened in the room, but then he heard Yan-Nibar's voice again.

"I don't have a drug problem. True, I have tried light drugs a few times, socially, for fun, or to help me through hard work. No big deal. Is there anybody in Andania City who has never used drugs?"

"I never did," retorted Sarpash. "But we know we're talking

about something more complicated ... deeper, right? It's not you taking drugs once or twice. In reality, you're hooked on drugs, and you're high most of the day. Correct? Right?" Sarpash insisted.

"I ... I'll deny it. Nobody will ever believe you. I'm the hero of this nation."

"You may be obliged to take a test, you know? But there is no need for that; I already have in my drawer the results of your periodic tests, which point to a state of deep addiction. And that's not all."

"Not all? What do you mean?"

"I also know about that girl last winter–what was her name? Dara, right? How old was she ... fifteen? Sixteen?"

"I didn't know ..."

"Of course, of course. How could you know? You were stoned out of your mind. I'm sure that you didn't even catch her name. So what will you say, Yan-Nibar? Are you going to stand by me in this effort to create a better future for Andania, or maybe the drugs have affected your brain to the point that you'll go against the best interests of your people?"

Silence fell again in the room. After a long pause, Yan-Nibar's voice was heard again, but this time, it was the voice of a beaten hero. "I'm ... with you," he said.

"I didn't hear you well," said Sarpash without trying to hide his satisfaction.

"I'll play along, dammit! You leave me no choice, you lousy blackmailer."

"Not really, no. And I don't mind if you feel like calling me names when we're alone, but we're best friends in public. Is that clear? Good. Don't forget it."

John heard footsteps approaching the door and quickly retreated to the other end of the room. The entrance to Sarpash's private office opened, and the minister stood in the doorway.

"Where is everybody?" he asked with surprise.

"They've gone to the office of the Deputy Minister, and I was ordered to wait here to see if anything is needed, sir."

"All right," said Sarpash, smiling broadly. "Tell them to come back. Tell them that we can start our planned meeting with the Head of the People's Council, who is waiting impatiently for our report on the plan's details, and to give us his blessing to continue with our successful project."

When, finally, John opened the door of his apartment, it was late. The endless meetings he had attended all day had sucked away all his energy. When he managed to escape, he wandered about town, drinking lightly at a couple of bars and killing time so he would not run into Tasha at the apartment. His anger and frustration from their trip to the lake were still stinging, and John was not yet ready to meet her. Clearly, he would have to face her eventually, and probably quite soon, but he still needed to allow some time to pass to look at her from the proper perspective.

The craving for a hot shower and a soft bed had become strong, and the hour was late enough to make it safe to return to the apartment. He couldn't help but admire Barak's stamina; he not only attended the exhausting meetings without apparent fatigue but looked as if he relished them. To John, this kind of activity was exhausting.

He closed the door behind him and stepped into the small anteroom that led to the living room and bedroom. Tasha was seated in the dark on the small sofa, and John almost didn't notice her. He wouldn't have become aware of her presence but for the whimpering sound from her direction.

"Tasha!" he cried with a mixture of surprise and concern. "What happened? What's the matter?" All the anger and bitterness he had carried around with him since that night at the lake disappeared at the sight of the crying girl. He sat beside her on the sofa, but they didn't speak or look at one another. They kept sitting in the semi-darkness, in silence, for what seemed to John like an eternity.

"I don't want you to be mad at me," said Tasha, at last, almost in a whisper, and something in her voice made John turn and look at her. She raised her head, and he saw big tears in her eyes, like a little girl who had been fighting to keep them back but had now given up and let them run freely. Instinctively, John took her hand in his and tried to comfort her.

"What happened? Why are you crying? It's not like you." He dried her tears with his other hand, but his touch only made them flow stronger, and she sat sobbing and chewing the corner of her lower lip. John felt an aching need to protect her, to cheer her up. He pulled her gently toward him, and she didn't resist. She put her head on his shoulder and hugged him with a strength that surprised him. They sat in silence for a few minutes until Tasha's moans stopped, and then she straightened up.

"Why did you leave like that? It hurt so much," she complained.

"I hurt you? You're kidding. I took the hint and took off."

"What hint?" Tasha asked, looking surprised.

"You ... with that Dor."

"Oh, with Dor ... you mean, at night? But," she continued emphatically when John nodded, "that doesn't mean anything. Dor and I are good friends, old friends. It's just ... it means nothing," she added.

Her face was now close to John's, and her eyes were locked with his as if to supply proof of her statement.

"I don't think so," he said at last, heavily. "Even if you don't attach any importance to it, the fact that you wanted to be with him after you invited me to go there with you ... it shows how you feel about me. Nothing can change that."

"I ... I," Tasha tried to say but couldn't continue.

John took her hand again and looked at her. He waited

patiently for her to go on, massaging her hand with his fingers to encourage her. After a while, when she spoke, it was in an undertone. "There's no choice, then," she said decidedly, "I'll tell you everything. I'm not who you think," she said.

"What do you mean? You're not a student?"

"Please let me explain without interrupting. I am a student, but I'm not really a cleaning woman. I work for Rippel, the chief of security for Yan-Nibar, and he sent me here."

"What?" John was astounded. "You're here to spy on me?"

Tasha nodded and continued.

"I didn't know you. I didn't know who you were," she said apologetically, new tears showing up at the corners of her eyes. "Yan-Nibar and Rippel are certain that Sarpash and Yabalan are planning to betray him; maybe they're planning a military coup to seize power in Andania. They trust nobody, particularly those who work for Yabalan. As a friend of Barak's, you were especially under suspicion because Rippel thinks that Barak is the brain behind Yabalan's moves."

John sat in silence, flabbergasted, and after a brief hesitation, Tasha continued.

"My job was to follow you after office hours to see where you go and who you see. Rippel arranged for me to work at your apartment to make it easy for me to follow you closely and look at suspicious documents you may have. That's it."

John let go of Tasha's hand, which he had kept holding without noticing. "What do you mean, 'that's it'?" he asked angrily. "You're telling me that you've come here to spy on me, like ... like a serpent in my home? And your invitation to the lake ... Ah! That's the icing on the cake! That way, you were doing your job but didn't have to work hard since we were together at the end of the world. Very clever," he added bitterly.

"No! It's not like that. Not at all," said Tasha forcefully. "Why do you think I'm telling you all this?"

"I don't know. Out of stupidity, perhaps?" said John and

immediately regretted it.

"Because I've fallen in love with you," she whispered, choking at the end of the sentence. John opened his mouth but found that he didn't know what to say. After a few seconds, she went on. "There, I've said it. I didn't know what to do. Can you see that?"

She was no longer able to control herself and started sobbing again. John pulled her gently toward him, and they hugged in the dark. Tasha's sobs subsided as John kept stroking her head and whispering in her ear, "It's okay, it's all right." After a while, she sat up, wiped her tears with both hands and spoke steadily.

"When I realized what was happening, I had to get away from you and not let it happen. Then I thought that if you saw me with somebody else, we'd remain friends at most, and nothing would happen to complicate all this. That's why I behaved that way down at the lake."

"Then you knew that I'd seen you that night?" John felt embarrassed asking, but he had to know.

"Yes. Sure. I made certain that you'd see it. I'm so sorry," she hurried to say, perhaps because of John's sad expression, and raised a hand to caress his cheek.

"So, what happens now? Are you going to tell Rippel?"

"I don't know what to do," she said in despair. "If I tell Rippel that I've blown my cover, not only will he punish me–that's sure–but he'll send me somewhere else, and I won't be able to go on seeing you."

"But you don't have to tell him, do you?"

"Mmm ..." said Tasha noncommittally.

A troubling thought occurred to John. "Do you still suspect I'm one of the bad guys?" he asked.

"No, stupid! Of course not. I know you aren't," she answered heatedly.

"Well, then, we can go on like this. You can keep following me and reporting about me to your superiors. Nobody needs to know that I know who you are."

"But what if they find out?"

"They won't unless we tell them. And we won't tell them."

They sat silently, hugging and enjoying each other's comforting warmth. After a while, Tasha lifted her head and gazed at John. "And you," she asked, "how do you feel about me?"

John didn't answer. Instead, he pulled her closer and kissed her gently and then increasingly passionately. "This is how I feel," he said when, eventually, their lips parted.

Time no longer had meaning for John. They sat on the couch, kissing and hugging until Tasha finally got up and pulled him gently toward the bedroom. "Wait a second," she said and went out. John lay on the bed, his senses in a state of complete ecstasy and unable to believe his luck. Since his forced separation from Dana, he had never felt so strongly for a woman. He tried hard not to draw comparisons with Dana, his lost love, and his first true love, but the feelings that boiled inside him had a strong ring of *déjà vu*.

As the water ran in the shower, John's expectations for Tasha's return kept growing. He sat on the bed, counting the seconds, then switched off the leading light and turned on the small night lamp that diffused a more pleasant, softer, and subdued light.

After a while, the water stopped running in the shower. Tasha appeared in the doorway clad in a towel, just as he remembered secretly seeing her that night. But this time, she didn't go to the chair in the corner; instead, she stood before him by the bed. John lifted an eyebrow, and she raised her hands, letting the towel drop to the floor.

"Move a little," she said, smiling. "Make some room."

John slid a little to his left, keeping his eyes riveted on her. Tasha's left knee pressed on the mattress, the right one followed, and John shut his eyes, concentrating on the sweet taste of her moist lips and allowing himself to become completely lost in her scent.

CHAPTER 16

"Can you answer the door?" Tasha shouted to John. "I'm in the middle of cooking the omelet."

John had just finished shaving. He washed his hands quickly under the faucet and went to the door. It was already nine in the morning, and they both had overslept ... little wonder after the previous night's excitement. This morning, opening his eyes and seeing Tasha's smile was one of the happiest moments of his life. At last, he felt things had started to work out for him. The loneliness that had haunted him since he had lost Dana had been ousted by the happiness Tasha had brought him.

On the doormat, he saw two men dressed in the gray uniform of the Security Police.

"Yes?" John asked, surprised at the sight of the officers. Since his arrival in Andania, he had had no dealings with the Security Police, although he had run into them at work now and then.

"Lieutenant John Hektor?" asked one of them, a blond man in his thirties.

"Yes. What's the matter?"

"Is your cleaning woman at work, uh ... Tasha?" he added after consulting a paper in his hand.

"She's here," said John, "but perhaps you won't mind explaining what this is all about?"

John stood in the doorway, blocking the passage into the apartment. His body language made it clear that he wouldn't move until the matter was explained.

"I'll explain immediately, Lieutenant," said the blond policeman. "My name is Yorg. We must ask Tasha about a very sensitive matter, and she has to come with us for questioning. I must ask you to move aside and let my colleague go in and bring her out. Oh, here she is," he added when Tasha appeared behind John. "Are you Natasha Araid?" Yorg asked.

"Yes," she said. She looked genuinely surprised by the presence of the policemen.

"You must come with us to be questioned about the attempted assassination of our leader, Yan-Nibar."

"Attempted assassination?" John gasped, astonished. "What attempted assassination?"

"I'll explain in a second," said Yorg dryly. "Take her to the car. I'll be right there," he ordered the second policeman, who hadn't bothered introducing himself to John.

"Wait a second!" said John, aggressively standing between Tasha and the policeman who had made one step toward her, "Nobody's going anywhere before I know what this is all about."

"Step aside, Lieutenant," Yorg ordered quietly. "If you interfere with our duty, we'll have to arrest you too. This is a dire situation, and I have no time for bullshit."

"That's okay, John," Tasha intervened. "I don't know what they want, but it must be some mistake because I have no idea what they're talking about. It will be better for me to go with them and get it clarified quickly."

John moved aside, letting Tasha pass. "All right, then. Call me and let me know what happened," he added, hoping to sound as detached as possible to avoid giving away their intimacy.

"I'll do that," she promised, answering with the same detached tone. She walked out of John's ground-floor apartment toward the police car parked near the building.

John turned again to Yorg. "Now explain, please. Do you want to come in and sit down?" he asked with belated politeness.

"No, thanks, Lieutenant, I must rush. I'll explain briefly. Yesterday afternoon, an unknown assassin shot Yan-Nibar several times."

"Did you catch him?"

"We're not sure yet."

"What happened to Yan-Nibar? Is he hurt?"

"He was badly wounded, and they rushed him to the hospital. The doctors say that his life is not in danger."

"Thank God," murmured John.

"Yes, but he is in a coma, and it's not clear when he'll come out of it ... or if he'll ever come out of it."

"That's terrible!" John's concern ran deep. "How come we didn't hear anything about it? It should be public knowledge by now if it happened yesterday afternoon."

"It was decided to keep it secret for the time being, to see how Yan-Nibar fared, but also to not interfere with the investigation. I haven't slept all night," he added. Yorg both looked and sounded tired, and John had no trouble believing him.

"I understand ... but what does all this have to do with my cleaning woman?"

"The assassin managed to access a secure area of the State Building," Yorg explained, "using a pass with the highest security clearance–in fact, your pass, Lieutenant."

"Mine?" John exclaimed in amazement. "But, I have mine on me all the time ..."

"We know. We also know that you were in the Ministry of Commerce building at the time of the assassination attempt and had your pass on you. We checked all the computer records, and there is no doubt about it. You're not under any suspicion in this matter, but we suspect that someone managed to duplicate your pass and use it."

"Still, what does that have to do with my cleaning woman?"

"Look," explained Yorg patiently, "the only time you don't need your pass is when you're not at work. We assume you adhere to the security instructions and don't leave the pass at home when you go out." Yorg watched John, who nodded in assent and then continued. "The most reasonable assumption at this time is that someone who has access to your pass when you are at home took it, duplicated it, and put it back before you noticed that it was missing. Do you understand now why we need to interrogate your cleaning woman? Okay. I appreciate your cooperation then," concluded Yorg, and walked to his waiting car.

John's eyes followed the car as it disappeared in the distance, his mind in turmoil with worry; he picked up his bag and left quickly for the Ministry. At work, at least so he hoped, he'd learn more details and find a way to help Tasha clear herself of all suspicion. He didn't fear that she might get hurt while in custody, but the thought that she was under arrest and surely frightened and that they were kept apart was unbearable.

"Where have you been?" Barak asked impatiently when John entered his office.

"I was at home. I told Eva that I'd be late today," he apologized.

"You picked the right day to be late," said Barak, shaking his head in despair.

"Well, I didn't know what had happened," John pointed out. "Nobody bothered to tell me. How's Yan-Nibar?" he asked with concern.

"He'll live," said Barak, "but so far, he's in a coma, and it doesn't look like he's going to come out of it shortly. The doctors say that the longer the coma, the smaller the chances that he'll get back to normal. Well," he sighed, "nothing that we can do about it. But there is also a bright side."

"I'm happy you can find a bright side to it," said John bitterly. "What can be good in that?"

"What's good, with all the sadness arising from the sorrowful situation of our beloved leader, Yan-Nibar," said Barak, "is that Sarpash will fill in for him." John had the strange feeling that he almost saw a smile of self-satisfaction trying to surface on Barak's lips. "Sarpash's temporary appointment will be approved today by the People's Assembly, which means that all we've been working for won't get stuck as I feared—on the contrary, the process will be accelerated. Sarpash has already ordered us to anticipate our trip to Earth. We leave in three days," he said simply.

"Meaning ...?" asked John, who had not yet digested the news.

"It means, my friend, that you and I are running to pack," Barak said happily. "After all these years, I'm curious to see how the old place has changed."

"It's a little sudden, isn't it?" asked John.

"The truth is that I think Sarpash is right. We need to exploit the momentum and avoid wasting time. He can't join us now that he's taking Yan-Nibar's position. However, his spirit will accompany us," he said, still smiling. John again had the strange feeling that Barak was playing a joke on him—or somebody, anyway.

"And the Deputy Minister will sign the agreement in his stead?"

"Of course, of course," said Barak, but he looked already far away as if running ahead in his mind in anticipation of the coming trip.

The two friends stood there, each deep in his thoughts, and after a two-minute silence, John summoned the courage to tackle the issue that worried him.

"Ahem ..." he said. Barak gazed at him and waited patiently for John to speak. "You know, I have a problem with my cleaning woman, Tasha ..."

"Ah, yes," Barak said immediately. "The security police have picked her up as a suspect in the assassination attempt. Don't worry," he reassured him, "finding a replacement will be no problem. I'll tell Eva to take care of it immediately, and you'll have a new one even before we leave for Earth."

"Thanks, really, but don't bother. I'm sure you have more pressing things to deal with right now, and I can look after myself for a few days."

"That's no trouble, really," interrupted Barak. "All I have to do is to give instructions to Eva–a matter of a second–and it's done. You must get used to getting what you deserve because if you don't look after your rights, nobody's going to spoon-feed you."

Barak got up from behind his desk and started pacing the room restlessly. John watched him, trying to find the right approach to Tasha's problem without giving away how important she was to him.

"Yes, yes. Thanks," he said heatedly, "but this is more of a matter of principle. The poor girl has been serving me well and needs this job. And I got used to her. Besides, she's done nothing wrong, and having her arrested just like that isn't right."

"You're taking her case very much to heart, my friend," Barak commented, giving John a surprised look.

"Of course! I can't stand injustice, particularly when it is directed against an innocent girl."

"Let me tell you something about your 'innocent girl,' John," Barak interrupted. "She's not innocent at all. She's one of Rippel's agents. Yes, Rippel–Yan-Nibar's security chief. This Rippel is no small pain in the ass, and he's put agents on everyone who works for Yabalan, hoping to find something incriminating to be used against us. Understand? Here's your 'innocent girl' ... you should be happy to be rid of her."

John looked at the floor, afraid his reaction might reveal his prior knowledge of Tasha's identity. "But what can she spy on me about?" he asked. "I'm a soldier, and I only follow orders."

"This Rippel is a nut!" Barak snarled. "That's why he suspects everybody of everything. There is some justice in the fact that it is one of his agents who is accused of involvement in the assassination attempt."

"I don't believe she did it!" said John heatedly.

"I agree with you, John," said Barak quietly. "I'll tell you more—I'm sure she has had nothing to do with it. But until that is fully clarified, my friend Rippel will sweat hard, and that's a big gain."

"Can you make them release her?" John asked directly.

"I can, but I won't. What's this exaggerated concern about your cleaning woman?"

John understood that going farther might be dangerous. Undermining his position would mean being unable to help Tasha.

"I gave her my word of honor when they came to arrest her at my apartment, that I'll find out what this is about and help her. You know me—once I give my word, I must do everything I can to keep it."

"Okay, my friend. But this time, it's not only up to you. She'll have to remain in custody until we return from Earth. I don't want Rippel to get in the way of my plans, and the best way to neutralize him is to accuse one of his agents of the crime. It puts a question mark on his involvement, too. It's perfect!" he added with open satisfaction.

"Then I've got to speak with her, to tell her that I haven't forgotten my promise. Will you arrange for me to visit her?" John pleaded.

Barak looked silently out of the window. He stood so for a long minute, his hands behind his back. John would have given all he possessed to know what was going on in his mind, but he knew his friend well enough to understand how mysterious he was. He waited patiently, and finally, Barak turned toward him and nodded.

"All right," he said, "but only because it's you. I wouldn't do it for anybody else in the world. But I want your word of honor that you won't say or hint at anything I told you."

"Of course, you've got my word," said John quickly. At that moment, he would have promised anything to see Tasha again.

CHAPTER 17

"You have ten minutes, Lieutenant. After that, I'll be back to let you out."

John didn't respond, and the policeman shrugged and opened the small cell door. Tasha stood in the center, twisting her hands nervously and gazing at him. John didn't speak until he heard the steps of the policeman fading away.

"Tasha ..." he started to speak emotionally, but something stopped him. Tasha's fingers moved slightly but quickly and attracted his attention. Her eyes went to their left corner as if to point at an object behind her.

"Lieutenant," she said, speaking in a detached voice, "thank you for your interest. I appreciate the time you have taken to visit me, but you shouldn't have."

John understood immediately that Tasha was trying to tell him something, and he searched feverishly for some explanation of her behavior. Slowly, hoping that he wasn't being obvious, he looked in the direction that he thought Tasha was indicating. Sure enough, his eyes fell on a little hole in the corner of the room, which told the story. A camera! Someone was eavesdropping on them and possibly also recording their meeting.

John checked his impulse to get close to Tasha, touch and comfort her. Instead, he forced himself to be distant, knowing that Tasha understood what he was going through.

"You don't have to thank me. I'm an officer, and I am responsible for those who work for me. Therefore, as I promised you, I'll keep in touch. You've been doing a good job for me," said John, hoping that Tasha would read into that lame sentence all his feelings for her. "Why were you arrested?"

"They questioned me as if I knew anything about the attempt to kill Yan-Nibar. They tried to force me to admit that Rippel has something to do with it."

"Rippel. Yan-Nibar's Chief of Security? What does he have to do with you?"

"I ..." she started to say and then stopped. John was forced to admire her acting skills. But perhaps she'd also been using them to manipulate him? Could it be that there was some substance in their accusations? John chased those troubling thoughts away immediately. No matter what, certain feelings can't be faked, and what had passed between them only a few hours before was real and of a strength that left no doubt in his mind.

"Yes, girl? Speak up!" John ordered. He surprised himself with his ability to play the part.

"I used to work for him in the past, but not now."

"What does that mean? Were you spying on me for Rippel?"

"No, no!" Tasha's eyes begged him to believe. "I worked for him in the past, but not now. Not now, I swear!"

"I believe you ... at least for the time being. But if I find that you lied to me, you're on your own. Do you understand?"

"Yes, yes ..." she whispered with a despair that was perhaps faked but sounded real. She sat on the small cot in the cell's corner and put her head in her hands.

"What did they say they would do with you?" John asked dryly, aching inside from the distance.

"They didn't say anything," she murmured through her

fingers. "They only kept asking questions ... all the time, the same questions. I'm so tired."

"Shape up," John barked at her. He knew he had to play the game, or he would break down and take her in his arms.

She raised her head, an expression of surprise in her eyes.

"I'm going to Earth in three days," said John, and the despair on her face was almost unbearable. "I don't know for how long I'll be gone, but I guess it'll be for a few weeks, and by the time I'm back, I'm sure everything will have been sorted out. I'll try to be in touch and keep updated, but in any case, when you get out ..."

"If I get out ..." Tasha whispered weakly.

"When you get out of here," John insisted, "leave a message at my apartment and let me know where I can reach you. You're a good employee, and I have no intention of giving you up. When I return to Andania, I expect you to show up for work. Agreed?"

"Yes, Lieutenant," she answered docilely.

The noise of a key turning in the cell's lock told John that his time was up. He stood by the door and looked at her for the last time. "Do you need anything?"

She shook her head. "Only to be let out of here," she said, smiling bitterly.

"I'll try to contact you before I leave to see if you need anything else. If you want to get out as soon as possible, I suggest you cooperate with the investigators."

He walked out without looking at her again, and the policeman slammed the door behind him, with}} unnecessary noise.

"Are you busy after work?" John asked.

Sammy moved her gaze from the papers on her desk and looked at him with surprise. "What's the matter? Do you suddenly need a date?" she asked.

"Let's say I need a friend willing to spend a few hours with me."

"Ah ... a friend. Doesn't sound exciting."

"We can try to make it interesting," John said seriously.

"You've managed to arouse my curiosity, John Hektor. What about a preview?"

"No previews. Contain yourself, woman!" said John, smiling. "When do I pick you up?"

"Come to my house at around seven. Now get the hell outta here," she ordered, smiling back, "I've got work to do."

"You know, it would help me a lot if you gave me the address before you throw me out," he suggested.

"Men ..." she said between clenched teeth. She wrote something on a piece of paper and handed it to John without looking at him.

"I asked you to come because I wanted to let you know that we have arrested Rippel," Barak said to John.

"Are you serious? You don't really believe that he has a hand in it."

"You're right," Barak sighed, "but sometimes you need to take steps you dislike for a just cause."

"I'm not sure that any cause can justify accusing an innocent man of being involved in an attempted murder," John commented.

"Well, we're not accusing him of anything specific, and eventually, he'll be found innocent. But meanwhile, he can't get in the way. By the way," said Barak, "I appreciate it that you advised that cleaning woman of yours to cooperate with us. If she gets the hint, it'll be much better for her, and she'll be out in no time."

"How do you know that I advised her to cooperate?" asked John, faking surprise. "Did she tell you?"

"I know," Barak said simply.

"But how?"

"I know ... let's leave it at that," he concluded and seated himself behind his desk, a clear sign that the conversation was over.

Sammy's house was located in one of the most beautiful areas of Andania City, in a one-story building with a small garden. John stood by the door, about to ring the bell, when a sudden thought froze him—he hadn't brought anything, not even a token gift like a bottle of liquor! Coming empty-handed was embarrassing, but it was too late now to find someplace to buy a present for Sammy.

His dilemma resolved itself when the door opened, and Sammy appeared, dressed in a green evening dress and sporting a hairdo that had obviously required some real work. John gaped at her. Until then, he had always seen her only at work, wearing functional clothes, and this improved version was a complete surprise.

"Hi! I thought I'd heard something," she said, looking amused. "Were you planning to ring the bell, or would you rather spend more time gaping at it?"

"I'm sorry," John said apologetically, lowering his eyes. You're stunning in that dress."

"Thank you, sir," she laughed. "Perhaps you'd like to come in all the same," she said, making an inviting gesture with her hand.

John stepped into the broad living room, tastefully furnished in soft colors, and looked around. It could have been a man's living room, practical and cozy at the same time, and he liked it.

"I'll get you a drink," said Sammy, and disappeared in the direction of what John assumed to be the kitchen. In three minutes, she returned with two glasses containing a green liquid with a pungent smell. John took his glass and seated himself in a soft armchair. Sammy sat on the sofa before him and sipped her drink slowly, throwing quick glances at him while she drank.

"So, what's the matter?" she asked at last.

"Nothing special, really," John lied. "I just wanted to spend some time with you before I leave for Earth because I didn't want to leave behind any awkward feelings after that night at the NNO camp. I want us to remain good friends," he said with a passion that was as real as his feeling of friendship for Sammy. Who knows, he thought suddenly, if they might not have been more than only friends had Tasha not come into his life. Probably they would, he concluded.

"Clean slate? We forget what happened?" she asked, smiling at him.

"Only what we'd rather not remember," said John, smiling back. "This drink is strong stuff, and my head swims," he said after a while. "Would you like to stroll outside a little?"

"Stroll? Where?"

"Anywhere. The weather is nice, and I feel like walking. Why don't you show me around your neighborhood?"

"Oh, okay," she said, sounding unconvinced. She stood up, took the glasses to the kitchen, then returned and stood by the door. "Shall we?" she asked, and John got up. Outside, Sammy locked the door behind them and started walking.

They strolled side by side for a few minutes without touching each other until Sammy stopped and looked at John. The night was pleasant, with a nice, cool breeze. The lights from the houses along the street they were walking on illuminated their path well—a perfect night.

"So, what's the matter, Soldier?" Sammy asked quietly.

"I don't know how to explain to you ..." he started. She waited patiently for him to continue. After a short pause, he continued: "When I was back on Earth–after I tested positive, I mean–I was nervous about speaking freely in places that might have been wired. That's when I made it a habit to go on long walks with the few people I trusted and talk about everything. Can you understand it?"

"I'm not familiar with the situation you describe because I was born here, in total freedom, but I get the picture. Still, what does that have to do with this evening?"

John fought his impulse to change the subject, and after a while, he asked bluntly, "Can I trust you, Sammy?"

"With what?" she asked with surprise.

"With things that are unusual ... that I wouldn't tell anybody but a real friend."

Sammy took John's upper arm in her hand and squeezed lightly.

"I'm your friend and more. You know that," she said accusingly as if to express her offense that John hadn't taken it for granted. He nodded in assent, and her serious expression relaxed a little. "Then tell me what kind of trouble you have got yourself in."

"Not me. I'm not in trouble ... I hope. But maybe we're all in trouble, the whole of Andania."

Their walk took them to the end of the street, where a low stone wall bordered an empty lot. Sammy stopped and sat on the fence. "Come here, sit by me," she said, and after John obliged, she continued. "Who gave you the strange idea that someone may be listening to what is said in my house?" she asked.

"I don't know. Maybe I'm just paranoid, but I don't know what to think anymore. Listen," he continued before she could say anything, "I have reason to believe that Yabalan is behind the attempted murder of Yan-Nibar."

Sammy gaped at him, motionless for so long that John wondered if she would ever react to the bomb he had dropped.

"That worm? Are you sure?" she said at last.

"Of course, I'm not sure," said John nervously. "He hasn't actually told me so. But I did the math on all kinds of allusions that Barak made. He was winking to me, to let me know without actually saying so openly ... I no longer know what to think."

"What about Sarpash?"

"I can't say for certain, but I don't think he was directly

involved. I think the plan was to make sure that Yabalan would go to Earth alone to meet with the representatives of the New Nations; God knows for what purpose. Think about it," he added after a brief pause, "now it's perfect—Yan-Nibar is out of the picture, and Sarpash got the position he's been eyeing all his life. Now, he'll have to remain in New Australia while Yabalan goes to Earth to sign an agreement with the Newists. Perfect!"

"Do you suspect Yabalan to have a plan unknown to Sarpash?"

"I'm pretty sure, and I'll tell you why. I heard with my ears how Sarpash blackmailed Yan-Nibar and forced him to agree to his plan for an agreement with the Newists. That is the plan I know from our discussions at the Ministry of Commerce, and Yan-Nibar had to accept it, although he thought it was crazy. In this situation, it makes no sense for Sarpash to try to kill him. On the contrary, if Yan-Nibar supports the plan, it will be much easier to make the public accept it. If something goes wrong with it, Yan-Nibar is the perfect scapegoat. No, it wouldn't make sense for Sarpash to be involved in the attempt to assassinate Yan-Nibar."

"Do you understand what you're saying?" said Sammy heatedly. "If even a small part of what you have told me is right, this means that Yabalan is planning something so crazy that he doesn't have a chance of selling it even to Sarpash."

"That's what I think," agreed John.

"But you know that the worm Yabalan can sell virtually any plan to Sarpash, who doesn't care about anything except his hairdo and how he will go down in posterity. If you're right, it means that Yabalan is planning a betrayal of a magnitude that even Sarpash would turn against him if he happened to get wind of it."

"That's what I worry about."

"And what about the wiring? I'm not aware that someone eavesdrops on the ministry employees. Why are you worried?"

"I know for a fact that Barak knows what was said in a private conversation in which I participated," he explained. He didn't feel comfortable telling Tasha's story to Sammy. He preferred to be vague about the actual circumstances of the case. "But what's freaking me out is that he isn't making a mystery of it. I have the feeling that since Yan-Nibar was shot, Barak feels free to do and say whatever he pleases."

Sammy's expression became serious, and she sat silently, gazing into the dark. After a minute, she turned to John and asked quietly, "Do you want to see the YYBZ files?"

"But you said that it's impossible to get into those files without the code and that only Yabalan has it."

"True, that's what I said."

"And ..."

"And I was the one who planned the security system for those files to be so perfect that nobody—including myself—would be able to access them. I did so under specific orders from Yabalan."

"And ..."

"And the worm Yabalan isn't as smart as he thinks."

"I'm shocked, Sammy," said John with a broad smile that said the opposite. "Does this mean you and I can go through those files?"

"Aha," Sammy nodded.

"Now?"

"Now, too, but we need to find a place that is definitely not wired to hook into the system. If they catch us, that's the end of us."

"What do we do, then?" John asked in despair. "We can't go to the office at this time of night because that will immediately arouse suspicion—besides, our offices are wired for sure. The terminals in our apartments are out of the question for the same reason. It's hopeless."

"Mmm, you're right ... but wait a sec! I've got an idea," she said, excitedly jumping to her feet. She pulled John after her, and he got up. "Come with me," she ordered, starting to walk quickly.

The large corridors of the university building were empty. John and Sammy's steps echoed loudly as they walked along the third floor, which was badly lit by small wall lights placed at even distances from one another.

"What are we doing here exactly, if you don't mind my asking," whispered John.

"This is the building of the faculty of Computer Sciences of the University of Andania," Sammy whispered back.

"I can read," John retorted ironically, "and this incredible piece of information is written on the front door."

"Yes," she continued without taking notice of John's irony, "but this is not just a university. Here's where I did my research work, and I'm still in touch with my advisor. I help him sometimes when I can find the time for it. That's why I have a key to his lab," she added with a smile of self-satisfaction, showing John a plastic card. "What's more important is that in the past, I arranged for the computer in the lab to connect with our system so that if something comes up while I'm working here, I can take care of it. Understand now?"

"I do, indeed. You're a genius, Sammy!" John whispered to her enthusiastically.

"I know, I know. I've always been. But why are you whispering?" she whispered.

"For the same reason that you're whispering," John said, and he was going to discuss the topic more but gave up when Sammy stopped by a brown door and opened it with the plastic card. They entered the dark laboratory quickly, and Sammy locked the door behind them.

John looked around. The room looked like any other computer lab, with three different workstations on small separate stands and many books and papers lying around.

Sammy approached the nearest terminal, turned it on, and sat by it, hitting the keys quickly. Seconds later, the familiar symbol of the Ministry of Commerce appeared on the screen. "We're in," she said quietly.

"Do you have an idea of what we're looking for?"

"No, and I can't search by keywords because the search will be recorded in the system and may even activate an alarm."

"So, what can we do?" John wondered.

"I can display the files without physically opening them, which will leave no trace, but we need to guess which one is the file that may interest us. Here, look," she said, pointing at the list of files displayed on the screen. "For instance, here's a file entitled 'Newists: Influences and Conditions.' Let's see what it is."

The files' contents were immediately displayed on the screen and turned out to be a geopolitical background of different groups within the Newist population. "This is garbage," said John, and Sammy moved on to the following file.

File after file, they saw reports and summaries concerning topics that were too boring even for the Ministry of Commerce.

"There's nothing of value here," said John after a while. "We have thousands of files here, and the chance of hitting the right one in a reasonable time is nil."

"It's worse than that," said Sammy. "We'll have to stop our screening in five minutes; otherwise, the control system will pick us up and lock all the files until further notice. We won't be able to go in again for five hours."

"Are you sure?"

"I built this, remember?"

"Then let's forget about it," said John in despair. "Anyway, I can't find anything of interest here."

"Wait!" Sammy ordered. "Think a little. The worm Yabalan hasn't gone to all the trouble to create a foolproof system–all right, all right," said Sammy, noticing John's lifted eyebrow, "except, of course, for whoever built it. He didn't do that just to store statistics on the feeding habits of the northern Newist tribes. There has to be more. Come on, pick a suspicious one."

"How can I tell that it's suspicious?"

"Here, let's look at this, for instance, in the folder 'Correspondence.' Look at the name of the file."

John looked at it. The file was named DMYLETT 13899A67B65Z. The only suspicious thing was that the file had a code name instead of a descriptive one, contrary to all the files they had checked before. Sammy clicked on it, and the system displayed the contents. It was a short letter written on the letterhead of the New Nations Organization. John and Sammy read it together.

"My God!" John exclaimed when he reached the end of the letter.

"I don't believe it!" Sammy echoed.

The letter left no room for misunderstandings.

To the Hon. Deputy Minister Mr. Yabalan:

The Council of the New Nations Organization has studied your revolutionary proposal to change the geopolitical situation in New Australia. The Council finds your proposal very interesting and commends you on its inception.

We believe that mixing the population of Andania with the Newist population will likely produce the desired result. The Council has taken under advisement your proposal to announce a blockade of New Australia for forty-eight months, counted from nine months after the borders on New Australia are abolished in practice. This will be announced at the New Nations Assembly before the parties' representatives to confirm your assumption that the danger of an epidemic no longer exists and to ensure that, should an epidemic occur within the mixed population, it will not spread beyond New Australia.

The Council admires your rare courage and willingness to assume responsibility for the future of New Australia. Therefore, we hereby undertake in writing to appoint you a lifetime member of the New Nations Organization with the rights of a special observer if, as it's hoped, will be proved beyond any reasonable doubt that creating mixed populations with D-positive and D-negative elements no longer represents a threat to public health.

Giba Garnol, Chairman of the Council of the New Nations.

"Now we know," said John slowly.

"One thing is for sure," said Sammy emphatically, "he has to be stopped!"

BOOK THREE

"I'd like to get away from Earth awhile
And then come back to it and begin over.
May no fate willfully misunderstand me
And half grant what I wish and snatch me away
Not to return. Earth's the right place for love:
I don't know where it's likely to go better."

Robert Frost–"Birches" 1916

CHAPTER 18

John stood on the bridge of the ship that was about to land him on Earth. He was pensive, but not because he was about to see his former home again. True, the preparations for landing had conjured up the illusion that Dana might suddenly appear at his side despite all his efforts to avoid thinking of her. The question of how he could manage to find her–and, more importantly, what would happen when he did–kept nagging throughout the trip. But he was realistic enough to know that finding her on Earth would be near impossible, considering how little he knew about her. Besides, she could be anywhere in the universe, on a passenger ship. And why would she talk to him if he did find her? She must be convinced he had deserted her for selfish reasons without bothering to say goodbye. She must hate him.

And Tasha? She suddenly was so far away that he missed her a little less, and then he felt guilty because of all those inconsistent thoughts and tried to chase them away. He did not doubt his love for her, he reassured himself, but the distance between them was too great for a relationship that hadn't had time to evolve, and he shouldn't be thinking about her so much.

He shook his head, shaking away his thoughts about Dana,

and turned his mind to the pressing problems before him. The news from Andania was alarming, particularly in light of the uncensored information that Sammy managed to give him.

Sammy! Thinking of Sammy always caused a smile to appear on John's lips. She was doubtless not only practical and smart but brave as well. He remembered their last meeting a few hours before his ship left Andania. They had sat in her garden at a safe distance from the house and any bugs it might contain.

"Take this," she had said, pressing a small object into his hand.

"What's that?" he had asked, looking obliquely at it.

"It's a coder-decoder. If you connect it to your computer when you talk to me, we can exchange secret messages."

"How does it work?" John had asked with amazement.

"It's straightforward. It's a clever little stick that connects to your computer's input port. You plug it in before you contact me on the video channel; it adds some additional information to the carrier wave of the transmission. The information is modulated with encryption that matches only our two sticks. Without one of the sticks, there's no way anybody can figure out the information."

"And the video channel, does it work normally?"

"Of course. We'll communicate by typing on the keyboard. The stick encrypts only what comes through the keyboard. Nobody will pay any attention to our exchanges because the amount of information we add is negligible compared to the video transmission. So if anybody is listening in, he'll see some quite normal spikes in the video channel, which can be attributed to background noises and transmission disturbances."

"It's sheer genius, Sammy!" John had said enthusiastically.

"Yep. I must agree that I'm pretty good. By the way, be careful not to point the camera at the keyboard while you communicate in this way because that'll give us away. Can you type blind?"

"Of course."

"Then there's no problem. Just try to look relaxed while we

correspond and stay as still as possible to avoid arousing suspicion in anyone watching us."

They had sat on Sammy's garden bench in silence while John worked up the courage to talk to her about Tasha.

"I need a big favor from you," he had said at last.

"Ask away. I've already broken all the laws I know for you, so you can't scare me. But," she had added pensively, "why do you look like a mischievous puppy?"

"I don't look like anything of the sort."

"You do, but never mind."

"Oh, all right. You see, I have this girl who cleans the apartment for me ... Tasha."

"Yes?" she had prompted him when he paused.

"Poor girl," he had said, trying to sound distant, "she's been arrested for questioning, but she's not connected. She has nothing to do with Yan-Nibar's case, but for his own purposes, Barak uses her in his internal battles with Rippel."

John had paused and looked far away. He had waited for some sort of response from Sammy, but she had merely kept glancing obliquely at him, waiting for him to go on.

"I promised her that I would be in touch, to try to help–but now, with this mission ... could you see what's going on with her while I'm away?"

"Is she important to you, this Tasha?" she had asked directly.

"Not really ... but she works for me, and they arrested her at my place. She's a good kid."

"So she's important to you," had been Sammy's verdict.

"To some extent," John had guardedly admitted.

"That's a good enough reason for me to take an interest in her on your behalf," she had said without a moment's hesitation.

"You are a good friend!"

"A good friend, hmm ... Yes, that'll be me. I have no control over it," she had said, smiling sadly.

"I wanted to visit her before I left, and I asked Barak to arrange a visit, but for some reason, the topic gets on his nerves, and he won't hear it. It'll surely be much easier for you when Barak is away."

"No problem. Leave it to me. Now, you'd better go and get ready."

"Yes," John had agreed, getting to his feet. He had taken Sammy's hand and squeezed it warmly. "I'll miss you," he had said, meaning it.

"Don't worry. We'll talk a lot via video link at the expense of the Ministry of Commerce," she had laughed.

"Every day," he had replied, nodding in agreement.

"And John," she had added, smiling mischievously and pointing at the garden, "we must stop meeting like this."

John was worried by the news coming from Andania. Yan-Nibar was still in a coma, and the doctors were unanimous that he was likely to remain in a vegetative state forever. Several functionaries of the Ministry of Commerce and other governmental institutions had been secretly arrested, Sammy reported via their secret communication channel and had been charged with conspiracy in the attempted murder of Yan-Nibar. According to Sammy, those people had no connection with the affair but had been on Yabalan's blacklist for a while. The impression John got was that the attempted murder was being exploited to the maximum to purge the government corridors of undesirable elements–undesirable according to Yabalan's views, of course. John was preoccupied, although Sammy also had some good news for him.

She had found a very convenient way to communicate. She prepared long reports concerning neutral topics, which she transmitted to John together with a few comments scattered along the transmission. This method allowed them to concentrate on their exchanges and justified their long silence, during which they communicated via the secret channel. This time, it was the turn of an instructive lesson on the etiquette of the New Nations.

"You must explain this to your whole team," said Sammy, speaking importantly.

Your cleaning woman has been released, and the letters Sammy typed ran at the bottom of John's screen.

When? John typed excitedly.

"I'll be sure to show it to them as soon as possible," he said aloud.

Yesterday, said the letters at the bottom of the screen. *She signed a confession that incriminates Rippel, and then they released her.* A confession? John frowned. How could she sign a confession if she'd done nothing? And if she did sign a confession, how could they let her go?

Have you seen the confession? he typed.

"Notice the order in which they shake hands," said Sammy.

Who do you think I am? The Head of the Secret Service? retorted Sammy. John felt that her typing was restless. *Obviously, I've not seen the confession. This is only a rumor that I'm passing on to you. We only get rumors nowadays. No reliable info. Take it with a grain of salt.*

"Yes. That's peculiar. I'm glad you passed this tip on to us. We wouldn't have known how to behave without it."

John hesitated, unsure of what his next step should be. Finally, he typed, *Can you go to talk to her?*

What??!! came the answer.

I can't explain right now, but it's very important to me that you see her and tell me what's going on with her. Can you do that?

Why do I feel exploited? Sammy asked after a few seconds. *Never mind. I'll try. Now we have to stop. We've transmitted too much already, and someone may notice. Watch to the end of the report and say goodbye to me nicely.*

The short movie ended half a minute later, and John addressed Sammy in a distant manner. "Thank you, Sammy. I'm sure that the

Deputy Minister will put the information you have provided today to good use. Keep sending us good material."

"You're welcome, John," said Sammy, speaking in a similar tone. "I'm happy to be able to assist the Deputy Minister. I'll get back to you soon with additional important information."

Additional important information? She must have meant about Tasha, thought John. He felt embarrassed that he had to ask Sammy to check on Tasha, but there was no other way, and he had to be reassured that all was well with her. Sammy was too smart, anyway, and had undoubtedly already guessed that something was going on between him and Tasha. Still, she had agreed to help him despite her declared feelings for him. John resolved to find a way to make it up to her, to make amends for being unfair to her.

Later, he told Barak that Sammy insisted on passing on useless information to them, such as tutorials on etiquette, but he couldn't ask her to stop because he didn't want to hurt her feelings. On the other hand, he didn't want to waste the Deputy Minister's precious time with details of that type. Barak had nodded in approval, and there, the matter had rested.

CHAPTER 19

The landing was uneventful, just as the trip had been. The government of Andania's ship was parked in the middle of the somewhat deserted airport, a short distance from the New Nations' capital, not far from what used to be Houston, Texas. The vast metropolis of Nations City had slowly swallowed the once well-defined city. One side of the metropolis lay along the Bay of Mexico and extended a distance that seemed endless to the naked eye. John grew up in a neighborhood in Nations City, still known by its historical name, Victoria.

John felt weird. This was a sort of homecoming to a place that was not home. He stood on the concrete next to the ship in his white uniform and inhaled the air from the hot ground. The air tasted different but not strange. John's senses identified it without difficulty. Suddenly, he recalled the similar feeling he experienced when he first landed in New Australia, years before when the taste of the Andanian air had made itself known to him for the first time. Then, he had attributed the strange feeling to the extended stay in the closed ship, but now he understood that the difference was substantial. The air was different from that of Andania, and its familiar smell brought past sensations back to John suddenly and without prior warning.

He stood near the ship hatch, patiently waiting for the deputy minister to emerge. Barak's head suddenly appeared from within. "Have they come yet?" he asked.

"Who?" John asked.

"The NNO officials who must meet the deputy minister–who else? He's getting impatient, but he can't leave the ship before they come to meet him. That's the protocol. I can't understand what's keeping them," he added angrily.

"Do you want me to go to the terminal to find out?"

"Yes, good idea. Go. I'll go back to Yabalan. Boy!" he added, "I want out of this box already."

John smiled to himself and walked toward the official car that was parked near the ship. The driver, who had seen him coming, got out of the car and waited for John by the open door.

"Good morning," John said to him. "Are you supposed to drive Deputy Minister Yabalan?"

"Yes, sir," he answered politely. "Where is Mr. Yabalan? He is expected at the terminal."

"Who's expecting him?"

"Erian Graziani, senior assistant to the Minister for Natural Resources."

"Why didn't he come to greet the deputy minister at the ship?"

"I'm only the driver, sir," said the man, smiling apologetically.

John returned to the ship and entered the dark corridor unhappily. The last few minutes had been sufficient for him to appreciate the difference between the ship's stale air and the natural air outside. Going into the ship again gave him a choking sensation. Barak was waiting for him at the end of the corridor that led to Yabalan's quarters. "Well?" he inquired impatiently.

"There is a car outside, waiting for Yabalan. It is not planned to have a receiving party here at the ship, but the senior assistant of the Minister for Natural Resources is waiting for him at the terminal."

"What? Didn't Valerie come in person?"

"Who's Valerie?" asked John, who hadn't heard the name before.

"She's the Minister for Natural Resources. Yabalan was expecting her to meet him at the ship. What am I going to tell him now?"

Barak looked worried, and John tried to encourage him. "Well, it's not your fault," he said, but Barak made an impatient gesture with his hand and disappeared into Yabalan's room.

John concluded he was not helpful inside the ship and walked out, finally positioning himself next to the entrance. Their luggage had already been removed from the ship, hopefully, to be taken to their hotel. A few more minutes passed before Yabalan emerged from the ship, looking enraged. The driver immediately went to open the door for him, and Yabalan quickly got into the back seat with Barak. John sat in front with the driver, who nodded in assent when he questioned him silently, pointing his finger at the front door.

The trip to the terminal only took two minutes, and the group was directed to a side door that opened into a small room. A man of about thirty was waiting for them, with a young woman holding a sheaf of papers. Yabalan, still looking upset, stood before him and waited.

"Welcome, Mister Deputy Minister Yabalan," the man greeted him. "Welcome to the New Nations," he added, including John and Barak with his eyes in his greetings. "My name is Erian Graziani, and I am the Assistant Minister of Natural Resources. Valerie Namkov, the official host of your delegation, apologizes for not being able to meet you here due to circumstances beyond her control."

Yabalan's expression softened a little. "Thank you for your words of welcome, Mr. Graziani. I am obviously disappointed that

Ms. Namkov is not here to meet me, but I'm sure we will meet soon. Meanwhile, where is the press conference going to take place?"

Graziani looked embarrassed but answered quickly. "No press conference is planned for the time being. The first part of your visit, until matters are finalized, has been defined as 'private.' Therefore, we have not released any information concerning your delegation."

Yabalan's face took on a deep shade of purple, and John feared he might have a fit. Eventually, however, he calmed down and spoke in a thin, metallic voice. "This is not what was agreed. Not at all. I'll have to talk about it with the person responsible, but clearly, you are not the right person to talk to. If this is how it is, please take us to our hotel so I can contact the appropriate person."

"Of course, sir," Graziani answered politely. But maybe the honorable Deputy Minister will allow me to outline the plan for the next few days so that you are fully informed?"

"You don't say. We have a plan!" Yabalan exclaimed scornfully. "Do you imagine we would have come all this way *without* a plan?"

"Of course not, sir. But there are a few technical changes, and I think I should update you, sir, and your party about them."

"All right, all right, get on with it," conceded Yabalan impatiently.

"Here are the arrangements, sir. Nothing is planned for today, and we are sure you'll want to take the time to settle down and rest after such a long journey. Therefore, I'll escort you to your hotel and will leave. Tomorrow, at noon, there will be a tour for you at the NNO building, including meetings with NNO Council members. Several members have voiced keen interest in meeting with you, sir."

"How many meetings are planned?" asked Barak.

"Ahem ... at this time, two," said Graziani without gazing at his guests.

"Two!" Barak repeated in disbelief. "You mean to tell us that out of four hundred and sixty members of the NNO Council, only two are interested in meeting the deputy minister?"

"Look, Mister ..."

"Barak. And this officer is Lieutenant John Hektor," said Barak curtly.

"Look here, Mr. Barak. We can offer meetings with visiting personalities to the members of the Council, but we can't force them to meet with the visitors. Anyway, the next day, the program calls for a visit to a prison for positive prisoners. We understand that misleading reports have reached Andania regarding conditions in the prison, and the NNO is keen to have the Deputy Minister see for himself and report to his government. Regarding the remaining days, the plan is, so far, skeletal. Here," he added, and the young woman, who had stood in silence until then, took a step forward and handed over copies of the papers she was holding. Yabalan, who looked furious, waved her away in the general direction of Barak. To his mind, Deputy Ministers had other people keeping papers for them. "The schedule is, of course, still open to changes. If you have no more questions, I suggest we go to the hotel."

The group left the terminal through a side door without having to go through any control. Before they left, the young woman handed them diplomatic passes, giving the one intended for Yabalan directly to Barak. Apparently, she was a fast learner.

The car that had driven them from the ship was waiting outside, together with an additional identical vehicle. Yabalan and Barak hastened to sit in the back seat, and John, who remained outside, turned to Graziani. "What about our gear?"

"Don't worry, Lieutenant. It has been taken care of, and we will wait for you at the hotel. Are you traveling in the Deputy Minister's car?"

"Other options?"

"You can come with me if you want. I'm with the other driver."

John accepted the invitation gladly. A trip with Yabalan, in his present state of mind, didn't appeal to him at all.

The cars moved away from the terminal, and Graziani looked more relaxed and friendly than before. "How was your journey?" he asked with a warm smile.

"'Twas fine. A little boring, perhaps. Tell me, Mr. Graziani ..."

"Erian," his host corrected him.

"Erian ... all right, I'm John, then. I wanted to ask you ... my mother lives not far away from here, in Victoria. I haven't seen her in years, and I'd like to visit her very much. Is there anything planned I should know about, or perhaps I can get away tonight?"

"As I said, we've left the whole day free for you to settle down. Now it's ..." Erian squinted and looked at the clock on the dashboard, "two in the afternoon. I guess it'll be four o'clock by the time you are organized at the hotel. I can ask the driver to stay with you and drive you wherever you want."

"That's too generous!" John protested. "I don't want to take your car ..."

"Don't worry," said Erian. "I'll take the other car, which is available anyway, and I don't need my driver again today 'cause I'm going straight home from the hotel. You can take him for as long as you need him."

"I don't know how to thank you, really," said John honestly. "You're too kind."

"I'll tell you how you can thank me. Next week, I host a dinner for a few intimate friends at my house. On that evening, there is no official engagement planned for you. Perhaps you'll agree to join us? My friends would love to hear first-hand reports about Andania, especially if they come from an officer like yourself who can talk about his own experience and is also a native of our area who understands our mentality. So, what do you say?"

"I'll be happy to come. Thanks for the invitation."

"It's agreed, then. Here's the hotel." The car stopped near an elegant building, and a doorman hastened to open the door for them.

John stepped quickly out of the car. Holding his briefcase, he stood by Yabalan's car. When Yabalan and Barak emerged, Erian led the way toward Reception, where the hotel manager awaited them.

"It's a great honor! A memorable day for our hotel, Mister Deputy Minister ..." he greeted them.

"Are the rooms ready?" Erian interrupted him.

"Of course. Of course, come this way, please."

The rooms were allocated quickly. Yabalan got a large suite with a spacious bedroom, a little kitchen, a small office with a desk, and a sitting area. Barak and John each were assigned a nice room adjacent to the suite. John was glad to find his luggage waiting for him there, and he unpacked it quickly.

Having gotten organized, John treated himself to a mineral water bottle from the minibar and sat to relax in the armchair that faced the window. The room was on the fortieth floor, and from his window, he saw the familiar roofs of the endless metropolis. Despite the familiarity of the scene, he felt distanced from his surroundings.

A light knock on the door heralded Barak's arrival. He approached the minibar, poured a glass of liquor, then sat in the armchair next to John's and sighed.

"They did a number on us, didn't they?" he said, sounding amused. "Yabalan is having a hysterical fit. He thinks he hasn't been treated with respect and has already told me he won't join us for dinner. He's going to lie down and nurture a headache. Let's hope he'll stay in bed until morning."

"So what are you going to do?" asked John.

"Me? I have to stick around in case he wants anything, so I guess I'll take a little walk–half an hour or something like that–and then you'll find me either at the bar or in bed."

"I was planning to go out. Are you okay with that? I really want to see my mother."

"Sure, sure. I understand you. Go. No problem. You won't be needed tonight. Actually," Barak almost whispered to himself, "the shape things are taking, it looks like we won't need you at all in the near future."

"Thanks. Then I'll go out in a little while."

Barak took another sip of his drink and looked out of the window. John wondered what his friend was thinking. Perhaps he remembered his family that he couldn't visit or thought about his street friends. He looked pensive, but John didn't ask questions that his friend, perhaps, didn't want to ask himself. They sat silently until Barak suddenly got up and, with a short "see you," left the room.

Erian's car stopped outside John's parents' house. "Is this the place?" the driver asked.

"Yes. I'll go inside in a minute," said John. His heart was beating fast, and he had to wait until it returned to normal. He was about to revisit the world he had thought he'd never see again and feared what he was about to find there.

Eventually, he got out of the car and strolled toward the door of his old home. He looked around at the building and its surroundings. It was all as he remembered as if time had stood still on the day he had left Earth, except for the little garden in front, which was unkempt. His father had always cared for the small patch of grass that ran parallel to the house's path, planting seasonal flowers and mowing the lawn to perfection. Now, John assumed, his mother no longer had the strength–or the will–to take care of it.

The house was dark; only a little light came from the kitchen. When he was a child, John remembered, lights had been kept on throughout the house all day, and the place looked different that way. It was only eight o'clock when he arrived, too early for his mother to be in bed. After a brief hesitation, he rang the bell. A noise came from within, and his mother's voice called faintly.

"Who's there?"

"It's me, Johnny."

"Johnny?" a noise of shaken keys came from the other side of the door, followed by the ring of metal falling on the floor. A few seconds later, the door opened, and his mother stood before him. "It's really you, Johnny? I'm not dreaming?"

John took a step forward, unable to find words, and took his mother in his arms. "It's me, Mommy," he mumbled. "It's really me."

"Johnny ... my Johnny," she wept. Deep moans came from her throat as if she was unable to bear her happiness. Many thoughts raced in John's head, but one was overwhelming–his mother had shrunk. She had become thin and fragile. This strong woman, who had always run the house and the family with an iron hand, now looked as if her flesh hung from her bones without the intervention of muscles. John thought she seemed so tiny and weak as if the fire that had always burned within her had been put out.

They stood on the doormat, hugging until his mother finally stepped back. "Come, let's go in," she whispered, pulling him inside, into the dark house. Once inside, she turned on a small light in the sitting room, and then she stood, facing John in silence, as if unable to believe he was there.

"Look at you!" she said at last. How beautiful you are in uniform—more than I could tell via the videophone. And you've put on some weight. It's good that you did ... it means you're eating well. Are you hungry? Come to the kitchen, and I'll fix you something. How long are you staying?"

"Mom ... I'm not hungry. Thanks. I only want to see you, to hear how you're doing. You look good," he lied.

"Anyway, I want to make tea. I have the cookies you like. Stay here; I'll be right back. Wait here."

John sat and waited patiently. He knew that arguing with her would get him nowhere. Five minutes later, she returned with cups and a plate of cookies. She sat by him and watched him drink and eat as if to ensure he liked the cookies.

"So, how long are you staying?"

"I don't know, Mom. A few days, but it's not up to me. I've just arrived, and I came immediately to see you. Now tell me, how are you doing?"

"I'm doing well. The cost of living has become a little higher, and sometimes it's tough, but your father left me enough to live on. Still, I'm a little lonely. Your Aunt Claire, bless her soul, passed away two years ago. Until then, we saw a lot of each other, but now I'm alone."

"But ... what about my brothers? Don't they come often?"

"Often?" His mother paused and looked far away above his shoulder as if to search for the answer there, then continued. "Not often, no. But they always come on my birthday. And, of course, they came to your father's funeral."

"That's it? They don't come every week? But do they call you, at least?"

"Sometimes. They're so busy, you know. They're big managers, and you can't expect ..."

"What? To have time for their mother? I thought that they'd take care of you and Father."

"Your father was a wise man. He understood much earlier than I did that we're unimportant to them. He said that to me after you left. He said, 'If they treat their brother this way, in his hour of need, you can be sure that they'll get rid of us the moment we'll need them.' And he was right! They didn't even bring their wives and children the last time they visited. I can't remember the names of some of my grandchildren anymore."

John gazed at her. She was crying again, and he went to sit next to her and hugged her tightly without speaking. He didn't know what to say. His mother started to cry uncontrollably and to shake in his arms, sobbing and weeping. "I want to die, Johnny. I can't go on anymore. I've been left with nothing. Nothing ..."

"It'll be all right, Mother. I'm here with you. I'll take you to Andania with me." Brave words, but meaningless. At her age, his mother would never be able to exchange the house where she had lived all her life for a faraway place where she knew nobody. But those words were the only consolation in his power to offer. He was talking from his heart, not his head.

After a while, she calmed down and went to wash her face. When she returned to the sitting room, she was a different woman, and for a moment, he saw his mother as he had known her, strong and hiding her feelings behind a straight face.

"Tell me about your work in the army," she said.

They sat for a long time, chatting aimlessly and pushing aside the pain and the fears until John got up. "I've got to go, Mom. I'm supposed to keep myself available for my deputy minister, and he must be looking for me now and asking himself where I've disappeared," he lied. "But I'll come to see you again soon, the minute I can get away."

"Promise?" she asked, sounding worried.

"Promise," said John, meaning it.

Back at the hotel, John went straight to his room to check his messages and was happy to discover that nobody had looked for him. He undressed and went into the shower, where a long soak under the running water reestablished a little of his composure. Despite the fatigue of the long day, he wasn't yet ready to go to bed, at least not before he found a way to unwind a little.

He opened his bag, took out civilian clothes, dressed in them, and went down to the lobby, where he followed the quiet music coming from the bar. He had to stand for a few seconds to let his eyes become accustomed to the low lighting. He scanned the room and immediately noticed that Barak had a stool in the bar's corner and was bent over a glass. John sat on the chair beside him, and Barak raised his head.

"Hi," he said, sounding tired. "How did you enjoy your visit with your mother?"

"It was ... weird. Sad and also unsettling," said John without thinking.

"You sound like you had fun," said Barak in a flat voice, nodding in understanding.

"You, too, look really in the pink," John commented.

"Yeah, the situation stinks, I'd say. I just realized that I'm fed up with the whole thing."

"It's not like you," John reproved him. "I guess you've drunk too much."

"If anything, I haven't drunk enough. I made a mistake when I decided to come to Earth. I should have remained in Andania, but my boss wouldn't have any of it. Perhaps I should have quit–I should've done everything not to return here, as I had promised myself. Did I ever tell you that I swore I'd never return on the day I left here?"

"No. I didn't know that. But we all swear to do things that, examined with hindsight, are stupid."

"This is not stupid. I should have kept my vow. Well, let's forget about it now. It's too late for it anyway." He got up slowly and looked at John. "Are you staying in the hotel now?" he asked.

"Yes. I'll sit here for a while and then go to bed."

"I'll go out then. If our boss needs anything, tell him I'm dead, and you're filling in for me. I'll see you in the morning," he added without waiting for John's reaction.

"Are you alone?"

John gazed in the direction from which the question had come. A young woman was standing by him. She looked lovely, he thought, if perhaps a bit too skinny for him. She wore a Bordeaux-colored dress that accentuated her figure, and her hair seemed too perfect to be natural. Without waiting for his answer, she climbed onto the stool that Barak had vacated. "I thought you might want to buy me a drink," she said.

John looked at her with surprise. She seemed a regular person, his image of the girl next door, but her intentions were quite obvious.

"Sorry," he said, "but I'm not in the mood for this. Here, buy yourself a drink," he added, leaving enough money on the counter to pay for ten drinks. Without another look at her, he got up and left.

CHAPTER 20

Council Member Zijan Chan met his guests in his NNO Center office. The room was small and sparsely furnished, which fit the host's unimpressive appearance well. Chan was thin, small, and young, although John wouldn't have guessed his exact age. He greeted them, smiling and bowing.

"A great honor, a great honor," he mumbled mechanically while shaking everyone's hands. "Please do sit down," he said, turning to a small, round table that occupied the best part of the room.

Four chairs stood by the table. Yabalan and Barak chose theirs, and Chan sat after them. John ignored the fourth chair and stood a short distance from the table next to Erian, who acted as their escort for the day.

The tour had started late. Erian had come to the hotel at half past ten, as planned, but they had all waited for Yabalan to join them in the lobby. After a restless night drained him, John was grateful for the late starting hour. At first, he hadn't been able to sleep; after he had finally managed to doze off, troubling dreams had awakened him twice. Most of his dreams were now only a confused memory, but he did remember that his brothers played a significant role in them. His father had been in his dreams, as had the woman from the bar, but the logic behind their appearances eluded him.

The visit to the NNO Center began with a guided tour of the enormous building. A professional guide walked them around, explaining the many architectural, artistic, and technological wonders. The trip took almost an hour. It ended near the corridor that led to the Councilors' offices, where Erian stepped again into the role of guide. Two minutes later, they were knocking on Chan's door.

"I'm very interested to hear your position on the overexploitation of Andania's mines," said Chan after seating himself ceremoniously before his guests.

Yabalan blinked and swallowed quickly, "Overexploitation? What overexploitation?" he asked.

"Yes, yes. It's all in here," said Chan enthusiastically, reaching behind him to pick up a hefty volume, which he slid on the table toward Yabalan. "This is my thesis, my master's work at Beijing University. I carried out extensive research on the ecological dangers that New Australia faces because of the intensive exploitation you make of the mines. It's all clearly explained here. I think the NNO must take steps and reach an agreement with your government to solve the problem. So, what can you tell me about it?"

"The truth is, Councilor Chan," Yabalan answered patiently, "that the problem you refer to has never been brought to my attention, and, therefore, I'm unable to comment on it now. But of course, given your enlightening comments, I'll study the matter in depth and will be in touch with you on the subject. Is there anything else you would like to discuss at this time?"

"No. This subject is close to my heart. That's why I insisted on meeting with Your Honor. I'll be very grateful if you give the matter proper consideration."

"He's a bloody fool," Erian whispered in John's ear, "but we couldn't refuse to let him meet the deputy minister."

John nodded, surprised by the intimacy of Erian's comment, but said nothing. Two minutes later, after a few more pleasantries, the group left the room.

"Now you'll meet with Joseph Brown," Barak informed Yabalan. "He's a councilor who's a great friend of Andania and favorable to D-positives as a group. It's important to make good contact with him."

Councilor Brown's office was much larger than Chan's and richly and tastefully decorated. John wondered what the criterion by which the NNO allocated space to its council members was. Joseph Brown was a hearty old man, slightly bent and hard of hearing. He stood inside his office, leaning on an antique-looking wooden stick, and greeted them warmly.

"Welcome, welcome!" he said. "It is a great pleasure for me to host such an important minister from Andania."

"Deputy Minister," Erian whispered in his ear, but loud enough that John heard him.

"Ah?"

"Deputy Minister, not Minister, sir," Erian repeated louder, keeping a straight face.

"All right, all right. It doesn't matter. You're welcome anyway." He extended his hand and took Yabalan's. "Who are these young men?" he asked.

John and Barak were introduced, and everybody sat down. Brown and Yabalan were facing armchairs, and the rest were on a soft sofa. Brown turned to Yabalan. "Tell me, what is the situation out there?" he asked. "I support you wholeheartedly and make no mystery of my views. On the contrary, I'm outspoken. Quite outspoken. You need to get rid of those barbarians, the Newists. Exterminate them entirely. And good riddance, I say!" The ancient councilor raised his voice and hit the floor with his stick.

"We are very appreciative of your support, Councilor," said

Yabalan, "but my government believes that it is possible to find a way to live in peace with the Newists ..."

"Nonsense!" Brown interrupted him. "What's that–are you a wimp? There's nothing to talk about with them!" he concluded.

"Perhaps you'll allow me to give you a brief review of the political situation in New Australia," said Yabalan desperately. When Brown nodded in assent, he went off on his preferred lecture.

After a few minutes, Yabalan stopped mid-sentence and stared at Brown in disbelief. "He's sleeping!" he exclaimed angrily toward Erian. John gazed at him and saw the nice old man sitting with eyes closed, his thorax rising and falling rhythmically. Councilor Brown, undoubtedly, was asleep.

"Ahem, Mister Deputy Minister," said Erian softly, "I believe we will all be spared embarrassment if we leave quietly and go on with our program."

That advice was clearly sound, and the group got up as quietly as possible and left the office, leaving behind their host, peaceful in his sleep.

The moment the group reached the corridor outside Brown's office, Yabalan went off like steam that had been kept under pressure for too long. He made it a point to speak pompously, as was his habit, in a way that, at least, so it seemed to John, was designed to help him emphasize his higher position. "Mr. Graziani," he said authoritatively, "I want to speak immediately with Valerie Namkov. Kindly get her for me at once."

"I'm afraid that isn't possible, sir."

"Look here, mister," Barak intervened, "too much is enough, and what's happening here is too much. Now you have two options: make the connection between the Deputy Minister and Valerie Namkov happen right away, or arrange transportation to the airfield, and we'll head back to Andania today. You decide."

Erian stood, looking embarrassed and unable to decide what to do. John felt sorry for him but had no way to hint to him that Barak was bluffing. John could have bet there was no way Yabalan would return to Andania empty-handed after being sent on such a crucial mission. Eventually, Erian gave in. "Wait for me here, please," he said. "I'll see what I can do." He walked away quickly, and John saw Yabalan and Barak talking in low voices a little farther away. Once more, he wondered why the deputy minister had brought him along since, clearly, he and Barak had no intention of sharing their secrets with him. The distance they kept from him bothered him so much that John had asked Barak a direct question during the flight to Earth. Still, all he had managed to extract from him was the dry answer: "You'll be precious to our mission yet. Don't worry," he had said. He then turned away, clearly showing that that was where the discussion ended.

Five minutes later, Erian returned and addressed Yabalan. "Miss Namkov is now visiting a location far away from here. She asked me to tell you, sir, that she would be pleased if you would agree to meet her for dinner tonight at seven if that fits the plans of the Deputy Minister."

"It does, it does." Yabalan smiled with self-satisfaction. "You see, with a little effort, everything can be fixed," he added.

"Yes, sir. One more thing, if I may. Dinner will be a private function; unfortunately, your aides won't attend. I apologize."

"No problem," said Barak, "I can use the free time."

"Don't worry about me," John added. I'll be happy to have another opportunity to visit my mother."

"Anyway, we need to discuss matters of state that are not for your level," Yabalan concluded. He appeared satisfied at his moral victory.

You're not as smart as you think you are, John thought. A hand touched his elbow, and he turned. Erian was standing beside him.

"Would you like to go out for a little fun after seeing your mother?" he whispered in John's ear.

"With pleasure," John answered, hiding his surprise at the invitation.

"I'll talk to you later," Erian concluded, still whispering, and started to walk toward the exit. "If you'll please come with me," he said to the group.

John opened the vehicle door and sat beside Erian, who was waiting outside his mother's house. This visit had been even more depressing than the first one, and apparently, it showed on John's face.

"Wasn't too good, then?" asked Erian.

"Ah? No, 'twas okay. I got to eat a lot of cookies, and we spoke a little. After such a long separation ..."

"I can imagine. Are you ready for a drink?"

"That's Nice of you, thanks. It may brighten me up a bit. But don't you have to get home or something? I feel bad taking up so much of your time."

"No, really. My pleasure. No problem. I'll be happy to spend time with you. I don't get to speak with someone like you every day."

They drove through streets that were only partly familiar to John. He was silent throughout the ride, lost in his private thoughts, and glad that Erian wasn't trying to make conversation. They eventually stopped near a door framed by bright-colored lights and got out of the vehicle.

When Erian pushed the door open, quiet music and soft lights greeted them. He was apparently a habitué because a waiter approached him immediately. After a brief exchange, he led them to a booth in a quiet corner of the bar. They sat without speaking until the waiter brought their drinks, and Erian lifted his glass.

"To your health, John. Tell me a little about life in Andania."

"What would you like to know?" asked John unenthusiastically. He didn't like to speak about himself.

"For instance, how was it like moving from here to there?"

"It's a very different place. It's difficult to explain."

"Do you like being in the army?"

"I guess that 'like' is not the right word. It's a meaningful job, and I think that I perform well. There is no little satisfaction in what I do."

"How does a field commander like you work for the Deputy Minister of Commerce?"

"How do you know that I am a field commander?"

"How? You must've told me."

"No, I didn't."

"Then, I must have assumed it ... perhaps because of your military countenance."

"Mmm ... Do you know what I'm thinking?"

"No. What?"

"I think you have been ordered to befriend me and learn things about us. It explains why you're being so nice to me and investing so much time in it."

Erian looked at John, smiling. "Is that a trait you have in New Australia, that you are so direct?" He seemed amused, but perhaps he only smiled to hide his embarrassment.

"Could be. We don't have much time for nonsense and niceties. It's much simpler to be straight talkers. It saves everybody valuable time."

"Good, then I'll be direct with you, too. The answer is no. Nobody instructed me to spy on you. But naturally, I'm interested in my guests. Besides, I'm sorry to disappoint you, but I like you, so I'm investing time in you. And, in your case, I'd particularly like to know more about you."

"Why 'particularly'?"

"I'll tell you sometime, but it doesn't matter right now. And while we are being direct, do you believe me or think I'm trying to fool you?"

"I lean toward believing you, but I reserve the right to change my mind."

"Fair enough. I can live with that. Tell me a little about what happened to you when you first got to Andania."

John was surprised to discover that talking to Erian was easier than he had anticipated. As time passed, he opened himself to the young man who sat with him in the booth and felt he liked him more. He told him about how he had been forced drafted into the army and hadn't been able to get in touch with the girl he loved and thus had lost her forever. The expression of sympathy on Erian's face was deep and sincere.

After three rounds of drinks, Erian checked the time. "It's late, you know. I'd go on chatting, but tomorrow, a long day awaits us–the jail and the long trip to get there–and I think we both need to get some sleep before then."

"Yeah. My head is heavy from all the drinks anyway. And you–are you sober?"

"I may have drunk a little too much, too," Erian laughed, "but I'm sober enough to get you to your hotel in one piece."

Erian insisted on paying the bill, and, that concluded, they walked heavily to the vehicle. They parted like old friends at the hotel, and John went straight to his room and into bed. This time, he fell asleep immediately.

CHAPTER 21

The trip to the military camp, which had been converted into a jail for D-positive criminals, took almost two hours. They were driven there in a large vehicle, not the car that had picked them up at the airfield. John sat in the back while Erian chatted like a tour guide, pointing out to Yabalan interesting areas, buildings, or natural structures they saw along the road. John was grateful for the opportunity to doze off for a few minutes and catch up with some of his lost sleep.

The jail was located in a dry valley–a scorching place that appeared to have been selected to create the most uncomfortable conditions possible for the inmates. At the gates, the vehicle stopped for a few minutes, and Erian disappeared into an adjacent low building, from which he emerged with papers and signaled the driver to drive on. The papers were shown to the guards at the gate, who waved them through, and the vehicle drove on for a few meters and then parked in a guest space. Erian approached a small man in a khaki uniform who had emerged from a three-story building next to the parking lot. They shook hands and exchanged a few words before turning to the guests' vehicle to greet Yabalan, who hurriedly exited out of the door that the driver had opened.

"Honorable Deputy Minister, allow me to introduce Warden Abed," said Erian, pointing at the small man.

"Pleased to meet you, Deputy Minister," said Abed, bowing slightly while extending his hand. "I'm at your service, entirely at your service, for as long as you choose to stay. Does Your Honor have any particular questions before we begin the tour of this facility?"

"Yes, Mister Abed," said Yabalan, importantly. "Where is your toilet?"

"Oh!" said Abed, looking abashed, "I should have suggested that you take time to get refreshed. How inconsiderate of me. Of course, of course. Forgive me. Here, this way," he added and led the group toward the building from which he had come. "I'll show you my private bathroom."

"I'll wait here," said John to Erian and moved a few paces into the comparative shade of the building. Barak also stayed, and after everybody else had disappeared into the building, John tackled the subject that had bothered him since their visit to the NNO Center. "What happened yesterday at the meeting between Yabalan and Valerie Namkov?" he asked.

"Mmm ... nothing much, I guess," said Barak, unusually candidly.

"What do you mean? Yabalan attached great importance to the meeting."

"Let's say that he didn't fill me in on what passed between them, and this usually means that nothing notable was said or done because Yabalan doesn't keep anything from me. What did happen—and this is of no lesser importance—is that we managed to keep face and force Namkov to meet with Yabalan, and we dictated the timing. It's vital not to be perceived as spineless by the NNO."

"I understand," mumbled John, who didn't. The more he thought about it, the less he saw that the waste of energy needed to stroke Yabalan's ego was justified.

The delegation returned from the toilet, and all grouped

around Warden Abed. "I would like, if you'll allow me, to explain the layout of these facilities briefly. Here," he continued when nobody protested, "the inmates are D-positives who have been found guilty of serious offenses, all connected with the fact that they are positives. As you know, from the point of view of public health, those criminal offenses are considered to be the most hazardous ones, and, therefore, the prisoners here are considered dangerous prisoners. Nevertheless, as you will see for yourselves, the conditions in this jail are very humane. Very humane, contrasting sharply with the malicious rumors that reckless elements have spread." The warden continued to explain his case with an obviously well-planned methodology. "The NNO doesn't consider the imprisonment of these criminals to constitute a punishment, but only a means to prevent them from perpetrating their crimes further in a manner that may harm public health."

"How do you know," John interrupted him, "that what they meant, or mean to do, may be harmful to public health? Sorry, Warden Abed," he added hastily, "I haven't introduced myself. I am Lieutenant John Hektor, and I'm the military secretary of the honorable deputy minister."

A chilly silence fell on the parking lot, and Yabalan stared at John angrily. Later, he'd tell him that his question had been rude, unprofessional, and lacking diplomacy, but at that moment, he tried to convey all that by lifting his eyebrows and shooting invisible arrows from his eyes. Abed glanced at John and answered icily.

"It's not our place to criticize the decisions of the lawmakers and the courts of the New Nations. Our role is limited to carrying out their policy according to instructions received from time to time."

"I see," said John, undeterred. "Only one more question, if you will, sir."

"John ..." Barak started to say, but Abed nodded and waited for the question, prompting John to continue.

"Wouldn't it be more efficient and cost-effective to dispatch all those positives who didn't act lawfully to Andania instead of keeping them in jail?"

"You may perhaps be right, Lieutenant. However, jailing them not only achieves the goal of keeping them away from society but, it is assumed, deters others from committing similar criminal acts. That's why we can't give every criminal a prize and set him free—we have stringent conditions for releasing prisoners from this place to Andania. It happens very seldom; I haven't had a single case in the seven years I've been here."

"Warden," Erian intervened, "I think we should start with the tour. There's only one detail that we need to arrange. According to Valerie Namkov's instructions, I promised the deputy minister that his team members would be able to speak freely and alone with prisoners of their choice. Thus, they will verify that the conditions here are humane and that all the stories that have been invented about this facility are only lies. We must ensure they can return to Andania and report the truth about it."

"No problem, Erian. You know that we've nothing to hide. What I suggest," he added, speaking directly to Yabalan, "is that we review a roll call of the prisoners in the courtyard. Each of your men will select one prisoner to talk to and take them to a corner of the courtyard for a one-on-one interview. Is that acceptable?"

"Fine," Barak said on behalf of everybody.

"Let's start the tour, then. The noon roll call will be in twenty minutes, and while you're waiting, you'll be able to see the facilities."

Abed guided them through the buildings and proudly showed them the kitchen and mess hall, laundry, two-person cells in the men's and women's wings, and even a small sports hall. Having completed the tour, he took them to the courtyard where about eight hundred prisoners stood in two separate blocks—one for male and the other for female prisoners. Armed guards stood on the courtyard walls, and Abed motioned his guests toward the prisoners, showing confidence in the efficacy of his security measures.

John thought a mutiny would carry a heavy price even with all the armed guards. Abed led the guests, now and then stopping by a prisoner and asking, "How's the food? How do you feel? Are you treated well?" and the answer he got was invariably, "Very good, sir."

The inmates of both sexes stood at attention, wearing grey uniforms buttoned up to the neck. The silence in the courtyard was complete except for the visitors' footsteps. The uniforms and the military-like stances almost canceled the different identities of the prisoners, and John found it difficult to remember the faces he had just seen. Suddenly, he stood astonished, a shiver running along his spine when a familiar face almost jumped at him from the second row of female prisoners. Could it be that Maya was there? Her hair was short and her face pale; her lowered eyes no longer showed the intelligent and effervescent expression that once had captured John's heart, but he had no doubt–that prisoner was his Maya.

"Okay," said the warden right then. "I think you got the idea, so if you want to interview anybody here ..."

"Yes, Mister Abed," John jumped ahead of the others and earned a poisonous look from Yabalan and a surprised one from Barak for the second time that day. He should have known that the boss always comes first, but the protocol was the farthest thing from his mind right then. "I'd like to interview this prisoner," he added, pointing at Maya.

"Fine, Lieutenant. Go with her to the northern side of the courtyard, where you can sit under the shade. You!" he barked at Maya, "step forward and wait for the lieutenant by the shade."

Maya stepped forward, still gazing at the ground. John started to walk with her, but the warden grabbed his arm and stopped him.

"Wait, Lieutenant. Our rule is that the prisoner always goes from one place to another, keeping a distance from us, and they must wait for the warden there."

"I'm not a warden," John pointed out.

"Still," Abed said dryly, "you need to abide by our rules."

John gazed at Maya, who walked heavily toward the shade far from where they stood. Once she got there, she turned around and stood at attention. John walked quickly to her.

"Maya ..." He realized he didn't know what to say.

Maya glanced at him quickly and lowered her eyes again. "It's really you, John," she said, speaking distantly.

"Yes, it's me. But what are you doing here? Come here. Sit down. Sit down and tell me."

Maya sat on the bench under the shade, and John sat beside her.

"There isn't much to tell, Lieutenant," said Maya, without looking at him, "I committed crimes against the state, and my deserved punishment is imprisonment here."

"I don't understand ... what are you saying? You weren't D-positive!"

"I committed crimes against the state, and my deserved punishment is imprisonment," Maya repeated monotonously.

"Maya, look at me!" John touched her chin and lifted her head. "Please, tell me what happened."

"I committed crimes against the ... Oh, John." Maya's voice broke, and large tears poured from her eyes. "No," she stopped him when he tried to get closer and comfort her, "don't come near me. It's forbidden. If you touch me again, I'll be punished."

John turned his gaze to the courtyard. Yabalan stood before a male prisoner, and Abed stood next to him. Barak sat with another prisoner in another corner. It looked like nobody was paying any attention to them.

"Tell me, then," he ordered.

"It's very tough. I knew that I was D-positive, and I have known since I was a little girl. My father tested me privately–he had friends and the means to do it–and I always knew I would find a way to fool the test."

"Then, when I came to you after my test, you already knew you were positive. I don't understand why you rejected me, then. We could have built a life together."

"When you told me that you had tested positive, I panicked. I immediately realized I had to get away from you because remaining attached to a positive would have awakened suspicion ..."

"But ... but what did it matter? We could've been together. On the contrary, it was a perfect solution."

"You don't understand. I can't ... I couldn't think I would be branded as a positive and lose all the social status I deserved; I simply couldn't."

"So, what did you do?"

"When the time of my test came, I was ready. I had studied the situation and knew there were ways to fool the test. It cost a lot of money, but money was no object. I bought a kit that was said to be reliable. I paid the man his money, and then the police came and arrested me. The man who sold the kit to me was an undercover police agent who framed me. I've been here since."

"Until when?"

"For life. Mine are crimes against humanity."

"We have to get you out of here. I ... I'll do something."

"Don't make promises you can't keep, John. Nobody can help me. Nobody."

The tears started to flow again, and her shoulders shook uncontrollably. John felt powerless and sat, gazing impotently at her. Suddenly, a warden appeared behind them. "Get on your feet!" he yelled at her. Maya got up like a robot and stood at attention. "Walk," the warden ordered, and they both disappeared, leaving John in turmoil behind them.

Yabalan and Barak had already completed the interviews with their selected prisoners and stood in one corner of the courtyard. Abed and Yabalan were talking animatedly, and Barak stood aside and listened. John approached him and touched his shoulder. "Barak!"

"Not now!" Barak hissed between clenched teeth.

"It's urgent!"

"You've managed to embarrass us sufficiently today. What do you want?"

John motioned him aside, out of reach of Abed's hearing, and explained. "The girl ... the prisoner that I interviewed, I know her. She's okay. I need your help to get her out of here."

"Out of the question!"

"Why? The NNO representatives are going out of their way to make us happy, and I'm sure that if Yabalan asks them, they'll agree. Tell them we'll take her to Andania immediately or send her on the next ship. I'll pay for it if the need arises."

"Listen to me very carefully, John," said Barak impatiently. "Having one of these prisoners released is mission impossible. If it's at all doable, it will require a huge effort on Yabalan's part, and I'm telling you that he'll never agree to use up the favor that the NNO may be willing to grant to ingratiate themselves with him, which he may need down the road, for some prisoner that you know. You're wasting your time."

"You don't understand," said John painfully, shaking his head in disbelief at his friend's words. "Have I ever asked you a special favor? This is the first time that I've asked for something out of the ordinary."

"You have a short memory, John. What about your cleaning woman?"

"Yes, all right," John admitted, "but that was small. I understand the favor I'm asking now is huge, but I must."

"I'm sorry, John. It's not realistic to think that it can be done. Forget it."

With those words, Barak turned his back on his friend and joined the conversation with the warden. John gazed at him with amazement but realized that Barak wouldn't help him. He walked behind Abed to where Erian was standing and touched his shoulder.

"Yes?" Erian asked politely. John motioned him away from the group, and when he felt that they had got far enough from them, he explained his problem.

"I don't believe that there is anything we can do about it. I'm very sorry about your friend."

"I can't accept it!" said John angrily.

"Listen," said Erian soothingly, "wait a little while. Perhaps you'll find a way."

"How?"

"I can't tell you right now, but there are ways ..."

"Do you know anything that I should know?"

"No, no. I've already said too much. Please forget what I said. It'll be better for your friend and you. But please, be patient and don't do anything rash. You're on an official mission and can't behave like a private citizen. There are some things ... that may complicate and cause damage. Trust me," he hastened to conclude. The discussion between Yabalan and Abed had ended, and Erian approached them.

"Did the honorable Deputy Minister see everything he wished to see?" he asked formally.

"More or less," said Yabalan.

"Then, I suggest that we head back to the city."

They parted from Abed, who was obviously happy to get rid of them, and got in the vehicle. Throughout the trip, John sat silently, now and then gazing at Barak, who smiled and listened to the compliments Yabalan was showering on Erian for the humane management of the jail.

CHAPTER 22

John's fingers played quickly over the keyboard of his computer. Sammy's face appeared on the screen.

"Hi, John. How's your visit going?"

Why are you looking like someone who's been hit on the head? Sammy's question ran at the bottom of the screen.

"I'm sure that our deputy minister is doing a great job. I don't have much to do, but I expect my turn will come in due course."

What's the matter? she insisted.

Nothing ... personal stuff. Doesn't matter. I'll tell you when I see you.

"So, how can I be of assistance, John?"

"I wanted an update on what's happening at home. How's Yan-Nibar?"

"His condition hasn't changed. I have prepared a summary of the news of the last few days, which you'll see in the movie I'm about to transmit to you. Please transmit this information to all members of the delegation."

"Of course," John nodded, and Sammy started to transmit.

I need information about a certain Erian Graziani. He's the assistant to the Minister of Natural Resources, Namkov.

How urgent is it?

Extremely urgent!

I can get hold of the info pretty quickly, but how can I get it to you? If we talk again too soon, it may raise suspicion ... wait! I've got it!

The transmission of the movie stopped abruptly.

"What happened? It stopped midway," John asked, managing to sound surprised.

"I'm sorry. Technical problem ... perhaps the file is corrupted. Wooff! This has never happened to me before. I'll fix it and call you back. I fear you'll have to re-record it all for the delegation."

You're a genius!

Yessss ...

"All right. I'll wait for your call, then."

John didn't have to wait long; Sammy's face appeared again on the screen in less than twenty minutes. "Here, I fixed it," she announced. "Start recording."

Something weird is going on here!

What?

Your friend's name indeed exists in our database, but all the information about him has been deleted.

Deleted! How can it be? The information is protected.

It's protected against accidental deletion, not against authorized changes. The person who erased the data had the appropriate permission–which had to be the highest.

So there's nothing that you can tell me about him?

Nothing. Zilch.

Mmm ...

I'll see if I can think something up, but it won't be soon. We have to sign out. The movie ends in a minute. Anything else?

Only ... have you heard anything about Tasha?

I tried to discreetly get some information on her. She's gone back to her apartment, where she lives with a junkie boyfriend. I couldn't find out anything else. If it's essential, I can investigate some more.

Still, it may be dangerous because I'm taking an unusual interest in her. You don't want to do anything unusual nowadays and attract attention to yourself.

No, no need. I don't want you to take chances with this. John felt that the less he asked about Tasha, the better his peace of mind would be.

"Okay, John. That's all," said Sammy when the movie ended.

"Thank you very much, Sammy. You're doing a great job. Talk to you soon."

Don't do anything stupid, you understand?

"Goodbye, John."

"I understand ... I mean, goodbye."

John stood before the mirror in his hotel room and checked every detail of his gala uniform. Tonight, at Erian's, he was the guest of honor and felt as if he represented the whole Andanian army. He also started to understand how a circus attraction felt. Erian had said to him openly that he meant to make John the attraction of the evening for his guests. John liked him well enough and didn't mind going along with it, but something in Erian's approach to his visit bothered him, as did the fact that someone had deleted his record from Andania's database. He didn't know what to think.

Erian's driver was waiting for him outside the hotel, and John climbed quickly into the vehicle. The drive took almost half an hour. Ultimately, they pulled up outside an extensive and impressive mansion that stood apart from neighboring homes in a pleasant area. Broad stairs led to the entrance, and the ornate entrance door opened as if by magic once John started to climb them. The driver had probably announced their arrival, or someone was watching out for John. Erian stood in the doorway, richly dressed, and greeted him with a warm smile.

"Welcome, John. I'm happy that you could join us tonight."

"This is some home you have here, Erian," said John, appreciatively.

"It was my parents' house, and I inherited it. I'm glad that you like it. Let's go inside. I want to introduce you to the other guests."

Erian led the way through an impressive entrance, along a high-ceilinged corridor, and toward a broad door through which the chatter of many voices filtered. Once in the room, John noticed about thirty people scattered around in groups, holding cocktail glasses and deep in conversation. Two waiters moved around, bearing trays of inviting-looking appetizers, the like of which John hadn't seen for a long time.

Erian stopped by an amazingly beautiful girl in a black evening dress who was talking to an elderly man. "Aline," he addressed her, "please meet our guest of honor, Lieutenant John Hektor."

John stiffened and bowed politely. "Nice meeting you, Aline," he said.

The young woman sized him up at length, studying him openly until John felt himself blushing in embarrassment. "I thought you'd be less formal, Lieutenant," she said, extending a hand for him to take. "I expected something less ... how to say, respectable. Something more savage."

"I regret disappointing you," said John, who didn't know whether to laugh or be offended, "but we, the Andanians, are boringly normal. I guess that you confused us with the Newists. They are the savages."

"Pay no attention to Aline," Erian laughed. "She always enjoys embarrassing young men. She's so beautiful that she knows she can get away with it," he added. John watched her listen to Erian with an amused look in a sort of decadent society game and wondered whether this was a place for him. Erian gestured him toward the older man standing beside her, who looked about sixty years old.

"Meet Doctor Charles Bening." The two men shook hands, and Erian continued with the introduction. "Doctor Bening is the Chief Scientist of the Ministry of Natural Resources. Anything he doesn't know about natural resources isn't worth knowing. Yes, what?" he asked inquisitively when a waiter approached them and stood before him.

"Mrs. Graziani wishes to meet the lieutenant in the library, sir. She isn't well enough to meet the guests yet."

"Oh, right." Erian turned to John apologetically. "My wife isn't feeling well today–the flu or something–but she refused to cancel the party in your honor. Half an hour ago, she took something to relieve her migraine, and I'm sure that she'll be able to join the crowd later. Would you mind meeting her in the library? It's quieter there, and I'm sure she has many questions to ask you."

"Of course. No problem."

"Escort the lieutenant to the library," Erian ordered the waiter. "In the meantime, I'll circulate and see how my guests are doing. I'll see you later."

John nodded to him, turned around, and followed the waiter, leading him to the end of the long corridor. Once there, he pointed theatrically at the door and left. John knocked lightly, and when no answer came, he turned the handle and walked in. The room was beautiful, with large French windows opening into a well-kept and masterfully lit garden. The walls were covered with books of all sizes and colors, and an ancient writing desk stood in the middle of the room. A small, thin woman in a light evening dress stood by the window, her back to the door. When John closed the door, she turned around and gazed at him.

"Hello, John," said Dana.

John stood there like a stone, feeling that his legs had been nailed to the floor. He stared at Dana in disbelief.

"You ... you ..." was all he managed to mumble.

"I'm Erian's wife, yes."

She walked up to John, put a hand on his arm, and gently

pulled him toward the large sofa beside the desk. "Come, sit down," she said, speaking as though to a frail old man. He mechanically sat, and she sat beside him.

He gazed at her at length, looking for signs of time but finding none. And why should she have changed? It hadn't been that long, even though it felt like an eternity to him. "Sorry, the shock ..." he said at last when he had regained some control over his voice.

"I understand. That's why I didn't want to meet you in the hall before all the other guests, so I invented a headache and waited for you here."

"Do you hate me?" John asked with ill-concealed fear.

"I don't hate you," she answered forcefully as if to avoid any misunderstanding. "I did hate you for a while when I thought you had run away from me without a word of farewell. But later, I forgave you. I never forgot, but I did forgive."

"But I didn't run away. I need to explain, to tell you ..."

"I know everything. Erian told me. Oh, I'm so sorry ..." Her voice broke, and a tear appeared in the corner of her eye. John raised his hand instinctively to wipe the tear. His hand rested on her cheek, and he realized he was applying light pressure, pulling her face toward him.

"No!" she said quickly. John, startled, withdrew his hand.

"I'm sorry ..."

"I'm a married woman now. I can't ..."

Dana lowered her gaze and became silent. She twisted her hands until her knuckles turned white, silent witnesses of her predicament.

"Let's stop being sorry," said John quietly, trying to lighten the atmosphere but unable to control the sadness in his voice. "Tell me how you became Graziani's wife."

"As soon as I returned from my trip to Andania, I realized that life on a ship was not for me, and I looked for a job that would let me stay put. I took a job as a guide in the New Nations Organization building. That's where I met Erian. He courted me, we went steady for a while, and ... that's it."

"Are you happy?" John asked, with mixed feelings.

"Erian is a wonderful person, and we are in love. Yes, I can say that I'm happy."

"Erian is a likable person. I'm happy you're with him and not with some ... with some ... you know."

"I know," said Dana softly, smiling for the first time since John entered the room.

John's hand found a long thread sewn onto his cushion. He lifted it and played with it carefully, twisting it around his finger repeatedly. He applied his attention to the thread, avoiding Dana's eyes, which he felt oppressively on him.

"Tell me," he said at last, "did you think about me sometimes?"

"I thought about you all the time. What do you think?" she snapped angrily. "During the first months, I didn't sleep or eat. I became a shadow of myself ..." Her voice broke again, and she turned her face. Her hand moved quickly to her face to wipe a tear from her cheek.

John felt a huge lump in his throat that made speech impossible. "So did I," he managed to say at last. He felt like he, too, would cry in a moment, but he knew that Dana shouldn't be allowed to see his weakness. "During the first months, I couldn't stop thinking about you even for a second. At night, at roll calls, and during training. All the time. I wrote to you at the address of the company that runs the ships, do you know that? Actually, you couldn't know because the letter came back. I was devastated and didn't know what to do."

"And what happened then?"

"Life was stronger than my pain, and I moved on. But I never forgot you, Dana. I never forgot ..."

John felt that he was about to lose control. He got up and walked to the window. He stood there, letting the cool wind play with his face while he fought a battle with himself for control over his feelings. A minute later, he turned to Dana again. "Does Erian know about us?" he asked.

"Yes. I told him everything."

"Everything?"

"Everything he needs to know, and that's almost everything."

"When did you learn that I was on Earth?"

"Erian's office started to prepare for your visit, and he received a list of the delegation members, which he left one evening here, on this table. I saw it by pure chance, and your name was on it. My first reaction was, 'This can't be real.' It took me a long time to calm down, and then I told him about you ... about us."

"That was the first time you told him?"

"No. He knew that I'd had ... something with a positive. Perhaps I even told him your name once, but he certainly couldn't have remembered it–and that after my trip to Andania, I lost contact with him. He knew that the relationship had been mean-ingful to me and that it had taken me a long time to get over it. But I didn't give him any additional details. When I saw that you were coming and would meet with him, I had to tell him everything. It was a nightmare that I couldn't have survived without his support."

"I can imagine."

"I asked him to learn a little about you–what you look like now, what you do, what you went through."

"And that didn't make him jealous?"

"Erian knows I love him, and I'll never cheat on him. He has no reason to be jealous. He was deeply moved when you two met, and you told him about me. He ran home. I was asleep, and he woke me up to tell me what you went through. He likes you very much, John."

"I like him very much," said John truthfully.

"You'll know yet what a good man Erian is."

"I'm sure ..."

"You don't know ... yet."

"So, what happens now?"

"Now, you wear your charming smile and go back to the guests. Erian is counting on you to amuse them. I'll wash my face, powder my nose, and join you in a little while. Go now!"

John got up and looked at her with admiration. She touched his cheek gently with her finger.

"Go now," she repeated softly.

John relished the shiver that the touch of her hand had generated in his body and let it run deep inside before he turned away from her and left the room with heavy steps.

CHAPTER 23

John stood in silence beside Erian in the hotel's lobby, waiting for the members of the delegation to join them.

"The party was a success, thanks to you," said Erian.

"You are a fortunate man, Erian," said John, without looking at him, "but you should have warned me. For a moment, I thought I couldn't handle it."

Erian also avoided John's eyes and spoke softly. "I wanted to, but Dana wouldn't let me. She wanted to be the one to tell you." He stopped for a moment and then, still keeping his voice low while looking straight ahead, he added, "I think she feared that you might not want to see her because she's married, and she had to ... here they come," he said with a marked note of relief.

"Good morning, Mister Deputy Minister," he said, smiling so broadly that a bystander could have thought that he actually enjoyed seeing him. He nodded at Barak, who curtly nodded back, and the delegation left the building toward the vehicle that waited at the entrance.

The trip was a short one. After five minutes, they reached the Ministry of Natural Resources, where meetings were planned for Yabalan with some officials. Erian escorted them to a meeting room. Only when Barak took the chair at the head of the table did John notice that Yabalan was not there.

"Where is Yabalan?" he asked in surprise.

Before Barak could answer, the door opened. Two people John had never seen before walked in, introduced themselves and their position with the ministry and shook hands with them. Erian excused himself and left.

"He's at the real meeting," Barak whispered to John as they sat down.

John didn't have an opportunity to ask Barak what he meant by a 'real meeting' until their meeting ended after tedious discussions of clearly irrelevant matters. It was almost lunchtime, and their hosts walked them to the dining room, talking incessantly. John quickly approached Barak and whispered, "What do you mean, 'the real meeting'?"

"Not now," he answered dryly and turned to converse with one of their hosts.

Throughout lunch, John sat moodily, answering his hosts' questions only to the extent needed not to appear impolite. He was seething. Something was clearly going on under his nose, but Barak and Yabalan didn't trust him enough to tell him anything about their plans. He felt that he was being used, and he was so mad that he could barely control himself.

After lunch, the two ministry employees escorted them back to the same meeting room and departed, announcing that the participants of the next meeting would come soon. John turned to watch Barak, who stood with his hands in his pockets lazily examining a large map hanging from the wall. Barak's placid countenance somehow enraged him more.

"Barak!" he almost yelled.

"Yes?" Barak lifted an eyebrow at the aggressive tone of John's voice.

"I know this may be inconvenient, but please accept my resignation. I would be grateful if you could arrange my immediate return to Andania and my unit."

Barak gazed at John, who stood at military attention, fixing his eyes above his friend's right shoulder. "Don't be ridiculous," he said, laughing lightly.

"I'm glad you find it entertaining, but I mean it."

"What exactly is this nonsense about?" Barak asked.

The two friends confronted one another, their anger out in the open.

"I think you know," John said curtly.

"Obviously, I don't. What is there to know?"

"Then I'll explain. You brought me here to be involved in a mission that clearly involves all kinds of activities that have nothing to do with its official purpose. You and Yabalan disappear to go to 'real' meetings, and I'm here just as a cover or something. This is not why I left my platoon and my soldiers. You obviously don't need me here, so I'm asking to be returned to where I'm useful. They need me there."

"Sit down, John," said Barak quietly.

"If you don't mind, I'd rather ..."

"Sit!" Barak barked at him.

John sat down, and Barak seated himself in front of him. He looked at John for a long minute without speaking. When he did, his voice was quiet and soothing.

"You're right, John, when you say things are happening behind the scenes. What you don't know is that you are important–critical. Without your help, our mission may fail."

"How?" John asked with surprise.

"Your role is critical to the mission–but I can't tell you what that role is yet. For your safety and the safety of the mission and Andania, you must not know before it's time. Many forces here plot against us, and we must be cautious. The NNO helps us make believe that we are on a commercial mission, and we hope that Andania's enemies won't be able to discover what the plan is and stop us."

"Who are those enemies of Andania?"

"I'd rather not tell you, John. The less you know, the safer you are. We are working strictly on a 'need to know' basis. There is stuff that Yabalan knows and I don't know, and vice versa. But you'll know what you have to soon enough."

"When?"

"Soon."

"Are we in danger?"

"Only if we make mistakes. For the time being, the right thing is to behave normally. Keep visiting your mother and attend every party you are invited to. Normal behavior is the best guarantee for your and everybody's safety."

"So, what are we going to do now?"

"We'll have our afternoon meeting." Barak sighed, and with perfect timing, the door opened to admit more officials eager to discuss unimportant issues.

John paced along the path winding through the dark public garden. His watch, which he checked every few seconds, said that the time was twenty minutes past the agreed-upon time, ten at night. Lamps on both sides flanked the path, but only a few were lit. He had to strain his eyes to see the features of the rare passersby who walked through the garden at that time of night.

"John!" The whisper from behind a small recess in the bushes caught him by surprise. He walked quickly up to the figure standing in the dark corner between the low trees and the bushes.

"You're late, and you scared me," he complained to Dana, "but it doesn't matter. What matters is that you're here. Come, let's sit down." He pointed to a nearby stone bench, and they sat beside each other.

"What happened, John? When you called and asked me to meet you here, secretly, you got me worried. What's the matter?" she urged him again.

"It's simply ... I don't know what you'll think of me, but I had to."

"You *had to* what?"

"Look here, I know fate separated us, and things have changed, but someone must ask this. Can't we fix it? Is there a way to turn the clock back?"

He took her hand and slid closer to her. She looked at his face, her eyes wide open. "What are you saying?" she murmured.

"I'm saying that I love you, dammit! As if you didn't know. What do you want me to say? That I'm ready to do anything for you? You know that already."

John lifted his gaze, which he had lowered to find the courage to say what was in his heart, and looked at her. She was crying. Large tears ran down her reddened cheeks. He pulled her toward him, and she laid her head on his shoulder.

"I love you too, John," she whispered. "I haven't stopped loving you for a moment, but ..."

"Don't say 'but'! No buts," said John in panic.

"I'm married to Erian, and I love him. Can you understand that? It is possible to love two people in different ways."

The sadness in her voice made itself heard even in her whisper. Her words suddenly brought Tasha's face back to him. How right she was, he realized, that one could love two people at the same time. But the guilt he felt toward Tasha immediately drowned in the turmoil of senses that Dana's presence and scent had ignited in his mind.

"So?" he asked. Dana didn't answer, but her hand increased its pressure on his arm. Her head moved away and then again rested on his shoulder.

John sat there, petrified. He was afraid that moving or speaking would chase Dana and the moment away from him ... her light, quick breathing was a clear testimony of her turmoil. Slowly, her breathing became calmer and more uniform, and after a time that seemed to John to be both endless and too short, she straightened up and looked into his eyes. Her face was next to his, and he felt her light breath on it.

"It's hard, John, but we must put our feelings behind us. I'll always love you, but I belong to someone else."

"I understand," said John heavily and lowered his head again to hide his despair from her.

"No, John. You don't understand. I know because I realize how hard it is, but Erian is not only my husband; he's my friend, and I'll never do anything to hurt him, even if that means I will be hurt. Can you understand that?"

John, who couldn't find the strength to answer, only nodded. Dana gently took John's hand, moved it from her shoulder, and stood up. "I'll better be going," she said softly.

"I'll walk you," said John.

"No. Better not."

A thought occurred to John. "Will you tell Erian?" he asked.

"No. Not this time."

She stood for a moment in silence and then stooped and kissed him lightly on his lips. After a second, she turned away and disappeared into the darkness, leaving him sitting on that bench, feeling lost.

CHAPTER 24

The guard, who walked John along the empty corridors of the Ministry of Natural Resources, acted sleepy, which wasn't surprising at that late time of night. Barak's voicemail message in his room said, "Come immediately to the Ministry of Natural Resources and tell the guard at the gates that Mrs. Namkov has asked you to come. The guard knows your name and will take you to us." Still dazed from his meeting with Dana, John left immediately, jumped into one of the taxis waiting by the hotel entrance, and reached the Ministry of Natural Resources building close to midnight.

"You took your sweet time coming," said Barak; John couldn't tell whether he was angry or amused because of the half-smile he tried to hide without success. He moved aside and motioned John to enter a spacious office already occupied by Yabalan. Dinner remains covered a side table; by the look of them, quite a few people had partaken of the food, but nobody else was in sight.

"I came as soon as I heard your message. What's up?"

Barak didn't answer, but Yabalan, who had been standing with his back to John, turned around and smiled broadly.

"What's happening, Lieutenant, is that we got almost all we

hoped for. Almost everything. The mission is practically complete, and now it's your turn to play your part and bring it to a complete success."

John was surprised to see how openly pleased Yabalan was. He had no idea what he was talking about, but somehow, he appeared too smug for someone on a political mission. He kept explaining in a satisfied voice, "I know that we didn't let you in on our plans from the beginning, Lieutenant, but believe me–that was in your best interest."

"Yes, Barak explained that much to me, and he also said that I have a role to play at a later stage."

"Well, the time has come, and your role is indeed critical. Here," he added, pointing to a computer terminal standing on a large desk in one corner of the room, "I hope that you're as good as your record makes you and as your friend Barak seems to believe."

"I don't understand ..." John said, but Yabalan raised his hand to silence him.

"You certainly need to hear more if we want you to appreciate this great hour for Andania. I can tell you that two hours ago, we signed a full-scale peace treaty with the Newists in this room. It has been a tough negotiation and a difficult result, which required a lot of hard work from me–from us–but we got it. The agreement will come into force a few days after we do our part, and New Australia will enter a new era. No more wars, no more people hurting one another, but good neighborly relations and cooperation for the welfare of the people of New Australia."

Yabalan's voice reflected emotion, but John wasn't sure whether it was genuine or merely a theatrical speech–perhaps a rehearsal of his future address to the people of Andania.

"And what part do I play if the agreement has already been signed?"

"Explain," Yabalan ordered Barak curtly. He sat on a chair beside the table loaded with food remains, waved his hand at

Barak, and then brought it to his mouth to hide a deep yawn. John gazed at Barak and waited.

"Here's the thing," Barak began. "As soon as the peace treaty is made public, we will hand some mines over to the Newists in about three weeks and open the border to a free flow of people and goods. This is an important trust-building step. That's why we need to neutralize the FOS. Your job is to crack the code and, in due course, to turn the FOS off for us."

"Are you out of your mind? It's impossible! You know that to turn off the system, you need to use three keys: Yan-Nibar's, the one in the custody of the Chief of Staff, and the one kept by the president of the Supreme Court. There's nothing that I can do without those keys."

"I'm sure you can manage," Barak retorted with a smile.

"I can't, and even if I could, that would be sheer madness! The moment that the FOS stops working, the Newists will cross our borders with their entire army, not just as they do today in small groups, and it'll be a massacre. We don't stand a chance without the FOS to defend us."

"Lieutenant," said Yabalan, plainly annoyed, "you must put a little more trust than this in your government. Have you forgotten that the situation has changed, and the Newists are no longer our enemies? In a situation of peace, the Frontier Obstacle System will no longer be needed, simply because there will no longer be a frontier."

"Besides," Barak intervened, "it gets better than that. We agreed in our peace treaty that Andania and the Newists would form a joint government. The position of Head of State will rotate between our representative and the Newists'. Our representative will be the first head of the joint government. You see? We rule."

"What does Sarpash say about all this? Does he agree with every detail of the agreement?"

"Sarpash ..." exclaimed Yabalan dismissively. "Sarpash's career is nearing its end, and he does what I tell him. Of course, we did keep him advised of the general lines of the treaty, but he's not interested in details."

"And now, John," said Barak, "it's time to get to work. The terminal on that desk is connected to the NNO central system, courtesy of Mrs. Namkov. I'm sure you are familiar with the system from your previous work on Earth and that you are aware of its ability to break codes. With this system and with the files of data we have prepared for you, we expect you to generate a code-cracked control system for the FOS, which will make it possible for us at the appropriate time to turn the system off, as we have agreed to do in our agreement with the Newists, and to remove the obstacles to peace with our neighbors."

John shook his head in disbelief. "What data are you talking about?"

"All you need is found in a hidden folder in the YYZB files where the Deputy Minister has kept them safe for a long time. Here's the access code to those files," he added, placing a note with a string of numerals and letters before John. "Now start working," he ordered.

John took a step back and looked from Barak to Yabalan. "You're mad," he said at last. "What assurances do we have that the Newists will not invade Andania and kill us all? Without the FOS and with their numerical advantage, we don't stand a chance."

"I have the word of Tafa-Aru Sed, and he is a man of honor. He knows how to do business," said Yabalan simply, as if that clarified everything and left no question open for discussion.

"So you're asking me to rely on the word of a Newist barbarian and to gamble with the lives of the citizens of Andania? I won't take part in this game!"

"I was afraid that you might take a defeatist position like this," Barak sighed. As if by magic, a laser gun appeared in his hand, pointed at John. "Therefore, we arranged for 'insurance.' Your girlfriend, Dana, is presently kept by our men under surveillance, and she won't fare well if you don't deliver. And, by the way, I must say that you were adorable there in the garden. I almost shed a tear myself ... Ah-ah," he added when John stepped toward him, his fist raised. He took a step back and pointed the gun at John's heart. "Behaving stupidly will do her or you no good," he warned him.

"We're wasting too much time, Barak," Yabalan complained.

"The Deputy Minister is right, John. The schedule must be adhered to. Kindly go immediately to the terminal and get down to work."

John strode to the terminal, trying to organize his thoughts. He keyed in the code and found himself inside the YYBZ files. The amount of information presented to John was huge, and he started working rapidly. He was so busy that he almost failed to notice that the door had opened. Barak seemed surprised at the sound of the door opening and started to turn the gun he had been pointing at John toward it, but then John heard a cracking sound, similar to an electric discharge, and Barak fell to the floor.

Yabalan jumped to his feet with a speed that took John by surprise and leaned against the door, pushing it hard. Before he managed to lock it, John tackled him, and they both fell to the ground. John hit him only once, but that was enough since Yabalan passed out and lay motionless on the floor.

John grabbed the handle and opened the door to find the man who had shot Barak stooping there and massaging his face, which the door had hit. "Erian?" John managed to utter before Erian pushed him inside and closed the door behind them.

CHAPTER 25

A s soon as the door closed, Erian kneeled beside Barak's body and touched his neck. "He's dead," he said simply. "What about Yabalan?"

"I only hit him once, and not hard. I think he's all right, but what's going on? Thanks for helping, I mean, but ... what are you doing here?"

"Later, you'll get to ask all the questions–there's no time now." The urgency in Erian's voice was convincing. "We must get out of here quickly. All the rooms in the building are under continuous surveillance." Erian lifted Barak's body over his shoulder, which made him puff a little. "A minute before I came in, I turned off the cameras in this part of the building. Nobody has seen what happened here, but one of the night guards may notice it soon and turn the system on again, and then we're doomed. Pick up your boss, and let's run," ordered Erian. "Here, take Barak's gun and be quick."

"Wait a second, there's something I must do first," said John. He got to the terminal and started typing quickly.

"What are you doing?" Erian complained nervously. "There's no time, I'm telling you."

"One more second, and I'm done deleting all of Yabalan's files so nobody else can use them to cause damage. Those idiots thought I was complying with their demands while deleting all their data. Here, I'm done," said John. He approached Yabalan, who lay motionless on the floor. "Get up!" he ordered, shaking him hard. Yabalan stirred and tried to get up. John pressed the gun to his cheek. "I suggest that you get on your feet quickly and come with us peacefully, sir, if you wish to avoid unpleasantness' like a hole in your head, for example," he whispered viciously.

Yabalan rose without a word, acting disoriented, like in a dream. John placed a hand on his shoulder as a way to direct him and jabbed the gun into his ribs in a way that left no doubt as to the seriousness of his intentions.

"Let's go," said Erian urgently. He opened the door and started walking quickly along the building's winding corridors, turning right and left at junctions without hesitation.

"What ... what happened to Barak?" stammered Yabalan.

"The same thing that will happen to you if you don't shut up," answered Erian without looking back. "He's dead."

Yabalan started to shake so much that John felt the vibrations through his gun. He asked no more and walked submissively, following the pressure of John's hand on his shoulder.

At the end of the corridor, Erian stood before a green door, through which machinery noise could be heard, and pressed a tag on the door. It opened into a large, poorly lit room filled with equipment of various sizes. He dropped Barak's body near a big machine, and John and Yabalan stopped beside him.

"What now?" John asked.

Erian lifted a lever and opened a hatch that was the inlet to the machine, revealing it to be a giant garbage compactor. "Now we say goodbye to your friend in this nice garbage disposal facility—not you, you idiot!" he added when Yabalan started shaking uncontrollably. He almost fell when his knees failed to support him, and John had to hold him up straight. Erian lifted Barak's body, and John hurried to help. Together, they pushed the body through the small opening and slid it into an enormous container, only half filled with garbage bags. The body was heavy, but John was unaware of the weight; his head was too busy processing the information that it was his former good friend he was pushing into the garbage machine.

As Barak's body slid into the compactor, Erian shut the feeding hatch and pushed the "Mix/Compact" button. The noise from the machine, like tree branches snapping, sent a shiver along John's spine.

"It'll take them some doing now to find him if they can find him at all," said Erian with open satisfaction. "Come, quickly," he urged, leading them toward a door at the other end of the room. A brief touch of Erian's tag produced a click of the lock. He cautiously opened the door and examined the area outside. "Nobody in sight," he said, "we can go."

Passing through the door, they found themselves in a small backyard. Erian led them toward a small metal gate, which opened silently but painfully slowly at the touch of the tag. Erian's vehicle was parked nearby, and they got in quickly. "Sit with your boss in the back and watch him," Erian ordered. He slid quickly into the driver's seat, and seconds later, they were moving, leaving the Ministry of Natural Resources building behind them.

"Erian!" John suddenly panicked, recalling Barak's words.

"Yes, John?" he answered patiently.

"Dana ... she's in danger. They're holding her as a hostage."

"Yeah, I heard what Barak said. But don't worry–if they so much as touch one hair of her head, I'll rip the intestines out of this scumbag."

"We were bluffing. We didn't do anything," whined Yabalan.

"We'll know soon enough whether you're telling the truth," said Erian, turning the communication system on. Dana's face appeared almost instantly on the screen before them. "Hi, honey," said Erian, barely concealing his relief when her smiling face made it clear that everything was in order. "I'll be late tonight. The Honorable Deputy Minister Yabalan has asked me to stay with him and the lieutenant until we wrap up something we're in the middle of. Everything okay at home?"

"Everything's fine. Hi, John," she added, nodding in his direction.

"Talk to you later, then," Erian said, switching the communication off.

"You're a fortunate man, Yabalan," he said. "There's a chance that you may live."

Yabalan didn't respond, and John smiled to himself. All the air had left the balloon that had been his deputy minister, and he was showing himself for the pitiful creature he was. Erian left the main road at a small junction and turned into a narrow, unpaved road. After a short while, he stopped the car and turned to John. "We need to talk privately. Let's get out of the car," he said. He gazed intently at Yabalan and added, "But we'll watch you all the time. If you so much as move a finger while we're gone ...." He didn't specify what would happen, but no explanations were needed. Yabalan's spirit had been broken, and he merely nodded.

John and Erian got out and moved a few paces away from the car–far enough to make sure that Yabalan couldn't hear through the closed doors but close enough to be able to keep an eye on him. "Listen, John," Erian said, "we don't have much time. I'll try to explain briefly, but you must understand that we must act immediately."

"But how did you get involved in all this? I need to know at least that much."

"All right, I'll tell you. I work for Rippel. He recruited me a few years ago. My sister tested positive and ... but that's a long story. She eventually committed suicide. I met Rippel and signed up with him during one of his secret visits here. Does that answer your question?"

"Ah ha ... at least in part. You'll have to tell the whole story to me slowly sometime."

"Okay, sometime. Now, let's keep to the essentials. You heard Yabalan's plan, and he isn't alone in this. There's a long list of influential people helping him with this madness. Some are simply stupid, while others hope to achieve their ambitions. One of them is the president of the Andanian Supreme Court. Do you see the problem?"

"Of course. They want to stop the FOS, and the judge has one of the keys. But why do they need me if they're close to obtaining all the keys?"

"They're not certain they'll be able to obtain all three keys. One of them is in the hands of the Chief of Staff—he won't cooperate with those who seek to undermine the security of Andania, and getting the key from him may be a problem. The second key is now in Sarpash's possession. To him, they gave all kinds of crap that has nothing to do with what is in the so-called 'peace treaty,' and he can be manipulated as long as his ego doesn't get in the way. Yabalan's problem is that he's the one who's going to get all the honors, and Sarpash may want to throw a stick in his wheels. That's why they need the shortcut to the FOS that they hoped you would provide. They're desperate for an alternative."

"I see. That would have solved a lot of problems for them. But since it didn't work out, Yabalan will have to resort to the original plan and get hold of the keys."

"That's why he can't return to Andania," Erian concluded.

"So, what are we going to do?"

"We'll drive straight to the airfield where Yabalan will order the captain of your ship to take you immediately back to New Australia while he and Barak remain on Earth to deal with an important mission."

"And then what?"

Erian peered into the vehicle. Yabalan was sitting in silence and motionless.

"And then I'll make sure that he can never be found again," he said simply.

John reflected on Erian's words. The fact that he planned to kill Yabalan, a traitor who was plotting to bring ruin upon his people, didn't bother him at all. What he found difficult to digest was the fact that this pleasant and polite person discussed so freely his plan of committing cold-blooded murder.

"But what will happen to you and Dana? Come with me to Andania—you won't be safe here."

"I'm sure that we'll manage; don't worry. This is my home, and I don't want to leave it."

"Of course, they'll suspect you! They'll see that your tag opened the Ministry of Natural Resources doors and will get on to you immediately. Can't you see that?"

Erian smiled broadly. "Yes, indeed, Ms. Namkov will have some explaining to do about why she was passing through all kinds of corridors in the middle of the night. Poor Valerie! She probably hasn't noticed yet that her tag has disappeared."

"Then ..."

"I wasn't at the Ministry at all tonight. Don't worry. Now, we must rush before anything goes wrong." He walked back to the vehicle, opened the back door, and put his gun's muzzle on Yabalan's cheek. "Do you want to have a chance of living?" Yabalan nodded frantically, scattering around the tears of fear that ran down his cheeks. "Then listen up. We're going to the airfield, to your ship. My office has already notified your captain that you wish to meet him on the ship, ready to take off. We have taken care of all permits, and everything is ready. Is this clear so far?"

"Yes," Yabalan said faintly.

"Good. As soon as we get there, you'll order the captain to leave immediately with John, who will be in command for the length of the trip and return for you in six weeks."

"What's going to happen to me?" asked Yabalan, still trembling.

"You'll be a guest at the home of a reliable friend of mine, out of town in a quiet place, and in six weeks, you'll be allowed to board your ship and go back to Andania–if you behave yourself, that is, and follow instructions to the letter at the airfield. Otherwise, I'm afraid you'll be the first to pay at the first sign of trouble. Am I clear?"

"I won't give you any trouble. But how can I be sure that you won't kill me anyway?"

"I gave you my word, didn't I? You were satisfied with the word of the Newists, and mine shouldn't count less. Besides, if you make trouble at the airfield, you have my word that you'll die instantly. Perhaps we'll make it, but you won't. More questions?"

Yabalan shook his head, and Erian started his vehicle and drove back toward the highway.

As usual, the official vehicle was allowed into the airfield, and Erian stopped next to the Andanian ship. As required by etiquette, the captain stood beside the hatch and saluted them. "Welcome, Honorable Deputy Minister," he said formally. "What are your orders?"

"Hello, Captain. I am putting a critical mission in your hands, the details of which I can't reveal now. Lieutenant Hektor will travel with you to Andania on a mission on my behalf. Lieutenant Hektor's orders should be considered my orders as long as he is on the ship. Questions?"

John couldn't help admiring Yabalan's ability to act. Despite the tension and the fear that had shown clearly before–or perhaps because of the fear–he acted normally, sounding pompous and powerful as usual. And maybe acting was all that politics was about, he reflected.

Erian kept himself one step behind them, and John knew that

the hand in his pocket pointed a gun at Yabalan's back, touching him lightly now and then to remind him of its presence.

"At your command, sir–and yours, Lieutenant," said the captain, nodding politely at him.

"I'm afraid that you have a hard job on your hands, Captain. When you arrive at Andania, you will service the ship, refuel and restock, and return to Earth to pick me up. You must get here on time, exactly six weeks from now. Is that clear?"

"Of course, sir. Are we to leave immediately?"

"Yes, leave at once," ordered Yabalan.

"Goodbye, sir," said John. He saluted him, knowing only too well that he would never see him again.

When John turned before climbing into the ship, the last thing he saw was Yabalan's bent back, disappearing into Erian's vehicle.

CHAPTER 26

J ohn stood on the ship's bridge and watched the captain and his officers prepare for takeoff. A tired face appeared on the large screen facing the command seat.

"Hi there. Ready for take-off?"

"In five minutes, sir," said the captain. "We are completing the final checks."

"Look here, Captain," said the face on the screen, "you weren't on our schedule, and I was yanked out of bed in the middle of the night to see you off. I would really appreciate your getting the hell outta here so that I can go back to bed where I belong." His body language left no doubt he was not happy to be at work at this time of night.

"We do apologize, sir," John intervened. "My name is Lieutenant John Hektor, and I'm the military secretary of Deputy Minister Yabalan. The deputy minister and his private secretary, Mr. Barak, are busy in their rooms and can't come to the bridge. They asked me to apologize to the airfield officers for the unexpected inconvenience that we have caused. Let me assure you that the reasons for the deputy minister's request to leave right away for

Andania are serious, and this is not just a whim. And again, I apologize," he concluded.

The expression on the face of the flight controller softened a little. "Well, all right ... it's no big deal. I understand. Just let's get this over with as quickly as possible, please."

The captain pushed a button, and the legend "microphone muted" appeared at the bottom of the screen. "Why did you tell him that Yabalan and Barak are on board?" The captain asked, sounding suspicious.

"It's essential for the mission. Everybody must think that they are no longer on Earth, and perhaps they'll be able to complete their part of the mission without interference. You must also tell the crew that they are on board but have given orders not to be disturbed, and only you and I are allowed into their quarters. I'll bring them trays with food to make it look real."

"Okay. It looks weird to me, but I'm sure you know what you're doing." The captain pushed the mike's button again and announced, "Preparations completed, requesting permission to take off."

"Permission granted," sighed the tired flight controller.

John watched the city's lights grow rapidly dimmer as the ship accelerated. He watched them with mixed feelings because his trip headed toward the unknown, but the unknown was also the dangers incurred by the people he had left behind. His thoughts went immediately to Dana and Erian. In the short time they had been together since Erian had erupted into the room at the Ministry, and until his departure, John had had no time to think about his motivations and what must be going on in his mind since the events precipitated by Barak's death. He wondered whether Yabalan might already be dead. His thoughts went back to Dana—Erian's Dana, who had made it clear in her characteristically simple way that going back to their past was no longer an option.

He suddenly realized that he hadn't said goodbye to his mother and that she didn't know that he was leaving Earth. He turned to the captain. "I need to make a private phone call to Earth, Captain–I didn't have time to say goodbye to my mother because Yabalan's orders were issued without prior warning. May I make the call from the bridge?"

"You can make the call from my cabin, Lieutenant. You'll have more privacy there," the captain suggested.

"That's a great idea," John thanked the captain. The captain handed him the key to his cabin, and John seated himself in front of the large screen that hung on the cabin's one empty wall.

"Hi, Mother. I'm sorry that I'm waking you up," John apologized when his mother's sleepy face appeared on the screen.

"What's the matter, Johnny? Where are you?"

"I'm on our ship, Mom. I had to leave in a hurry to carry out a mission, but I'll be back soon," he said quickly, trying to dispel the expression of despair that had taken over his mother's features. "I promise. We won't be apart for long. I'll call you often. Okay?"

"Yes, Johnny," his mother said feebly, but her expression of disbelief was too deep to conceal.

"No, really, Mom! My word of honor. And you–look after yourself, okay? Promise?"

"Yes, Johnny."

"I must go now. I'll call you soon."

His mother nodded slightly as if unable to find the strength to talk, and John switched the call off. He sat in the captain's cabin in silence, in the dark, unwilling to move away from the blank screen. At last, he got up and went back to the bridge.

The captain stood on the bridge, studying the documents and dials before him. "Did you manage to make the call?" he asked when John handed him the key.

"Yes, thanks a lot, Captain," he answered heavily. "I'm a little tired now, and I think I'll retire for a while."

"Do you want to be called for breakfast?" asked the captain. John nodded listlessly. He felt emptied of strength and returned to his cabin with a bowed head.

Seven hours of sleep and a hearty breakfast did much to restore John's equanimity. He sat on his bed in the tiny cabin, fiddling with his keyboard while he waited for Sammy's face to appear on the screen.

"Morning, John!" Sammy's tone sounded reproachful. "You must be having fun on Earth and forgetting that there is work to be done. We haven't been in contact for three days now."

Is everything all right? Are you all right? The words ran at the bottom of the screen.

"I'm sorry, Sammy. I've been swamped these days. Deputy Minister Yabalan assigned me various tasks, and I simply had no time for anything else."

Don't ask. Find something to show me and give me time to write to you.

"I'm on the ship right now, on my way home. We left eight hours ago. I have orders from Deputy Minister Yabalan, but I can't brief you now because they are all classified. I have instructions that require me to brief you immediately on arrival, and I'll ask you to wait for me at the airfield, where I'll give you your orders from Deputy Minister Yabalan."

"Certainly, I'll be there. But you need to be updated on the latest events here in Andania, which you may want to relay to the Deputy Minister. Here, I've prepared a short filmed report." Images started to appear on the screen, but John paid no attention to them. He was too busy typing fast.

Sammy, the situation is dangerous and messy—it concerns the letter we both saw. It's all true. I need you to do something for me. Make an appointment with General Chang for me. I need to see him immediately when I arrive. Every hour is critical.

Oh, no problem at all. I'll simply stroll into General Chang's offices and tell him that Lieutenant Hektor asked him to clear his calendar so he could chat with him. No doubt they'll throw me in jail – if I can get to him, that is.

You can reach him if you tell him that Deputy Minister Yabalan has an urgent secret message for him. You are senior enough, and they'll believe you.

Yeah? And what happens when he finds out that I have no such message?

Here's what you tell him next ...

CHAPTER 27

The ship's hatch opened noisily, and John took a deep breath of the familiar Andanian air that hit his face. He stood at the hatch, squinting against the sun low on the horizon, to capture the scene's details. His eyes had grown accustomed to the ship's dim light during the last few days, and the pleasant breeze only partly calmed the burning feeling caused by the intense sunlight.

After a minute, his eyes adjusted enough to let him move, and he walked along the transparent sleeve that connected the ship and the terminal. Sammy waited in the arrivals hall and waved to him through the door. She seemed younger and more beautiful than ever, and John wondered at the change–maybe something in her hair–but he had never been good at noticing what women did to themselves.

The door of the arrivals hall opened, and he found himself face-to-face with Sammy.

"Welcome, soldier," she said, smiling broadly, and opened her arms invitingly.

John hugged her warmly. It was nice seeing his friend after the tension of the last few days. Only a few seconds later, when they stepped out of the embrace, did John realize they had never hugged before. It seemed natural, though, he thought, like old friends. Cozy, nice. There was nothing improper about it. That's how good friends greet one another after a long separation.

"You look great," said John spontaneously. "Are you blooming because I wasn't here to bother you?"

"Don't worry. You managed to make yourself felt with all the errands you dumped on me."

"Did you manage ...?" he whispered urgently.

"Yes, but he won't be able to see you immediately because he's out of town. He'll be back in five hours and will see us then. Tell me what's going on."

"Not now, Sammy. I've got something urgent to do. Can I borrow your car?"

"You'll have to drop me off at home first ... but, you know, I'm sort of fed up with all your secrecy. Get over it, will you? I'm dying of curiosity."

They stopped at Immigration, and John handed his documents to the policeman at the stand, who checked them briefly and returned them to him. "Not here, Sammy," he said, speaking nervously, "later." They left the building, and John stopped a few paces from Sammy's vehicle. "The situation is extremely dangerous. I can't talk anywhere that might be wired, including your car. Let's just exchange pleasantries during the trip, and I'll explain everything later."

"All right, soldier, but when you get to it, it had better be good and convincing 'cause you're freaking me out with all this."

The trip from the airfield to Sammy's home took about fifteen minutes, during which Sammy drove prudently, and John allowed himself to relax in the passenger's seat. He told her about his visits to his old home and the meetings with his mother. John described the elegant parties to which he had been invited and told her about the strange feeling of returning to Earth as a visiting stranger. Finally, for the benefit of any potential eavesdropper, he told her how amazing it had been working with a genius such as Deputy Minister Yabalan and how their boss and his good friend Barak had remained on Earth to complete a critical and secret mission.

When the car stopped by her house, Sammy glanced at him quickly and asked, "Where are you going, John?"

"I ... it's something private. Not work-related, Sammy. I won't be gone for long."

"You're going to look for Tasha, aren't you?"

"Sammy ..."

"Is that what you're going to do?"

"Yes," admitted John, keeping his gaze down.

"Don't go now, John, please," she pleaded. "You should know ..."

"What?"

After a few moments of silence, she spoke, her eyes looking far away. "Nothing, John," she said. "But trust me, and don't go today. Not today, okay? Go tomorrow. Go after your mission is accomplished. Not today, please? For me?"

"I can't, Sammy. I'm sorry. I have to." He opened the vehicle door and circled to the driver's door. Sammy got up and stood a few centimeters away from him. "Don't go," she said again, sounding desperate, "for your sake ..."

John moved past her without speaking, got into the car, and in the driver's seat. He drove away quickly, leaving her standing.

Once he reached Tasha's neighborhood, John drove slowly, looking for the street to which she had directed him on the day of their trip to the lake. The road and the building appeared to his left, and he turned, cutting the engine at the curb near the entrance. A shiver of anticipation ran through his body, and he took a deep breath. The expectation of his forthcoming encounter with her after their long separation filled him with images of Tasha that ran in his head as an imaginary movie.

Two minutes later, he got out of the car and walked into the building. He had to look for the right floor because Tasha never told him which one she lived in—or if she had, he had forgotten it. The small entrance was dark. He had to squint to read the faded stickers that bore the tenants' names, some of which had been written over the names of earlier inhabitants that had been crossed out. One almost illegible note that said, "Dor & Tasha," sent a pang of jealousy through John's heart. The glue had dried up, and the sticker hung half curled up. Without thinking, John tore it off and threw it into a corner, ashamed of his childish reaction.

He climbed the steep stairs to the door marked "4" on the second floor. Another "Dor & Tasha" sign was on the door, but this time, it was a handsome sign hand-painted on a piece of metal. John pushed away the instinct to vandalize it and knocked twice on the door.

Silence. No sounds came from the apartment, but John was convinced it was not empty. Someone was inside and was trying to move around silently, but he was there. He knocked again, and this time forcefully. "Open up, it's me, John. Tasha! Tasha!" he cried out loud. He put his lips to the crack between the door and the lintel and tried to make himself heard within.

A louder noise came at last from inside the apartment, as if someone was dragging a chair across the floor, and painfully slow steps came closer to the door. At last, the door opened, and a young man, almost a boy, appeared in the doorway. John recognized him as the same Dor he had met at the lake, but he was much thinner as if he hadn't eaten for a long time. He stood bent back in dirty clothing, shaking vigorously every few seconds. He looked at John but didn't seem to recognize him.

"I'm John, Tasha's friend. Do you remember me?" asked John. "We met at the cabin on the lake."

The young man's obtuse features were lit for a second by a flash of recognition, and he nodded, then turned around and dragged his feet toward the inner part of the apartment. John didn't know how to behave and remained standing at the door. Dor walked to a closed door and turned around. "Come," he said, making an inviting gesture. John entered the apartment and approached.

The room into which they walked was a bedroom with a small double bed. The sheets on the bed were filthy, and a poignant smell of sweat, perhaps mixed with spoiled cheese, hit John's nose. Dor sat on the bed and stared at the floor. John found a chair, dragged it close to him, and sat down.

"Thanks for letting me in," he said, smiling encouragingly to get the young man's attention. I'm looking for Tasha."

"Tasha?" Dor exclaimed, immediately choking on the word. He let his body drop on the bed, lying on one side, and started to weep. "Tasha, Tasha!" he cried, and every few seconds, he kicked the air with a strong kick.

John jumped to his feet, feeling helpless. The young man was undoubtedly stoned and in no shape to make conversation. He left him on the bed and went to look for the kitchen. A few glasses and one or two plates rested encrusted in the sink, but John found a reasonably clean mug and filled it with a teaspoonful of coffee. He waited for the kettle's water to boil while looking around. Knowing Tasha's obsession with tidiness, John knew she wasn't living in this filth. He reasoned that she must have left the apartment she had shared with that miserable creature and moved somewhere else. Now, all it would take was to wake Dor up enough to get the new address from him.

Five minutes later, John returned to the bedroom with a hot mug of coffee. Dor lay on the bed, still on one side, his eyes wide open and his lower lip trembling as if praying. John pulled him to a seating position by his shoulder, and he didn't resist. He made him drink the coffee, and Dor swallowed it, choking and coughing. After downing most of the hot liquid, he looked a little more coherent and sat stably on the bed without John's help.

"Give me Tasha's address," John asked politely when Dor appeared to be able to focus, "and I'll go and leave you in peace."

"Tasha?" Dor said again, his eyes filled with tears. John feared that he was about to have a new fit, but he only wiped the tears with the back of his dirty right hand and kept gazing at infinity. "They said that the government agents did it to her, but it's not true. I know; I was there."

"Did what to her? What did they do to her?" asked John, suddenly panicking. Did anybody hurt his Tasha? When Dor didn't react, he shook him so forcefully that some of the coffee that remained in the mug held in his left hand spilled on him.

Dor looked at the spilled coffee in disbelief. "They did nothing to her. I was with her. She sat here, where I am now, and I said, 'Tasha, honey, you're overdoing it with that shit.' But she didn't listen. She never listened to me; she only laughed and laughed and took some more. And suddenly, she wasn't laughing anymore. She lay here and didn't laugh. And I wasn't laughing either."

John stood before him, shaking uncontrollably. "What are you saying? What are you saying?" he yelled at him. "What happened to her? Where is she?"

"You don't know? I thought you knew. She overdosed. I called for help, but it didn't help, didn't help, it didn't … I called for them immediately, and it didn't help … I swear I called immediately. Immediately, I called them …"

Dor went on and on monotonously, but John wasn't listening anymore. He turned around slowly, feeling that his legs were too heavy—he found it hard to walk, but he had to get out of there, to get away, and hear no more.

"… didn't help. She didn't move. And I called …" Dor's

mechanical voice continued from afar, but John had already closed the apartment door behind him.

John sat in the car outside Sammy's house, gazing at the sky, motionless. He couldn't say for how long he had been sitting like that; moreover, he had no idea how he had managed to get there. The car door opened, and a soft hand pressed lightly on his arm.

"I'm sorry, John," said Sammy quietly.

John turned his head and looked at her. "You knew!" he said.

"Yes. I tried to warn you, but you wouldn't listen. I couldn't tell you, just like that. Please forgive me. I'm sorry ..." Sammy's voice broke, and she barely managed not to burst into tears.

"It's not your fault, Sammy," said John sadly, "it isn't anybody's fault, except perhaps mine. She did it to herself–she and nobody else. Perhaps things would've been different had I been at her side ..."

"No! Don't blame yourself. You couldn't have done anything. Junkies don't think like us ... like regular people. This could've happened at any time, now or in the future."

"Maybe ..." He stopped and swallowed twice. His voice was flat, and he wasn't looking at her. "What a fool I was. How did I believe her when she said that she never touched drugs? Who knows what other stories she told me and how many times she made a fool of me! I'll never know."

His voice broke again, and he sat in silence, sagging in the driver's seat, until Sammy's hand, which she had kept on his arm, shook him gently.

"Let's go inside. We have three more hours until the meeting. Lie down and rest for a while. I'll give you a drink–a small one because we've got work to do. Come," she repeated, pulling at his arm again.

John felt like a child being led by his mother. He no longer had any will of his own, and he followed Sammy without thinking. He felt strange in a world without Tasha when he hadn't had a chance to say goodbye to her. That's my destiny, he thought to himself, to lose all the people I love, suddenly, just like that, without a last word or touch. Or maybe it's my curse, he wondered.

Sammy made him sit down on a soft sofa, and he closed his eyes. His inner exhaustion was so great that he fell asleep in a few seconds.

CHAPTER 28

The anteroom that led to General Chang's office seemed too small and unpretentious for the man who commanded the whole Andanian army but reflected military order and neatness. John was too nervous to sit in the small armchair provided for visitors; instead, he stood before a large map of Andania and studied it without seeing it. His mind raced between different ideas and topics while he planned the details of the forthcoming meeting with his commander and then went back and planned them again. This meeting would affect their fate–he knew that for sure, and that helped him concentrate all his energy on it. Thus, he managed to ignore the demons that dwelled in his head and kept showing him images of Tasha—Tasha making dinner ... Tasha smiling by the bed ... Tasha crying on the sofa and holding on to him ...

"We've been waiting half an hour already," he whispered nervously to Sammy. "I hope we won't have any surprises."

"I'm sure he'll see us," she whispered back. She was about to add something else but thought better of it and closed her mouth. During the last hour, since she had awakened him from his exhausted sleep, she hadn't tried to make conversation, and John was grateful to her for that. She knew that he needed to grieve but didn't have the time to do it, and she was giving him whatever little free time there was to keep to himself.

"The general will see you now," said the uniformed secretary seated behind an empty desk outside General Chang's office. As she got up, John noticed she was wearing an immaculate white uniform.

John and Sammy walked quickly to the door the secretary held open. They found themselves in a vast room, not in character with the unpretentious atmosphere of the building. General Chang stood before a large screen, his back to the door, and spoke into a military communicator. In contrast, John and Sammy stood twenty paces from him, as required of soldiers approaching senior officers, and waited patiently for him to notice their presence.

General Chang was short and chubby, and although it was late in the day, his uniform looked like it had just come off a hanger. He ended his conversation and raised his head. John, who had never met him before, was immediately attracted by his magnetic eyes and powerful countenance. He stood at attention and saluted; Chang answered with a careless salute that ended with a "sit down" motion toward the chairs before his large desk. He sat behind the desk and waited for John and Sammy to approach.

"Lieutenant John Hektor, sir!" barked John.

"I know who you are, Lieutenant—no need to shout. I know the lady, too. Sit down, please."

"I'm sorry, sir. Thank you, sir," John mumbled, embarrassed. He felt that he was blushing and glanced at Sammy. She was looking at Chang with an amused look in her eyes. But, of course, she wasn't a soldier, and things were different for her.

"You asked for an urgent meeting," said the general, looking at Sammy. "What is the urgency, and what does Mister Yabalan want from me now? He's become quite active lately."

"Sir," said Sammy apologetically, "I'm afraid I may have unintentionally misled you. This is not about something Yabalan wants, but something that has to do with him."

Chang's eyes had changed into two slits, and his expression was inscrutable. He moved his gaze to John, who chose his words carefully and began to explain.

"I must say, sir, that this is a matter of momentous importance for Andania. This could be Andania's and our doom. You are the only hope. We–everyone–is in grave danger now."

"Quit beating about the bush," ordered Chang, "and get to the point. I don't have all day."

"Yes, sir. The story is amazing, but it's all true. This is what happened ..."

Chang raised his head, which he had kept low in a listening posture throughout John's report, and looked at them. "If what you're telling me is true," he said gravely, "we're talking high treason, and Yabalan isn't the only traitor."

"It's all true, sir," said John earnestly, "and that's why we had to talk to you privately."

"But according to what you say, there is no immediate danger. Yabalan and his gang have been left without the files to disarm the FOS. So what's the rush?"

"We don't know who else is helping Yabalan, and particularly, we don't know how involved Sarpash is. We know from Yabalan that the President of the Supreme Court works closely with him, and if Sarpash is also involved... well, the only missing key is the one in your hands. If they didn't shy away from hurting Yan-Nibar ..."

"What did you say?" the general's expression darkened even more.

"I should have said that we suspect that they hurt Yan-Nibar. I have good reason to believe that's what happened, but there's no time for that now. We're apprehensive that they may try to take the key from you by force. The announcement is due the day after tomorrow, and they don't have much time left."

General Chang walked around the table to the communication system. "Simpson!" he shouted, and a few seconds later, the door opened, and a young colonel stood before them at attention.

"Twenty guards in full gear in fifteen minutes, two vehicles, and two officers. You're one of them."

"Yes, sir!" answered Colonel Simpson. Without asking any questions, he saluted and left, closing the door behind him. By his reaction, one could have thought he received that kind of order every night.

Chang returned to the communication system, and the secretary's face appeared on the screen. "Call Judge Labra and tell him I need to see him immediately–I have no time to explain, but it's important. He is to meet us at the courthouse in half an hour."

He looked at them with a satisfied smile. "I think we'll have no trouble stopping them from turning off the FOS," he said.

"On the contrary, sir," John hastened to correct him, "we must be able to turn it off."

The general cocked his head to one side and looked intensely at John. "I prefer to think you're out of your mind, Lieutenant. The FOS cannot be turned off under any circumstances because if God forbid, it stops working, we'll be exposed to an attack that we have no chance to counter with our limited forces. Certainly not without suffering terrible losses."

John smiled for the first time since he had walked into the room. "I'll explain, if I may, sir," he said, and when Chang nodded, he continued. "The plan that Yabalan has concluded with the Newists is that the day after tomorrow at noon, Sarpash will announce that a peace treaty has been signed with the Newists and that the borders have been opened. At the same hour, the FOS is supposed to be turned off. Yabalan was afraid that he might not be able to convince you to disable the FOS without first receiving proof and assurances against any attack, which he felt was 'unnecessary in time of peace.'"

"The little slimeball knows me well," exclaimed Chang.

"Therefore," John went on, "he had to be ready with an alternative plan. The plan involved convincing me to use the New Nations' computer system to break and turn the code off. So what happens if we don't stop it tomorrow? There is a good chance that Sarpash will be able to convince the People's Assembly that the long-hoped-for peace is in danger, that we are about to miss a once-in-a-lifetime opportunity, and that the Newists meant to keep their promises while we didn't keep ours–which will cause endless wars for all generations to come. In such a situation, sir, you may be forced to surrender the key, and then we'll be lost."

"You're right, Lieutenant. I should've seen it myself. If we turn off the FOS for a brief period, we'll see the real intentions of the Newists and, if they attack us, to turn it on again. Good plan. Good for you!"

Sammy had kept silent until then, slumped in her chair, and now she straightened her back and touched John's arm to silence him. "Aren't we forgetting something? You'll have to get the keys in Sarpash and Judge Labra's hands to do what you're planning. Turning off the FOS is permitted by law only if the three of you agree or by the People's Assembly decree. How do we get that?"

"By force, young lady," said Chang lightly. "It's called 'military coup' or something like that," he explained, smiling.

Sammy smiled back at him. "If you're okay with it, it's fine by me," she said but immediately turned serious. "I must ask you something, General. How come you're taking our story at face value? We came to you with a pretty amazing story, didn't we? And I wouldn't have been surprised if you had demanded some kind of proof from us."

"You're very right," General Chang said, "but I know a few

facts that strengthen what you're telling me. First, I think I'm a good judge of people and can tell you're telling the truth."

"We could be wrong, even if we believe we're telling the truth," commented John.

"Yes, but I know the persons involved, and I've already gotten some signals from other channels that something is cooking in Sarpash's pot ... something that needs keeping an eye on. Ever since Yan-Nibar's attempted murder, I'm being extra cautious. Besides, what you suggest entails no danger. I'll keep the keys and will have control over everything. And if everybody is wrong and the Newists come with the purest intentions, we will be in time to let this peace thing go on. So let's waste no more time."

"The soldiers are ready, sir," said Colonel Simpson, who had reappeared out of nowhere. General Chang, who had seated himself on the corner of his desk to talk to Sammy, got up and turned toward the door. "Are you coming or not?" he threw at them over his shoulder. John and Sammy ran after him, and Sammy linked arms with John. Her face was flushed, and she looked excited. "It's starting," she whispered in his ear.

Judge Labra's office was large and elegant, with a high ceiling and walls paneled with imported wood. John felt this excessive luxury was in bad taste and showed that the Supreme Court was out of touch with the people of Andania, who lived frugally. The judge met them wearing a black toga with red shoulders, which looked ridiculous outside the courtroom.

"Ah, General," said the judge, purposely sounding bored. "Who are your friends? Doesn't matter. I hope you had a good reason for getting me out of the house so late."

"I did. I did, Judge," said Chang, impatiently. "We want the key."

"Ah?" said the judge with surprise. "Key? What key?"

"The key to the FOS," said Chang simply. "Yabalan sent us to pick up the key so we may proceed with the plan. You know, don't you, that the day after tomorrow is the day."

The judge furtively looked around him, clearly embarrassed. "But ... Yabalan told me nothing about you coming here ... He said he'd come in person, he or his assistant Barak. What happened? Did anything go wrong with the plan?"

"Yes, Judge. What went wrong was that we have discovered that you and your friends are traitors!" said Chang simply and waited for Labra's reaction.

The judge took one step back and sat heavily in his elegant armchair. "Are you out of your mind, General?" he said accusingly.

"I'm not, but I can't say the same thing of you. We know all about your and Yabalan's plans."

"I ..."

"There's no point in denying, Judge. Yabalan gave it all to us."

"You don't understand, Chang. We are acting in the people's best interests—and who is better equipped for that than Yabalan, with his vision and innovative thought, and I, the one person in Andania who is guided only by Truth and Justice?" The judge stood as if lecturing, waving his hands to emphasize his words. "I'm sure you understand that the people don't know what's good for them. That's why they have leaders that lead them for their best."

"No," retorted General Chang quietly, "you don't understand. You don't understand that unless you give me the key immediately, I'll have to take it by force."

The judge froze, his right hand upraised, and stared at the general in disbelief. At last, his hand dropped, and his eyes became menacing slits.

"You've gone too far, Chang," he hissed between clenched teeth, "and I have nothing more to say to you."

"Colonel," shouted Chang, stopping the judge's sentence midway. Colonel Simpson appeared at the door and saluted.

"Colonel," ordered Chang, "take the judge to another room and lock him there. Put a guard on him. I'll tell you later what to do with him. Meanwhile, bring an engineer with some explosives."

"Explosive? What do you plan to do?" cried the judge.

"I'm only going to open that nice safe that you have there, in the corner. That's how I'll get the key, which I assume is there."

"You wouldn't dare!"

Chang didn't answer but motioned to Simpson with his head, and the colonel approached the judge and took his elbow. "No, wait!" pleaded Labra. "I have important and delicate items in the safe–artworks–you'll damage them. Let me open it."

"He got some sense, at last," John commented quietly. The judge approached the safe and hid the lock with his body. After a few clicking sounds, the door opened, and the judge closed it again almost immediately. When he turned toward them, a little purple box was in his hand. "Aha!" said Chang with satisfaction. He took the box from the judge's hand and opened it. "This is the key all right," he said, closing the lid. "Colonel," he ordered, "the judge is under arrest. One of the vehicles will take you to the base, and the other comes with me."

"But ... but I gave you what you wanted." The judge seemed to be about to cry.

"Judge," said Chang gravely, "you are under arrest for high treason, not because of the key. You'll remain in jail until the state of emergency is over, and it is decided how you'll stand trial. In the meantime, I recommend that you remove that ridiculous toga. You won't need it in jail."

Chang turned to John and Sammy, ignoring the judge's pleas that faded in the distance.

"General, you're my hero," said Sammy admiringly.

"Thanks," smiled the general, "but now we must get to Sarpash quickly. The news of Judge Labra's arrest won't take long to reach him. These walls have ears, and some court employees have witnessed the arrest; besides, his whining must have been heard in all of Andania City. Let's go."

When Chang and his followers arrived, Sarpash was sleeping in a room adjacent to his office. His private secretary, Victoria, received them. "The Prime Minister cannot be disturbed now. He's resting," she ruled.

"Then tell him that this is an emergency and that he has to see us immediately," said Chang impatiently.

"I have very clear instructions not to interrupt his rest," answered Victoria, sounding like a schoolteacher reproving a retarded child.

Chang looked at her for an instant and then simply circled her and, without a word, opened the door of Sarpash's room and turned on the light. Sarpash was in bed, wearing blue pajamas covered with drawings of birds. John recalled having pajamas like those as a child, but they looked ridiculous on an adult. Sarpash blinked and sat on the bed heavily. "What? What's the matter?" he mumbled.

"I'm sorry," said Victoria, sounding worried, "but I couldn't stop them. General Chang knows very well that you're resting after a hard day, but he crashed in without my permission."

"Yeah, complain about me later," said Chang curtly. "We need to talk to you now, Mister Acting Prime Minister" (Chang stressed the word "Acting"), "and in private," he added, throwing a glance to Victoria.

"It's all right, Vicky," Sarpash said soothingly. "If General Chang needs me urgently, I rely on his judgment. Just bring me something hot to drink, will you? Would you like anything?" he asked those present without addressing anybody in particular.

"No, thanks," answered Chang. John and Sammy shook their heads.

Sarpash got up and put on an ornate dressing gown that hung by a peg by the door. He then slid his feet into a pair of slippers and went into his office. His feet were thin and white, with blue veins running along them. John's eyes kept going back to those feet, and he had to make an effort to look elsewhere.

"Now, gentlemen, what seems to be the matter?" asked Sarpash when Victoria left the room after placing a hot drink before him. "Tomorrow, a long and hard day is in store for me; I've got to plan for the day after. The day after tomorrow will be a great day, you'll see that, and a very important one. Very important." A smile of satisfaction on Sarpash's face clearly said that he knew a sweet secret.

"We know everything about the day after tomorrow, sir," said Chang, "and at this very moment, the whole Andanian army is moving toward the passes to meet the enemy."

"What? What are you talking about? What is this nonsense?"

"We know that you plan to announce the peace treaty with the Newists at noon the day after tomorrow and that you expect the FOS to be turned off at that time. That is part of the plan developed by the New Nations Organization and the Newists, with the help of Yabalan, to invade Andania and destroy it."

"You're out of your mind, Chang! The treaty announcement is due the day after tomorrow, but what is all this nonsense about a diabolical plan? It doesn't make sense. Ask Yabalan, and he'll show you the guarantees that we have—"

"Yabalan is dead," intervened John, and Sarpash choked on his words.

Chang turned around and looked at him. "You didn't tell me that before. Are you sure?"

"Yes, sir. I apologize. I should've reported that before. I'm quite sure, although he was still alive the last time I saw him."

"But ... but I was told he's on his way here," mumbled Sarpash. "He should already have arrived."

"The report was misleading on purpose. No, he's not coming."

"Then it's the end. It's the end," whispered Sarpash to himself. The key to the peace treaty was in his hand. All the agreements and all the personal connections with the Newists—everything. Without him ... the work of my entire life is destroyed. Do you understand that? All I've been working for all my life! At this time, in two days, I should've been the elected president of United New Australia, and now ..."

"You have nothing to be sorry about," said John. "Yabalan's plan was not what he told you. He planned to be the one who would be appointed president of United New Australia, in rotation with Tafa-Aru Sed. You would've been left a puppet job."

"I don't believe you! I raised him. He owes me."

"Really," spurted Chang.

"We must hurry, General," Sammy reminded him.

"Yes, thanks for the wake-up call," he answered ironically. "I could've forgotten that we have work to do. Sarpash!" he called authoritatively, and Sarpash, who had been sitting with his head in his hands, straightened up in surprise.

"Yes, Chang. What now?"

"Now you have two options–you may become a hero of Andania or a traitor and a bad joke. Which will it be?"

Sarpash opened his mouth to speak and then closed it again. It took him only a few moments to get hold of himself and to ask the general, "What am I supposed to do?"

"You'll keep preparing for tomorrow as if nothing happened. That would give the army time to organize at the borders before the Newists noticed something was going on. The day after tomorrow, you'll announce to the people of Andania that you have reached a peace agreement with the Newists, and at noon, we will switch off the FOS exactly as the Newists expect."

"I don't understand."

"The small change in plan is that the army will be ready near the passes. We expect the Newists will invade Andania in great force soon after the FOS is down. When a part of the Newist army has passed, the FOS will start working again, killing everybody in the passage. Our army will destroy the forces already on our side of the border. In this way, you'll be able to tell the people about the Newist betrayal and about your wisdom in not trusting them and being ready for their move. See?"

"A great plan, Chang. You deserve great praise. I'll commend you."

"Do me a favor and don't piss me off," said Chang angrily. He extended his hand. "The key," he ordered.

Sarpash went to a cupboard and opened it without arguing. A minute later, he handed Chang a box identical to the one he had taken from Judge Labra.

"Colonel Simpson and his men will remain with you from this moment on to make sure that you won't 'forget' your part," explained Chang and turned his back to Sarpash. "Have I forgotten anything?" he asked John and Sammy.

"Only Rippel, sir," said John. "He's still in jail, and I think getting him out and here to help us is imperative."

"Did you hear him, Sarpash?" Chang asked threateningly. "Start working with that communicator of yours. I want to see Rippel here within the hour. Thank you, Lieutenant," he added courteously. Now, I need to rush. Come, Lieutenant. We've got a lot of work to do."

"Ehm ..." came the faint sound from Sarpash.

"Yes?" asked Chang, lifting an eyebrow.

"I'm afraid that Rippel is no longer ... how should I say ... there has been a sad incident, and he's ..."

"Dead?" completed Chang for him. Sarpash swallowed and nodded.

"This goes on your bill, Sarpash," said Chang flatly and turned away.

"Asking for permission to come with you, General," said Sammy militarily.

"I guess that you earned a front seat at the show. Any objection, Lieutenant?"

"Don't even think about it ..." Sammy started to say, but John smiled and extended his hand.

"Come on," he said.

"You're smarter than you look," she said, smiling back.

CHAPTER 29

"People of Andania." Sarpash's pompous voice was a good match to his ostentatious appearance. His face was radiant on the screen, and he had clearly invested a lot of effort in grooming himself to the last hair of his complicated head-dress. "Ahead of us, we see a new era–a time of peace with our neighbors and shared prosperity. I'm proud to tell you that my emissary, Deputy Minister Yabalan, who is right now on Earth, has signed a detailed peace treaty with the leaders of the Newists on my behalf.

"I won't tell you we could obtain this result without conces-sions, but the outcome is terrific. On the negative side, we are turning over, symbolically, the ownership of ten important mines to Tafa-Aru Sed today, but this will not affect our lives because we will continue to operate the mines for the next two hundred years. During this time, we will work to reach suitable agreements that will allow us to go on exploiting them.

"The transfer of ownership is needed to recognize what the Newists see as their legitimate rights on the territories in which the mines are located."

Sammy glanced at John, who watched Sarpash on a screen in

the middle of the command car they traveled. "Do you think he believes what he's saying?" she asked.

John waved his hand and shrugged without removing his eyes from the screen.

"This agreement and the symbolic concession I just mentioned," continued Sarpash, "allow us to begin a new era of peace. The borders between us and the Newists will be opened today at noon. Their leader, Tafa-Aru Sed, will arrive at the head of a peace procession in Andania City for the ceremonial signing of the peace treaty, which will be broadcast live to all of Andania.

"This agreement, you should know, includes establishing a joint government for all of New Australia, which Tafa-Aru Sed and I will head in rotation. It would be my honor to be the first president of the New Australian Confederation.

"Citizens of Andania," Sarpash theatrically paused, his eyes seeming to look straight into those of each of his citizens, "we are opening today a new era of peace and prosperity. Yesterday is dead; long live tomorrow!"

The transmission ended, and General Chang turned off the screen. "You must hand it to him; the bastard can talk."

"That's about all he can do," said Sammy quietly.

The command car climbed the winding road leading to the top of the hill where the control bunker of FOS3–the most important of all passages–was located. The bunker was dug behind the top of the hill. The exit from the passage could be seen from it; many cameras showed different sections of the passage. Every day, at least one animal would enter the passage and get hit by the laser rays activated randomly by presence sensors, and their carcasses were scattered along the path. Only when a Newist got killed did the rules allow for a temporary shutdown of FOS3 for a brief time, after special permission was granted, to remove his body together with the carcasses of the animals that were scattered around. A local shutdown of a single passage could be made using a local key after the appropriate forces were deployed at the border, but it lasted only half an hour. After thirty minutes, FOS3 was automatically reactivated; therefore, every cleaning operation had to allow for sufficient safety margins and required great proficiency to ensure that nobody got hurt.

Nevertheless, now and then, small groups of Newists succeeded in crossing the passage, but not before a number of them lay dead along the path. John was always amazed by their perseverance and lack of fear of death.

The command car overtook a group of soldiers marching in full combat gear on the right side of the road. John's heart leaped when he recognized his soldiers in them. "May we stop for a moment, sir? I see my men here, and I'd like to go to them. I can walk to the bunker later."

General Chang ordered the driver to stop, and John jumped down and ran to his soldiers. Sammy watched as they received him with handshakes and hugs, feeling jealous.

"He's all right, this boyfriend of yours," said General Chang, who had been watching the reunion.

"He's not my boyfriend," Sammy said flatly.

"Strange," said the general, "I would've thought ..."

The activity within the bunker was frantic. Chang's staff officers were there, and their helpers spoke simultaneously into different communicators. The noise in the small room, hardly suited to host so many people, was deafening. The large screens that occupied the room's longest wall showed different sections of the passage made of solid concrete from openings in which hidden launchers fired their laser rays.

John walked into the room in full combat gear, and General Chang shot an oblique glance at him. "Where do you think you're going, boy?" he asked.

"Requesting permission to join my men, sir. They are in an

advanced position, not far from here, and they are responsible for taking out any Newists who will make it through the passage before FOS3 is reactivated. My place is with them."

"Permission denied, Lieutenant. I need you here with me. They'll have to manage without you."

"But, sir ..."

Chang didn't answer, but one glance was enough to tell John his decision was final. He bowed his head, snapped the buckle of his combat belt open, and perched it with his weapon against the wall behind him.

"He's right, you know," Sammy whispered softly. "We need you here. I need you here more than your soldiers do ... never mind, not a good time now," she added quickly when an expression of surprise appeared on John's face. She turned her head and stared straight into the screen before her.

John didn't know what to say—or if he should say anything—and kept silent. A minute later, everybody's attention turned to General Chang, who stood at the room's center and requested silence. "The time is noon. I will now use the keys to deactivate the entire FOS system ... here, it's deactivated."

A tense silence ensued as everyone watched the screen showing the farthest section of the FOS3 passage. The room had been silent for a full five minutes when a moving object appeared on the screen; a minute later, it materialized into a procession moving slowly toward them. The parade was headed by an old, long-bearded man, who walked barefooted and in whom John identified a religious figure whose name had slipped his memory. Behind him advanced a large cart harnessed to two short-legged Newist horses. On the cart, a big sign said "Peace Procession," and a second one announced that "The Newist Nation Greets the People of Andania in Peace."

When the procession came closer, John saw hundreds of Newists walking behind the cart, holding flowers of many colors in one hand and walking sticks in the other. Among them rolled smaller carts with signs about 'peace and loving your neighbors.' The procession was colorful and so long that its end was still out of sight. There was no telling how many hundreds or thousands participated in the caravan.

"Could we be wrong?" Sammy wondered. "Maybe they are coming in peace?"

"Look," John whispered, "there are no women or children among them. Only men."

One of Chang's officers apparently raised the same question because his voice blared from the other end of the room. "Cut the bullshit!" he barked. "Can't you see that it's a trap? Look at this screen–check out the x-ray of the first wagon that entered the passage. What do you see? Right, weapons. Did you really believe that they were bringing us flowers?"

A tense silence fell upon the room while everybody tried to get a good view of the carts' x-ray images as they entered the passage, one by one. There was no doubt–all the carts were loaded with weapons, and the bigger ones also hid men, probably warriors ready for the battle.

"As soon as the first cart reaches the exit from the passage, we'll reactivate the FOS," said Chang matter-of-factly. "Obviously, some Newists will make it out of the passage. Perhaps those hiding in the carts are equipped with protective shields that will give some protection against our laser rays. Those will be dealt with by the units positioned outside. What's the situation at the other passages?"

A young officer stepped one step forward and saluted the general. "Passage One and Passage Five report similar processions, but they started later than here, and the first carts are only now entering the passages. Passages Two and Four report no activity."

"Those are the more difficult passages and are easier to protect, even without the FOS. I guess that the Newists have decided to go through the easier ones. All right, I'll reactivate everything, even if the Newists have not yet reached the end of the path at Passages One and Five. I'm not going to take any risks here."

General Chang and everybody else concentrated on the screen that showed the last section of the passage and the last turn before Andanian territory. The screen only showed concrete walls. General Chang held the control box of the FOS, which already had all three keys in it, and waited patiently. Suddenly, the screen became alive with movement, and the head of the procession appeared clearly on it. The distance between him and Andanian territory was only three hundred meters–less than five minutes.

"Now!" Chang announced. He pushed the red button on the control box and removed the keys. The people in the room fixed their eyes on the screens, waiting to see how the laser rays destroyed the fraudulent Newist procession. Nothing happened.

"Damn!" General Chang spurted. He pushed the button repeatedly, checking the screens after every attempt, but the FOS didn't reactivate. "Gentlemen, we are in trouble," he said at last.

"General!" someone shouted from the other end of the room. "Prime Minister Sarpash wants to talk to you. On the leftmost screen."

Colonel Simpson's face appeared on the screen, and beside him was Sarpash. "Sir," the colonel said, "you should see this."

The image moved to the right, to the large screen in Sarpash's office. On the screen, they saw Yabalan's unctuous face and, beside him, a big woman whom John recognized as Valerie Namkov, the Minister of Natural Resources of the New Nations.

"It can't be ..." John murmured to himself.

"Hi, Chang," said Yabalan with a broad smile. "I see you have a few of my good friends with you, ah? I think that someone's surprised to see me, right, John? Well, your criminal friends had the pretense of trying to get in the way of my plans, but I managed to get away–it wasn't easy, by the way, and I still hurt where I got hit jumping out of their car, but we'll deal with you all some other time."

"What do you want? I don't have time for you now," Chang replied scornfully.

"Yes, I'm sure that you're very busy right now. You're probably trying to reactivate the FOS, right? Don't waste your energy. As it turns out, our friends here at the New Nations decoded the commands that activate the FOS a long time ago–they're a bit more advanced than we are, you know? Anyway, we have deactivated the system from our end, and there's no way that you can turn it on locally. Sorry."

"You're crazy, Yabalan. The Newists are invading Andania right now with huge forces, and unless we turn the FOS on here and now, there will be a massacre. Reactivate it immediately!"

"Ehh ... make me," Yabalan teased him. "You military people see everything with the eyes of yesterday and just seem unable to see the big picture. We must give the Newists a little satisfaction to give their leaders the strength to go to their people and tell them they want to make real peace. People will indeed get hurt in the process, and I'm very sorry about that, but those will be the victims needed for peace. You'll build me a monument yet, I promise you."

"Yabalan, for God's sake," Chang implored him, "activate the FOS. Do it now!"

"Sorry," said Yabalan placidly, "even if I wanted to, it's out of my hands now, and besides, I don't want to. I'll be in touch."

Yabalan's face disappeared, and they were left gazing at an empty screen until the picture moved again, and Simpson and Sarpash reappeared. "Perhaps ... perhaps he's right?" stammered Sarpash. "Perhaps everything will calm down once they see they can prevail?"

"Simpson!" Chang ordered. "Lock that babbling idiot somewhere and make sure that he talks to nobody. And order Code Red for the defense of Andania City."

Simpson saluted without another word, and Chang turned to those in the room. "We are retreating immediately to the rear command position, ten kilometers from here. This place will be hell in five minutes, and we need time to organize the units. Everybody on board immediately! Transmit a heads-up on what's happening to your units on the way out."

The room emptied in a minute as everybody ran toward the vehicles. Sammy stood by Chang's command car when John, in full combat gear, approached her. "Drive fast, Sammy," he said to her. "I'll catch up with you later."

"But ... but the general said everybody's leaving," she said. Her voice was shaking, and so was she. Tears appeared in her eyes, and she held on to him with all her strength.

General Chang, who stood beside her, touched her shoulder. "Let him go, Sammy. He's right, and God knows that I would've liked to go with him. Quick, now!" he concluded, getting into the car.

John took Sammy's hand and got closer. "I'll be seeing you again," he said. "I promise."

"Don't promise," she wept.

John took her head into both hands and lightly kissed the corner of her mouth. "Go, now," he whispered. He turned around and walked toward the hills.

The battle was at its height, and John couldn't locate his men among the many units fighting the wave of barbarians crossing over the borders of Andania. Under a big rock, just below the top of the hill, he saw the crushed body of a soldier, apparently hit by a shell shot from one of the wagons, but his face was intact, and John recognized one of his sergeants. He ran, bent almost in two, toward a group of soldiers that were shooting from the top of the hill into the valley below.

His body was lifted, and his feet kicked the air as a blast he hadn't seen coming threw him upwards. His flight through the air seemed to last an eternity, but eventually, he hit the rock and fell to the earth.

I'm hit, he thought, but he felt no pain. A strange silence fell around him, and he heard voices from afar. Dana? No, Tasha? Surely, it was Tasha's voice calling to him.

A shooting pain in his left shoulder, which had hit the ground first, awakened him to reality, and he crawled painfully and with great effort to the top of the hill. On the slopes, on the other side, his soldiers were fighting face-to-face, outnumbered ten to one, against a never-ending flow of Newists. The clangor of battle and the noise of shells falling around them with monotonous rhythm were deafening. John managed to rise to his knees with great effort, his feet shaking and his eyes blinded by sparks of light at his every movement. The clamor of the battle faded in his head for a moment, and he felt light. He looked at the body of the soldier lying beside him as, suddenly, it took on his mother's face. "Mom ..." he tried to say, but her face faded ... leaving that of the soldier, resembling a sleeping child.

A familiar figure stood before him–Sammy. In his confusion, he couldn't distinguish between reality and imagination and wasn't sure if she was really there, on the top of the hill with him. "Don't promise," she wept. "Promise that you'll return. Don't promise ..."

John got on his feet and took a step toward her, but she disappeared. He turned around and saw, in the far distance, the military convoy driving away, fast, on the narrow, winding road to Andania City. They were so small that they looked like toy cars, and the Andanian Valley looked like a pastoral image on a postcard.

His vision cleared, and he took a deep breath of the air of Andania with the weird taste that he had grown to love so much. Then, he turned his back to the green Andanian Valley and walked determinedly over the top and down the hill toward his soldiers.

EPILOGUE

The sun was low over the horizon, but the air was warm and clean in the summer afternoon. A crowd of maybe a hundred people was assembled on the esplanade facing the Three-Years Monument, before which a stage had been erected. The solemnity of the place did not invite noise, so everybody spoke in a low voice, creating a hum resembling that of a bee swarm. Some somewhat sad music played in the background.

Sammy glanced at her son with a smile of satisfaction. At 7, he was growing to be strong and handsome like his father, but like him, he would never shut up.

"When is Daddy coming? Why is this monument shaped like a 3? Where is Uncle Erian? He promised to bring me a gift."

"One question at a time, Honey, okay?"

"Yes, but why?"

Her son was like that, impetuous and demanding, but she liked his thirst for understanding.

"Daddy is behind the curtains. You will see him when they call him on stage."

"They are going to give him a medal, right? But why here?"

"This monument is in memory of the three years during which Andania was dominated by the Newists, long before you were born. We visited here before, remember?"

"Yes, before Daddy killed all the Newists."

"The Newists were bad people, and your father fought them, but he didn't kill them all—there were a lot of them, and they did it to themselves."

"How?"

"It's a long story. There was a very dangerous epidemic that killed almost every one of them."

"I learned about it in school. It's the D-Plague. We in Andania can't get sick with it."

"You are right, but the Newists could, and they mixed with Andanians too much. That started an epidemic like the one they had on Earth many years ago."

"And it killed them all!" he insisted.

"Yes, it did," Sammy smiled.

"Where is my gift?"

"Uncle Erian had to return to Earth. He asked me to tell you that your gift will arrive on the next ship."

"He is an important person, Uncle Erian, right?"

"Very important, a minister. We will visit him and Aunt Dana soon."

"When is soon?"

"Before your eighth birthday. Now, quit asking questions. Daddy's next, look!"

The music stopped, and the constant murmur from the crowd died down. The master or ceremony's voice thundered from the loudspeakers. "The Medal of Honor will now be awarded to Colonel John Hektor for his brave fight for Andania. Colonel Hektor fought valiantly on the day of the Newist invasion, then organized men from different units who survived the battle into a guerrilla force that defended several agricultural units and prevented their fall into Newist hands. For this and other acts of bravery, he is now awarded the highest Andanian honor."

John marched on the stage toward the podium.

"Here's my Daddy!" the boy shouted, "He's a hero!"

"Yes, he is," Sammy said. She hugged her boy harder and allowed a tear of happiness down her cheek.

Pine Ten, LLC

205 North Michigan Avenue

Chicago, IL 60601

First published by Echelon Press 2006

ISBN: 978-1-938212-04-8

MEET THE AUTHOR

Kfir Luzzatto is the author of thirteen novels, several short stories, and seven non-fiction books. Kfir was born and raised in Italy and moved to Israel as a teenager. He acquired his love for the English language from his father, a former U.S. soldier, a voracious reader, and a prolific writer. He holds a Ph.D. in chemical engineering and works as a patent attorney. In pursuit of his interest in the mind-body connection, Kfir was certified as a Clinical Hypnotherapist by the Anglo-European College of Therapeutic Hypnosis.

Kfir is a member of the HWA (Horror Writers Association) and ITW (International Thriller Writers). You can visit Kfir's website and read his blog at https://www.kfirluzzatto.com. Follow him on Twitter (@KfirLuzzatto) and friend him on Facebook (https://www.facebook.com/KfirLuzzattoAuthor).

ALSO BY KFIR LUZZATTO

CROSSING THE MEADOW

THE ODYSSEY GENE

THE EVELYN PROJECT

HAVE BOOK, WILL TRAVEL
(With Yonatan Luzzatto)

AN ITALIAN OBSESSION

EXODUS '95

CHIPLESS

REWIRED (*The sequel to CHIPLESS*)

ONCE AWAKENED

The Tessa Extra-Sensory Agent series:

TESSA (Tessa Extra-Sensory Agent Book 1)

THE OTHERS (Tessa Extra-Sensory Agent Book 2)

HUNTER (Tessa Extra-Sensory Agent Book 3)

PHANTOM (Tessa Extra-Sensory Agent Book 4)

RUNNER (Tessa Extra-Sensory Agent Book 5)

The DEAD & BUSY series:

#1: ACCIDENTAL LAZARUS

#2: PHANTOM LOVER

#3: MICE

#4: THE ACCOUNTANT

Short Story Collections:

HIS DARKER SIDE

HIS LIGHTER SIDE